T0113829

Hearthstones

AFRICAN CLASSICS SERIES

1. *Secret Lives* – Ngugi wa Thiong'o
2. *Matigari* – Ngugi wa Thiong'o
3. *A Grain of Wheat* – Ngugi wa Thiong'o
4. *Weep Not, Child* – Ngugi wa Thiong'o
5. *The River Between* – Ngugi wa Thiong'o
6. *Devil on the Cross* – Ngugi wa Thiong'o
7. *Petals of Blood* – Ngugi wa Thiong'o
8. *Wizard of the Crow* – Ngugi wa Thiong'o
9. *Homing In* – Marjorie Oludhe Macgoye
10. *Coming to Birth* – Marjorie Oludhe Macgoye
11. *Street Life* – Marjorie Oludhe Macgoye
12. *The Present Moment* – Marjorie Oludhe Macgoye
13. *Chira* – Marjorie Oludhe Macgoye
14. *A Farm Called Kishinev* – Marjorie Oludhe Macgoye
15. *No Longer at Ease* – Chinua Achebe
16. *Arrow of God* – Chinua Achebe
17. *A Man of the People* – Chinua Achebe
18. *Things Fall Apart* – Chinua Achebe
19. *Anthills of the Savannah* – Chinua Achebe
20. *The Strange Bride* – Grace Ogot
21. *Land Without Thunder* – Grace Ogot
22. *The Promised Land* – Grace Ogot
23. *The Other Woman* – Grace Ogot
24. *The Minister's Daughter* – Mwangi Ruheni
25. *The Future Leaders* – Mwangi Ruheni
26. *White Teeth* – Okot P'Bitek
27. *Horn of My Love* – Okot P'Bitek
28. *God's Bits of Wood* – Sembene Ousmane
29. *Emperor Shaka the Great* – Masizi Kunene
30. *No Easy Walk to Freedom* – Nelson Mandela
31. *Mine Boy* – Peter Abrahams
32. *Takadini* – Ben Hanson
33. *Myths and Legends of the Swahili* – Jan Knappert
34. *Mau Mau Author in Detention* – Gakaara wa Wanjau
35. *Igereka and Other African Narratives* – John Ruganda
36. *Kill Me Quick* – Meja Mwangi
37. *Going Down River Road* – Meja Mwangi
38. *Striving for the Wind* – Meja Mwangi
39. *Carcase for Hounds* – Meja Mwangi
40. *The Last Plague* – Meja Mwangi
41. *The Big Chiefs* – Meja Mwangi
42. *The Slave* – Elechi Amadi
43. *The Concubine* – Elechi Amadi
44. *The Great Ponds* – Elechi Amadi
45. *The African Child* – Camara Laye
46. *Mission to Kala* – Mongo Beti
47. *The Trouble with Nigeria* – Chinua Achebe
48. *Hearthstones* – Kekelwa Nyaywa

PEAK LIBRARY SERIES

1. *Without a Conscience* – Barbara Baumann
2. *The Herdsman's Daughter* – Bernard Chahilu
3. *Of Man and Lion* – Beatrice Erlwanger
4. *My Heart on Trial* – Genga Idowu
5. *Kosiya Kifefe* – Arthur Gakwandi
6. *Return to Paradise* – Yusuf K Dawood
7. *Mission to Gehenna* – Karanja wa Kang'ethe
8. *Goatsmell* – Nevanji Madanhire
9. *Sunset in Africa* – Peter M Nyarango
10. *The Moon Also Sets* – Osi Ogbu
11. *Breaking Chains* – Dorothea Holi
12. *The Missing Links* – Tobias O Otieno
13. *I Shall Walk Alone* – Paul Nakitare
14. *A Season of Waiting* – David Omowale
15. *Before the Rooster Crows* – Peter Kimani
16. *A Nose for Money* – Francis B Nyamnjoh
17. *The Travail of Dieudonné* – Francis B Nyamnjoh
18. *A Journey Within* – Florence Mbaya
19. *The Doomed Conspiracy* – Barrack O Muluka and Tobias O Otieno
20. *The Lone Dancer* – Joe Kiarie
21. *Eye of the Storm* – Yusuf K Dawood
22. *Animal Farm* – George Orwell
23. *Stillborn* – Diekoye Oyeyinka
24. *Ugandan Affairs* – Sira Kiwana
25. *African Quilt* – Harshi Syal Gill and Parvin D. Syal
26. *The Dolphin Catchers and other stories*
27. *Black Ghost* – Ken N. Kamoche
28. *The Guardian Angels* – Issa Noor

Hearthstones

Kekelwa Nyaywa

East African Educational Publishers
Nairobi • Kampala • Dar es Salaam • Kigali • Lusaka • Lilongwe

Published by
East African Educational Publishers Ltd.
Shreeji Road, off North Airport Road,
Embakasi, Nairobi.
P.O. Box 45314, Nairobi - 00100, KENYA
Tel: +254 20 2324760
Mobile: +254 722 205661 / 722 207216 / 733 677716 / 734 652012
Email: eaep@eastafricanpublishers.com
Website: www.eastafricanpublishers.com

East African Educational Publishers also has offices or is represented in the following countries: Uganda, Tanzania, Rwanda, Malawi, Zambia, Botswana and South Sudan.

First published 1995

Reprinted 2015, 2021

ISBN 978-9966-46-872-7

Chapter One

It was a hot and muggy afternoon, as Chilufya and her long-time friends, Likande and Tengani, sat in the large and spacious screened verandah of Chilufya's ranch. The house was built on a hill overlooking a lush green valley, through which flowed a stream that provided water for irrigating their vegetable garden and orchard. In the orchard, a variety of tropical fruits, including oranges, pawpaws, bananas, lemons, guavas and tangerines were growing. Chilufya and her husband, Hambala, also kept chickens, rabbits and guinea fowls.

Chilufya loved going back to the sanctuary of her home after working long hours at the University Teaching Hospital in Lusaka. Their twenty-five acre ranch was only twenty minutes away by car from Lusaka, where she and her lawyer husband worked. But when they were home, it was as if they were in another world ... a world that seemed far away from the hustle, crowds and pollution of city life, and the human suffering that she dealt with every day in the overcrowded hospital.

Today was her day off from the hospital, and she was enjoying being with the two people she called her "best friends." She handed out ice cold drinks to Tengani and Likande while she kept an eye on her sons, six-year-old Mwinga and five-year-old Mwansa, who were shrieking and laughing as they splashed and raced in the swimming pool. Taking a long sip from her glass, she said, "You know, I can't really believe that it's been ten years since we were together, like this. Ten whole years!"

"Are you sure it's been that long?" asked Tengani, "I saw you when I came to the Convention and ... "

"I meant the three of us. Not just you and me," said Chilufya.

"I can't believe, either, that it's been ten years. How time flies!" remarked Likande.

"You're right, Chilufya. How can I forget the evening when I thought I had met the love of my life!" murmured Tengani.

"Oh, Tengani, don't tell me you're still carrying a torch for that creep! See what you did to our friend, Chilufya by inviting him to your house," said Likande, with mock seriousness.

"Me? I'm not the one who had invited him. It was my ex-husband. All I had wanted was a quiet dinner with the two of you, but Zelani wouldn't hear of it. For him, it was always huge parties and big splashes. He had such a long list of friends that I didn't know half of them. Who could have imagined that I would escape that terrible life and finally find happiness and peace of mind?"

"I remember your bitter custody fight over Zenai. What a terrible time it must have been for that poor child," remarked Tengani.

"I know. It was awful," said Chilufya. "He threatened me and tried to force me to go back to him, saying that if I didn't, I would never see Zenai again. If it weren't for my lawyer, I mean, Hambala, who ..."

" ... advised you not to go back, for ulterior motives, of course!" laughed Likande.

"Yes, courtroom romance," added Tengani, "lawyer falls for client and proposes marriage to her soon after the divorce! You lucky woman, you got yourself a big catch. Good looks and brains!"

"Now look here, you two. Things weren't that fast. I didn't even notice his looks or anything about him. All I wanted was for him to get Zelani off my back. The last thing I wanted was to rush into another relationship."

"We're only joking, Chilufya. So don't get all worked up. Besides, we've all had our ups and downs. I'm glad things worked out well for you in the end," said Likande.

"Sometimes, I wonder about our classmates. I'd love to know what they've been doing since we left school," said Tengani.

"Hmm ..." nodded both Chilufya and Likande.

"It would be fun to have a reunion and have everyone tell us how things have been for them," suggested Chilufya.

"Yah, I guess it would be interesting to find out whether or not their dreams came true, and whether they've done what they set out to do," said Likande.

"Might even be better to begin with ourselves, instead of asking others," suggested Tengani.

"Us? What do you mean? We're friends and already know what has happened to us!" pointed out Likande.

"I think it's a very good idea!" said Chilufya. "It would be fun to do it. Besides, it would be a wonderful way to prepare for the reunion."

"Shall we begin right now?" asked Tengani, getting quite excited.

"No, not now," said Likande. "It's already getting late, and I promised my sister I would be back in time for dinner. They have guests coming, so I had better go and help."

"Well, why don't we just think about this and then discuss it when we meet next?" suggested Chilufya.

"Sounds okay to me. Bye, girls," said Likande, as she rose from her chair.

They still called each other "girls," the way they used to way back when they were in Chipembi Girls' Boarding School. They were so close that the other students called them "The Three Musketeers." They went everywhere together. Whenever one of them was not there, the other two would be asked whether she was sick.

They were close friends, but very different in their temperament and personalities. It was strange how their friendship developed and grew despite their differences.

Chilufya had always been the one who seemed to know what she wanted in life and how to work towards achieving her goal. She was now a medical doctor and worked at the teaching hospital in Lusaka, juggling time between her work and her family.

Tengani was the free and restless one, impatient at the seemingly slow pace of life and the people around her. What she wanted was change; the power to change the world, especially her own country. She was a politician, but preferred to call herself "a full-time rebel."

Likande had been the "brainy one" at school – the one everyone had expected to end up a professor or a researcher in some university or as Tengani often teased her, "the nun, the missionary type." She dabbled in many things, and loved travelling and living in different countries with her husband and children. She often said her job was "working with people and communities, wherever I am."

The task for each one of them was to look into their past and how far they had come, and how life had treated them along the way...

Chapter Two

CHILUFYA

It's almost a week since we agreed to reflect on our past, and I've not done it yet, what with being on call at the hospital and attending to emergencies. But I can't go back on our agreement now. Besides, I was always the one who was expected to follow up on anything I said. It was as if I had this urge to prove myself to other people. My mother used to say it was because I was stubborn and inflexible. Maybe she was right, but I didn't agree with her at the time.

Anyway, if I had done whatever my mother wanted me to do, I wouldn't be where I am today. I certainly would not be a doctor. I probably would not even have finished my primary education. If she had her way, I would have left school at the onset of my menstruation, when I reached puberty and became "mature". She would have arranged for me to get married soon after that, as a kind of insurance against getting pregnant out of wedlock. I would have ended up a big mama with ten children!

You see, my mother grew up a typical African village girl, brought up to believe that women are in this world to be good wives and mothers. Her parents never sent her to school, although there was one called Mbereshi School near her village. During her time it was not compulsory for parents to send their children to school. Those who did often sent boys instead of girls, because it was considered a "waste of time to send girls to school", as they could learn all they needed to know at home.

Life for my mother would have gone on in the village the same it had since time immemorial, if she hadn't married my father and moved away to the copper-mining town of Luanshya, on Copperbelt. Even then, she still kept her ideas and beliefs. She physically lived in Luanshya, but spiritually belonged to the village.

My father was persuaded to leave the village by a visiting uncle who was a miner in Luanshya. He later told us that at first he didn't want to go. The idea of going underground scared him. Apparently, he feared he might die and said so to his uncle. "Supposing the whole mine collapsed? I don't want to die!"

"You won't. That is why I'm here to tell you about it," assured uncle.

He was finally persuaded to go. He insisted on first going alone so that he could check things out, so he left my mother in the village and came back for her several months later. My mother was already pregnant when they went to the copperbelt and I was born soon after she arrived in Luanshya, the first of four girls and one boy, all born in Luanshya.

Life in Luanshya for us kids was fun. We loved playing with other children in the mine compound. However, my parents didn't seem to really like it there. My mother missed her relatives and the close-knit village community. My father never seemed to stop complaining about the way African miners were exploited by the *basungu*, the white people. He started going to night school in the hope of improving his chances and climbing up the ladder, or, as he often promised, "so that he can get us out of this hovel."

What he hated most were the communal bathrooms and toilets. It seemed to him that the *basungu* didn't really care about the Africans, especially the uneducated ones. They seemed to believe that because Africans liked extended families and "being communal," they also loved to have everything in common. So an artificial "extended family" was created in the compound. However, the *basungu* did realize that the compound was not a village, where people spoke same language and shared similar cultural and ethnic beliefs and customs. My father told us that the only way out was education. He observed that the few educated Africans in the mines were treated differently from the uneducated ones. They lived in better houses, complete with their own bathrooms. They were not treated exactly the same as the whites, but were certainly closer to them than to the rest of the workers.

My father's belief in education rubbed off on me, much to the dismay of my mother, who could not understand "this obsession for education." For me, the real eye-opener to what my father was talking about came when I was nine years old. One day I accompanied an older cousin, Mwelwa, to her babysitting job at the home of "Bwana Gregson."

The word "Bwana" denoted deference to white men who in those days symbolized power. It was my first time to enter the home of a white family and the luxury surrounding their lives. These homes were popularly known as "Ma Yard" because of their large gardens and beautiful flowers and plants. It was Mwelwa's first experience too. She was asked to help by her friend who worked as a nanny at the Gregsons and who needed extra help, as there was a party that afternoon. The friend had been asked to help by the lady of the house, the "Dona," to "bring a reliable friend." I was of course thrilled when Mwelwa took me along.

I hopped, skipped and jumped, twirled around, did acrobatics on the way, and only stopped when we approached the large houses, where the continuous barking of ferocious-looking dogs sent shivers down my spine. I grabbed my cousin's hand and held it tightly, pleading with her to "please, take me back home, right now!" Her amused friend assured me that the dogs were safely behind the fences and would not jump over them. She also told me that there were no dogs at the Gregsons, "only cats." I let out a loud sigh of relief. Cats I could handle. They seemed to be harmless creatures who spent a lot of their time licking and grooming themselves. But dogs were different. I hated their growling, barking and menacing noises.

We finally arrived at the house and I followed my cousin's friend through the gates and into the yard. My mouth flew open at the sight before me. I just stood still, transfixed, like a statue, gaping at the sight of white children who were swimming and splashing away in the swimming pool. At that time I didn't know what a swimming pool was.

The nearest thing I could think of was a pond. I thought their house was built around a natural pond. Like someone sleepwalking, I moved slowly towards the children. A girl about my age, who was lying on a towel and drying in the sun, smiled and beckoned me. I was about to quicken my step when I felt firm, strong hands grab me by my shoulder and pull me away.

"Go in through the back door, you little .. , er ... er ... nobody! This is no place for the likes of you!"

I quivered with fright as he yelled at me and threatened to give me "a good spanking if I see you again stepping on my garden!" Despite my fright, I couldn't help glancing at his rugged clothes and wondering why he had called it his garden. He noticed my glance and in a softer voice said, "Er . . . it's not mine. But I'm the chief gardener here. I don't like it when little children like you come stomping over the lawn and flowers. Now off with you!"

My cousin, who had not noticed until now that I had not followed them to the back of the house, came running. "Where were you, you little fool! Don't wander off like that." She gripped me by the arm and led me away, holding me tight as if to make sure that I would not slip away again. When we got to the kitchen, a big, plump woman ordered us to wipe our feet on the rug by the door. I should have worn my Sunday-best shoes, I thought, the ones my mother had just bought for me. This woman would not have looked at me with such disgust, as if my feet were the filthiest in the world. When we entered the kitchen, the delicious smell of baking drifted in the air. I peeped at the tray full of cakes and pastries, but the woman impatiently shooed us towards the hallway. We tiptoed there as if walking on eggs. I couldn't understand why we were walking like that, but my cousin's stern glance warned me not to open my mouth. So I quietly followed along.

My cousin's friend opened the door where the sound of babies crying was coming from. There were four girls in the room, all clad in blue uniforms which were covered on the front by white aprons. They were busy chatting and giggling as they looked after the infants and toddlers in their charge. My cousin and her friend soon joined in the conversation that was going on. I found most of it rather boring chit-chat about their boyfriends, who was dating whom, and so on. Then the talk turned to scandals about some of the *Bwanas* and *Donas* and I leaned forward to hear better. Any conversation about these people who lived in such luxury was now of great interest to me.

One of the nannies was relating the story of her predecessor and how she was fired for having an affair with the *Bwana*. As the others listened attentively, she said, "Cook told me that Chanda was really beautiful and *Bwana* fell for her as soon as he saw her." Apparently, the Bwana started meeting the nanny after her work and also bought her jewellery. The *Dona* became suspicious and watched them closely.

"How romantic!" exclaimed one of the girls. "What happened next?"

"What do you think? She got what she deserved, of course," replied the girl who was relating the story. "She lost her job. Anyway, no one felt sorry for her because apparently, she had become 'too big for her boots' and was rude to everyone. Cook has also warned me to be careful. Bwana does have a wandering eye!"

The next story was about the white woman who left her husband for the gardener and went to live with him in the African compounds. I couldn't believe that anyone in their right mind could leave such luxury to live in those compounds. But, apparently, this woman did, and even took the trouble of learning the gardener's language and also got up early every morning to go to the market with other local women to buy food. The girl relating the story said that at first the local women shunned her and even laughed at her, so the gardener accompanied her everywhere. However, she soon made friends with some of the women, and they started accompanying her to the market.

When the family party was over, the *Dona* paid my cousin and her friend a lot of money. At least, it seemed a lot to me. She also gave me a bag full of sweets and biscuits. My cousin was also given a large piece of cake which she shared with me. I couldn't wait to show my mother the goodies I had been given by Mrs. Gregson!

That evening, when my father came home, my mother told him where my cousin and I had been that afternoon. She handed him a piece of cake and said, "The *Dona* seems such a nice woman. I hope Chilufya will soon be old enough to baby si…"

We stared in horror as my father snatched the little ceramic plate from her hand and smashed it against the wall, smearing it with cake, while bits of the broken plate lay scattered all over the floor. He then swiftly moved towards her and, in a voice that was almost hissing and choking with anger, said, "never, ever, bring crumbs and scraps from some *basungu's* table to this house! If you make any child of mine work as a nanny for anybody, I'll kill you!"

He then stormed out of the room, kicking a chair as he went and banging the bedroom door after him. Never before had I seen my dad so angry. Even my mother seemed visibly shaken and frightened. She stared at the bits of broken crockery on the floor, one of the handful of China that we possessed. Rarely did she use them except on special occasions. She had obviously made a special effort to please my father, but things had turned out terribly for her. Poor mama, I thought, she should have used our usual metal plates. Instinctively, I walked towards her and put my arms around her. Her quivering lips parted as she started crying, weeping as if her heart would break.

Much later, after she had cleaned up the mess and I was lying in bed, I heard her screaming at my father and demanding that he give her money for the bus fare back to her village. To shut off the angry sounds and screaming, I placed the pillow over my ears. When I woke up the following morning, I expected my mother to be all packed and ready to go. I took longer than usual to come out of my room, so as not to face what lay ahead. What would happen to us if she left? Who would help me get ready for school each morning? Who would prepare our meals? I knew that my dad would never let her take me and my younger sisters with her. But when I finally dragged myself to the kitchen, I found them standing close together, with dad's arm around her. There was no talk of going away. It was as if the incident of the previous evening had never taken place. Everything seemed normal again.

After that my mother never mentioned my going to work as a nanny, although she still did not believe in education for girls which my father did. He told me that girls could choose whatever they wanted to do in life. It was then that I told him that I wanted to be a doctor. You should have seen the look on my mother's face when I said that! She stared at me as if I were completely out of my mind.

My father however let out a hearty, joyous laugh. Patting me on the back, he said, "There's my girl! A doctor, eeh? Why not?"

Several months later, when we were at the Mine Hospital to visit my mother who had just given birth to my sister Bwembya, my father told the doctor who delivered her that I also wanted to be a doctor. The doctor gave me a big smile and said, "So you're the future doctor, hey? Well, begin by helping your mummy and daddy to look after the baby. Okay?"

I nodded vigorously. My father said afterwards that my baby sister Bwembya was very lucky to be delivered by one of very few African doctors in the country. He said, "This doctor is a beacon of light for us Africans. He is showing the *basungu*, that Africans are capable of looking after their own."

My father seemed to have this thing about *basungu*, the white people. At the time I was too young to understand the problems he and other African miners were facing. To me, he seemed unduly obsessed with *basungu*. As I grew older, I realized the terrible conditions under which he and other African men were working, compared to those of white miners. My father could see young, white boys, straight from school, quickly rise to high positions after being taught the basics of the job by men like him. They were now bosses of African men who were as old as their fathers. They didn't even bother to learn their names and, instead, called them boys. It really infuriated my father to be called "boy" by a young, inexperienced worker who got where he was in the system due to the colour of his skin. It made my father very upset to watch long -time miners who were even older than he was, being shouted at by these young people and addressed through words like, "Hey boy, *buya Lapa*! Come here!" Africans were treated like a mass of people without individual feelings and aspirations.

Soon the miners started organizing themselves to fight against the injustice and discrimination in the mines. The Trade Union Movement became the focal point, not only for workers' complaints, but also for the political fight in the country. My father, who attended union meetings, came home convinced that it was up to the Africans themselves to improve their lot. He would say to us, "what is important is what you think about yourself. If you don't believe in yourself, no one else will."

He loved telling us the story of "Tortoise and Hare," which went as follows: One hot and humid October afternoon, the animals had come for a drink at the only lake which still had water. The other small pond and wells had long dried up as the dry, rainless months dragged on. Hare, who loved teasing and embarrassing Tortoise in front of others, challenged him to a race. To the great surprise and amusement of the other animals, Tortoise agreed to race him. They laughed even louder when Hare quickly sprinted off, leaving Tortoise well behind. A few birds flew to the finishing line to wait for the winner. Monkey followed, hopping from tree to tree, while the other animals just ran through the forest towards the agreed finishing point.

Halfway through the race, Hare stopped under a tree for a short rest. He was dripping with sweat and muttered to himself, "Poor, silly Tortoise, why didn't he just admit that he was unable to compete with me? He would have saved us both having to race in this terrible heat! Why, I could win the race even if I was running with my eyes closed."

Feeling smug and pleased with himself, Hare leaned against the tree trunk. He closed his eyes slightly so as not to miss anything that was going on but the heat and humidity soon became unbearable for him "Maybe a short nap will give me more energy so that I'll run even faster than Leopard," he murmured to himself.

Hare fell asleep and soon started snoring. Then, he suddenly woke up at the sound of loud cheering. Rushing towards the finishing line, he came to a halt. From where he was, he could see slow, clumsy tortoise on Elephant's back, smiling and beaming at all the animals who were cheering him. With his head bowing low and his shoulders hunched, hare broke down and cried.

When someone asked, "Where on earth is Hare? What happened to him?" Hare quickly ran away, but the sounds of laughter and cheer followed him into the forest. The joke was now on him. Tortoise was the winner. He was slow, but sure. He would not give up easily.

That was the motto my father imparted to me when I left for Chipembi Girls' School. I was twelve years old when I went there. My mother was horrified at my being sent away so young, but my father had been told by one of the supervisors at his work place that it was a very good school. The supervisor had two daughters who were already in the school. He had been trying to convince my father that not every white person was bad. He told him that the missionaries who ran the school were dedicated people who treated the girls as if they were their own children. He also told him that most of the missionaries were not married and that they did not have children because they wanted to dedicate their lives to teaching the students and to bringing them up as the future leaders of the country. My father decided then that it was what he wanted for me.

My mother tried to talk my father out of sending me away. "What will happen to her if she becomes of age while she is at school? Who will show her what to do?"

For my mother, that was a crucial question. She wanted me to go through the same traditional rituals of puberty which she had experienced, way back in her village. There, at the onset of menstruation, a girl was placed in a secluded hut for a week or two, during which time she was told about the facts of life by older female relatives. They gave her lessons about what it now meant to 'mature,' not only in terms of physical growth and development, but in terms of what was expected as a future wife and mother. At the end of the seclusion period, there was a feast, a 'coming out ceremony,' marked by lots of food, drink and dancing all night to the accompaniment of drums, until the early hours of the morning.

But my mother's wishes and her plans for me could not be indulged. My father was determined that I should go, puberty or not. He brushed off her concerns by saying, "These missionaries are also women, so they'll know what to do. Besides, these puberty ceremonies are only an excuse for people to get drunk and to rush girls into early marriages." As soon as the letter of acceptance arrived from Chipembi, we rushed to buy the things that were on the list of clothing: six dresses, six underwear, two pairs of black or brown shoes, one pair of boots, two night dresses, soap, a toothbrush, toothpaste, slippers and so on. The list seemed to go on and on.

After the shopping was completed, I had more things than I have ever owned before. It was only much later, when I was older, that I realized what a huge sacrifice it must have been for my parents to send me to that school and to pay the fees.

The supervisor's daughters were asked by my father to look after me on the train. I had lots of questions to ask them about the school, but as soon as Mwaba and Chibuye saw their friends, they forgot all about me. Well, that's not exactly true. To be fair to them, I must admit that they did try to include me in their conversation, but I still felt out of place. How could I discuss things and people I didn't know? They were mentioning names of people I hadn't met and places I didn't know. One of the girls they were talking about was Mukando. But what did I care whether or not she was going back to school? The rumour was that she was pregnant and would not be returning to school. Apparently Mukando was often in trouble and had been called to the principal's office for trying to sneak out of the school grounds to meet her boyfriend.

After discussing Mukando, the conversation drifted to how they had spent their school holidays. The chattering of the girls, each trying to get their story heard, was deafening. The train was heading towards Broken Hill, so named after a place in Australia. It was also a mining town, producing mostly lead and zinc. It was renamed Kabwe after the country became the Republic of Zambia. As the train slowly pulled out of the station and gathered speed as it moved on, Chibuye told me that the next major stop would be Chisamba, where we would disembark. I looked out the window and let my eyes move with the savanna landscape that seemed to be racing with the train. I felt as if the large farms of corn, orange groves, and grazing cattle were speeding along with us. But the constant change of scenery of course meant that it was the train moving and not the whole landscape.

I knew when I heard the delighted shouts of "Chisamba" that we had arrived. Otherwise, the place looked small and insignificant.

There was a simple plaque that read, 'CHISAMBA.' A stampede followed as the girls grabbed their things and tried to rush off the train. I stayed close to Chibuye and Mwaba and later got onto the same bus as the girls were climbing onto any transport that was available, including lorries and other trucks. There were teachers trying to organize the students so that they did not rush in all directions or overload one or two vehicles.

The bus trip took us through more farmland with corn fields, potatoes, orchards of tropical fruit and cattle farms. The farm houses were huge and far between, surrounded by large tracts of land. Every now and then we spotted a farmer on a tractor or farm hands picking fruit.

When we finally arrived at the school, Mwaba offered to take me around and help find my dormitory. After we found out that I was in House 5, she accompanied me as far as the entrance and then said, "I'd better go now. Both Chibuye and I are in House 14. Let us know if you need anything."

"Thank you very much for everything," I said quietly, as I watched her go away. It was then that homesickness and an intense feeling of loneliness hit me. I stared at the door, one hand firmly gripping my suitcase, while the other clutched my handbag. I don't know how long I would have stood there, if the door hadn't suddenly swung open. Two girls came rushing out, and after making faces and nudging each other, one of them said, "another *puku*!" Then off they went, laughing and giggling.

I swore under my breath. How I hated that word, *puku*! – the derogatory term for 'New Girl!', which they used to taunt new girls on the train! I had seen and heard new girls being taunted on the train and had wondered how people could be so cruel and insensitive. Since the door was left open by the two girls, I drapped my weary and reluctant legs inside the dormitory. Once inside, I stood rooted to one spot, my hands still clutching my belongings. A girl who seemed to be eighteen or nineteen saw me and came forward, her hand outstretched in greeting.

"Hello, welcome to House 5. My name is Nguza, and I'm the House Mother. What's your name?"

"Chilufya."

"Well, Chilufya, please come with me. I'll show you your bed and locker." I followed her through the dormitory which was divided into several sections, with subdivisions containing beds, lockers and small closets for each girl.

As I started unpacking my things and hanging my clothes, I felt a big lump in my throat and tears in my eyes. Why cry? I sternly reproached myself. What good will that do? Will it change the fact that I was all alone with these strangers, in the middle of nowhere? The best thing was to stop wallowing in self-pity and get on with the business of settling down in this new place. I was almost done with my unpacking when another girl walked in. One could see from the noisy way she was dragging her suitcase and the deep frown on her face, that she was very angry about something. Throwing the suitcase onto the bed, she muttered, "I'm sick and tired of this stupid word called *puku*. If anyone calls me *puku* again, I'll bash them up."

There was a deathly silence as everyone stopped what they were doing and stared at her. The House Mother soothingly said to her, "I would just ignore them if I were you. We were all new once and were called *puku*."

A girl who was lying on the bed reading a novel said, "I wouldn't go around threatening people if I were you, or you'll be the one who will be bashed up."

There was laughter from the others, but everybody soon got back to what they had been doing. I gave the new girl a furtive smile and she smiled back. Then she said, "Hi! Are you also new here?"

"Yes. Hi," I said, as I stretched out my hand in greeting. But she ignored it.

"I'm Tengani," she said, and started unpacking her things. I watched her in silence as she grabbed handfuls of clothing and shoved them into her locker and hung others in the closet. A few minutes later she turned to me and asked, "What do you think of this place?"

"Er ... okay, I suppose. Too early to tell," I stammered.

"It's not okay for me. I wish I wasn't here."

But she did not say it as if she were nervous or worried about the new place, the way I was. There was an air of defiance and an

'I don't care' attitude about her.

After dinner, we all met in the living room and were told about the house rules. The House Mother explained the duty roster for cleaning rooms, cooking and washing dishes. She told us that the younger, inexperienced girls would be placed with the older ones so that they could help with the cleaning, while the older girls would be responsible for preparing meals. She ended by saying that bedtime rules had to be "strictly adhered to."

Later, when the lights went off to indicate bedtime, I was already in bed. My eyes were heavy with exhaustion. It had been a very long day. Just as I was about to drift off to sleep, I was jolted by a sharp scream from Tengani. Pandemonium broke out as everyone started screaming, jumping up and down on their beds, running in all directions and bumping into each other in the dark. Someone screamed, "It's a snake!" If there's anything that really scares me to death, it's a snake or the mere mention of that reptile. I jumped from bed to bed and quickly rushed out into the next room, just missing treading on an equally frightened frog that was heading in the same direction. The torch that the House Mother shone around revealed another frog. So there were shouts of "Frogs, frogs, it's not a snake!" But even the fact that it was frogs still had the girls running around in panic.

When I asked where the light switch was, someone said that the generator had been turned off for the night and that was why they were using torches. But someone else lit a lamp and there was more light. The House Mother tried to appeal for silence and calm, but her voice was drowned by the noise. Calm was finally restored when the teacher on duty, who rushed to our dormitory after hearing all the shouting and noise, blew a whistle.

"What on earth is going on here?" she shouted above the noise. "Two frogs jumped from Tengani's bed," explained the House Mother.

"Frogs? How did they get there, and who is Tengani?" the teacher asked.

"I am here," Tengani replied, her arms folded across her chest, her body leaning against the wall. That look of defiance was back on her face. Was this the same girl who had screamed in fright?

"Tengani, how did the frog get into your bed'?" demanded the teacher.

"That's what I would like to know. I think someone here did it."

"Which one of you played the silly prank on this girl?" asked the teacher, her eyes searching the room. There was absolute silence. No one moved. Not a word. Nothing.

"Someone here must have done it. Are you going to own up or should I punish everybody?"

There were murmurs of disapproval at the idea of everybody being punished for something they didn't do.

"I think I know who did it," said Tengani. All eyes turned to her. The air was thick with tension and suspense.

"Yes?" encouraged the teacher. "Well, who is it?"

"I said I thought I knew. Just a suspicion. I have no evidence."

"In future, don't open your mouth unless you know what you are talking about," snapped the teacher, and turning to the rest, she yelled "Get back to bed, all of you! If I hear any more noise, even whispers, you'll all be punished."

Things settled down, and after making sure that everyone was in bed, the teacher left. The House Mother went around the rooms checking every bed, and then retired to her own room. I was about to close my eyes when I saw Tengani get out of bed and walk towards Kabinda's bed. Kabinda was the girl who earlier on had warned her not to threaten others, or she would have her head bashed. I overheard Tengani's angry voice whispering, "I know you did it, you coward and fool! I only saved your skin because I don't tell on compatriots." With that she marched back to her bed. Compatriots? What on earth was she talking about? But I was just too tired to bother finding out. I soon drifted off to sleep.

The following morning, much to my pleasant surprise, Tengani asked me to walk with her to school. On our way, she started talking about the fight for freedom and independence. She complained that being at school was a waste of time.

"If all our compatriots stand united against the British, we shall win the war."

"But we are only kids, what can we do?" I asked.

"In times of war, there are no kids. You've got to grow up fast," she declared.

She was far too serious about things, I thought, far too serious. But I was still fascinated by her. We stayed close through Assembly, where the whole school gathered for prayers and announcements, and then on to our classroom. When we got to the classroom, we found most desks occupied so we couldn't sit together. I sat near the front while Tengani took the remaining space in the back.

"Hi," said the girl sitting next to me.

"Hi," I answered back.

"I'm Likande. What's your name?"

"Chilufya ..."

"Good morning, girls. My name is Miss Dale. I am your maths teacher."

Great! I thought to myself, my favourite subject!

"Oh, no! I hate mathematics!" whispered Likande in my ear.

"What I hate is history," I whispered back.

"But history is fun and so easy. It is my fav ..."

"Okay, you two. Quiet, please," called out Miss Dale.

History, fun and easy? How could anyone enjoy having to remember dates and events that happened a long time ago? Well, I supposed, each one for herself. She must be wondering why I like figures.

Chapter Three

TENGANI

It is a strange feeling to look into one's past. One wonders whether, given another chance, one would have done things differently. Nobody likes to be called names, the way I've been: pushy, crazy, nasty, and so on. I've also been called a revolutionary and a rebel: those I like. Neither do I mind being a hard nut to crack.

When my father sent me to Chipembi School at the age of twelve ... well, twelve and a half, to be exact, most girls were scared of me. They thought I was a bully and a trouble-maker. Many thought if they became friendly with me, they too would get into trouble. In what way was I a trouble-maker? For believing in freedom and independence for my country? Because I told my geography teacher that it wasn't David Livingstone, the British explorer, who discovered the mighty waterfalls locally known as Mosi O Tunya, but which he renamed the Victoria Falls after Queen Victoria?

I can't even remember the number of times I was punished for things like that. Being made to stand in front of the class for the whole period. Standing in one spot, like a statue. Not moving. Not shifting or turning. Just still, at the same spot. My arms, feet and legs ached. It was as if I was carrying heavy iron. Some girls giggled and laughed, stopping only when they were threatened with the same punishment. Sometimes I wished they would experience what I was going through. I'm sure they would never have laughed at me again.

I went through every kind of punishment that was available for naughty and difficult girls. I was made to water the vegetable garden and sweep floors. That was the worst punishment and everybody dreaded it. It was code-named H.L., for hard labour. When this didn't seem to work, they changed to mothering me. Sometimes I wondered which was worse, that, or H.L.

One day I was sent to the principal's office for having told the history teacher that I thought the tribal chiefs were tricked into giving up their land by the British. Her face turned a bright red. With her voice shaking and almost choking with emotion, she screamed, "Tengani, come here at once! Right now!"

Slowly I rose from the chair, and it made a screeching sound as I pulled it back. Then I sauntered to the front. Her knuckles were a deathly white as she continuously twisted her hands. Was it nerves, or was she imagining her hands around my neck? When I got closer, she said, "Likande, please keep order while I take Tengani to the Principal."

Likande! She was my friend, but how different we were! We were both sixteen years old then. She was a prefect, and I, the so-called trouble-maker. I often wondered why she remained my friend despite all the problems I seemed to cause. At first, I hated her do-gooder attitude, like a missionary out to convert a pagan. But I soon realized that, she was a genuine and sincere person. I also felt that she really liked me. She wasn't scared of me. She told me off if I did something wrong, but also defended me against those who attacked me. We were poles apart, yet something drew us together. We became a threesome, Likande, Chilufya, and I. "The Three Musketeers," we were called.

When we arrived at the office, Miss Brown explained what had happened and said that I was a "rude and difficult child." She wiped her face with a handkerchief and waved her hands in exasperation.

"It's alright, leave her with me," said the Principal. After the teacher left, she turned to me and in a soft, soothing voice said, "Tengani, what is it, child? What exactly is troubling you?"

My lip quivered, and I bit it hard to keep it from trembling. I was used to being punished and being told that I was a naughty girl. Threats and punishment I could handle. I was used to them. That put me on the war front. But this made me uneasy. Very uneasy, indeed. It played havoc with my emotions. My throat tightened and my heart ached. I quickly looked away…"

"Well, maybe you'd rather not talk about it now. Why don't we pray about this and ask God for guidance?"

I nodded and closed my eyes. She asked God to help me and teach me to be patient. God to help me? Where was He when I needed Him most? Where was He when I cried for His help? He let me down at the most crucial and desperate moment of my entire life. I'll never, never forget that day as long as I live, I said to myself over and over. The lump in my throat disappeared and it was replaced by a feeling of anger that seemed to consume my whole being. I closed my eyes tight that I began to perspire, and my heart started beating at incredible speed. I felt myself drifting back in time… the screams were getting louder and louder ….

I flinched as the man on horseback swung the whip and lashed against an old, wobbly man. I cried out to my mother, my eyes darting from side to side. Where was she? One minute she had been next to me and now she was gone. "Mummy, mummy . . ." I called again, tears pouring down my face.

Then I saw her, but she was waving me away. "Run, Tengani, run. Please go home …" There were people everywhere, running in all directions, screaming and crying out as the white mounted policemen continued lashing out. The air was filled with the smell of *Kashasu*, illegal home brew, pouring out of the huge containers that had been kicked down by the police. I almost fell into the sticky, slippery stuff. I spotted my mother again, as she was rushing towards me. However, before she could get to me, the hissing and cracking whip caught her. It cut her right across her big belly.

"You crazy monster! How can you strike a pregnant woman! You devil … you …" yelled my aunt Tilyenji, as she picked up a stone and hurled it at the man who had hit my mother. A cousin grabbed me by the hand and we ran into the cornfields and hid. Moments later, we heard the galloping horses speeding away. We made our way back to the village.

As we approached the village, I saw a crowd gathered around someone. A cold shiver shook my body when I saw her. It was my mother. She lay in a pool of blood, and two men were trying to lift her. My aunt was weeping and wailing, as was the group of women with her. I ran towards them as fast as my legs could carry me, but someone grabbed me midway. "Let go of me, I want mummy," I screamed. But they continued to hold me, shielding me from even looking at her as they carried her into my aunt's house. A few minutes later my aunt came out of the hut. I wriggled free from the hands that were holding me and ran to her.

"You poor baby," she cried, "your mother is gone. She's left us. She's dead, baby. Dead. Oh, my sister ..."

Dead? Just like that? Gone? How could she die like that, leaving me?

I couldn't believe that she was dead. I moved around in a daze, not really comprehending what had happened. Was that how people died? One minute she was talking to me, and the next she was gone. But my inner thoughts of anguish and torment were disrupted by the arrival of my father. Someone had rushed to our village to get him. My heart went out to my father when I saw him. His eyes were red from crying, and his voice broke as he moaned, *Mukazi wanga*, my dear wife, what have they done to you? How can you leave me alone? What will I do with Tengani? She's only eight years old!"

Tears poured down his face as he wailed. I had never seen my father cry before. Moving towards him and holding onto his hand, I murmured, "I'll be okay, pa, I'll be fine."

But he quickly let go of my hand as he angrily moved towards my aunt and shouted, "You're the cause of my wife's death, you brewer of illicit *Kachasu*! I told her to keep away from you, but she wouldn't listen. Look now what you've done ..."

"Please, Mr. Nvula calm down," appealed a man standing next to my aunt, "don't blame your sister-in-law for your wife's death. It's those colonial police. We must remove them from our country!"

My sixteen-year-old brother came running as soon as he heard the news. As he wept, he swore that he would go to the Boma, the provincial capital, then known as Fort Jameson, but later renamed Chipata. He said he would complain to the District Commissioner. People appealed to him to calm down and to "leave things to adults." But his anger and hatred for mother's killer shone in his teary eyes. I felt the same anger going through my entire body. I swore that whoever had caused my mother's death would pay. He and his people would pay, some day. When I grow up, mama, I'll make sure that they pay, one way or another, I promised.

After the funeral my brother left home. My father tried to stop him from going, telling him that he had to complete school first. But he wouldn't listen. He announced that he was quitting school and that no one would force him to stay. As he bade me farewell, he whispered, "Don't worry, Tengani, everything will be okay."

But things were not alright. The following months were the loneliest and most miserable that I ever experienced. My father told me that Mandarena, my mother's cousin, would move in with us, "to help with the house and taking care of you." I soon found out that I wasn't the one she had really come to take care of. Within two weeks of her arrival she moved her things into father's room. Six months later they were married. They didn't even have the decency to wait one year, the usual mourning period. As soon as Mandarena was officially Mrs Nvula, she started bossing me around and treating me like her little slave. "Tengani, look at the dishes you just washed. They're filthy. Wash them again!" or "Tengani, I told you to sweep the floor. Why haven't you done it yet?"

How I hated her! What a hypocrite! Shedding crocodile tears at my mother's funeral, when she couldn't wait to replace her. She had moaned and wailed over her "dear cousin," but as soon as the funeral was over, offered herself to "come and take care of Tengani."

Taking care of me, indeed? I should as well have had a stepmother from another planet than the so-called cousin of my mother. I begged my father to let me go and stay with my aunt, but he wouldn't hear it. "I don't want you killed, too," he said.

What finally saved me from my stepmother was the arrival of my brother. He came for a visit and told us that he was working as a security guard for a construction company. I begged him to let me go with him. At first he was hesitant, but when I told him how terrible Mandarena had been to me, he agreed to take me along. My father feebly argued against my going, but soon gave in. I suppose he was in a way relieved, as he was tired of intervening in the constant fights between Mandarena and me. However, he insisted on going with us to check out my brother's place.

Chenjerani lived in a two-room "bachelor's quarters" with a live-in girlfriend called Dora. My father strongly disapproved of the arrangement, and when Dora was out of earshot he lectured my brother about "these cheap street girls." Chenjerani explained that Dora was "no street girl," and that she first came to visit her brother who lived next door. Apparently, "one thing led to another," and she moved in with him after his roommate left.

After my father left I settled into my new life with Chenjerani and Dora. Dora was really sweet and treated me as if I were her own younger sister. For the first time since my mother's death I felt relaxed and happy. Dora even accompanied me to the local school to have me enrolled. She was only seventeen, but acted like a very responsible adult. "If there had been a school so close to my home, I would still be in school," she declared.

During my second month at my brother's place, I found out that his home was one of the meeting places for politicians and freedom fighters. They rotated the meetings, and once a month it was at my brother's house. Fifteen to twenty people would squeeze into the tiny room, some sitting on the floor and the bed. At first, he sent me to bed just before the meeting started, but later, allowed me to stay. Most of the talk was about the Federation of Rhodesia and Nyasaland, which was opposed by most Africans. They said it was imposed on black people by a small group of white settlers. They also argued that all the wealth from the copper mines and the farms in Northern Rhodesia was being used to develop Southern Rhodesia, the place the whites felt would be their future home. They never even imagined that Southern Rhodesia would also undergo political change, and eventually become independent and change its name to Zimbabwe. But this was the 1950's, and the problem at hand was the Federation. The question of independence was not yet major even though it was considered the goal by most Africans.

My brother was the leader of the Youth Wing of the Freedom Movement in our area. His job was to recruit young people for the party.

One evening, as the meeting was in progress, we heard loud knocks, followed by kicks on the door. Someone outside yelled, "Open up! Police!"

With a swift movement, Dora grabbed me by the arm and we ran into my room, where she pushed me under the bed and then quickly followed. We heard scuffles and shouts in the next room. Then someone said, "Chenjerani Nvula, you are under arrest, and so are all of you attending this illegal meeting."

Chenjerani said that it wasn't a meeting, but a party. The man shouted at him and said, "Do you think we're fools? Party, hey? Where's the music? Where's the food and drinks? You won't get away with this! We'll lock you up for good. You'll rot in prison!"

There were more scuffles, and then my brother's voice shouting, "Let go of my hand! You have no right to push me around. You've not charged me with anything. Where's your warrant?"

"We've been watching you, *kaffir* boy! You thought you were clever, but you got a nasty surprise, hey? We have our own informers."

"Wait, I need some stuff, clothes, toothpaste and toothbrush ..."

"Hah, hah! Since when did you Africans worry about clothes and toothbrushes? You used to wear animal skins and bark cloth!"

"Yes," agreed another voice, "we bloody taught you how to be civilized, and now you kick us in the face. Ungrateful niggers!"

"We'll complain to the United Nations. We'll also report you to the British Government," warned Mr. Bunga, who had earlier reported that he had just arrived from Lusaka.

"Come on, all of you. Get out or we'll shoot. Dead men don't talk. Not even to the United Nations! Hah, hah."

We heard several car doors being shut and then the cars moving away. I was trembling with fear. What would they do to my brother? First my mother, and now my brother? Where are you, oh God? Why are you letting these people treat us like this? I closed my eyes tightly as I prayed to God and asked Him to bring back my brother quickly and unharmed.

"Come on, let's go. Quick!" said Dora.

"Where to?" I asked as I crawled from under the bed.

"Just follow me." She knocked on the third door from ours. We saw someone peep through the window and then, as if to make sure, he asked who it was. After Dora identified herself, the door opened. The man of the house said he was sorry about my brother, but there was nothing he could do about it. He suggested we go to the Head of the Section of our area, who for some reason had not been at the meeting.

When we went to him, he informed us that there was nothing he could do at that time of night, but that we should all meet at the police station the following morning at ten o'clock.

There was a huge crowd when we arrived there. The Section Head had obviously done what he had promised to do, "to mobilize all the people." We stood right on the edge as there was no room to move closer to the police building. The crowd started off peacefully. They were singing political songs, demanding freedom, and chanting, "Let our people go! Let our people go!" But when nothing happened and two hours passed without any sign of the people who had been arrested, the mood of the crowd turned ugly. A few people started throwing stones at the police station and broke windows. Others followed suit, and there were more and more stones being hurled at the building. That was when the riot police arrived, supported by mounted police. There was panic and pandemonium as the crowd tried to disperse. Like someone caught in a horror film that kept being played over and over again, I heard the crack of the whips from the mounted police. It was now four years since my mother's death, but it was like yesterday. My whole body started shaking and shivering, as I covered my face with my hands to shut off the horrible sight.

"Come on, Tengani, don't just stand there," called Dora as she started running away. Being on the fringe of the crowd proved to be a blessing in disguise for us. Most of those up front were caught between the police building and the crowd behind them. They had no room to move and were being squashed from the back and front.

We later learned that some people were hospitalized as a result of the injuries they sustained in the stampede. It was a miracle that no one died. We also learned that my brother and the other people were moved away to another town, to avoid further demonstrations. Nobody seemed to know exactly where they were taken, or for how long.

"Dora, what will happen to me now?" I asked.

"You'll go to school, as usual. And we'll wait for Chenjerani."

I was about to ask her how we would live since Chenjerani was the one working, but decided not to say anything. She seemed so sure of everything that I was sure things would be fine.

I was back to school the following morning and everyone was talking about my brother. Since he was a Youth Leader, he had tried to recruit people from nearby schools and communities and was therefore, quite well known. But he was no hero to everyone. Some called him a trouble-maker, and their parents forbade them to go to the meetings which he organized. But most kids in the area liked him, and being his sister made me quite a popular girl in school. However, few seemed to want to be too close to me after he was arrested. Even people I considered my friends were cool towards me. That was when I realized how fickle human nature could be. They were friends when things were going well, but chickened out at the first sign of trouble.

As if things at school were not bad enough, more awaited me home. My heart sank as soon as I saw my father. He was sitting outside on a chair, looking flustered and waving his arms about. Dora was sitting on a reed mat next to him, her head slightly bent down, and gave my father an occasional nod or shook her head every few minutes. She appeared to be under intense interrogation.

I stood and watched them for a couple of minutes as I debated whether or not to retrace my steps and run away or join them. But where would I go? My so-called friends had just deserted me.

"Oh, there she is!" boomed my father's voice, almost making me jump.

"Hello, papa," I said in a soft meek voice.

"Come here. You see, now, what I warned you about your brother, but you wouldn't listen. No one listens to me. Not you, and certainly not your brother. You've both been nothing but trouble since your mother died. Chenjerani thinks he was born to save the world. Well, let's see now whether he will save himself from the trouble he has gotten himself into. As for you, you had better start packing your things. You're coming with me right now. Quick! We have a bus to catch."

"But my school ..."

"Dora will tell them that I came to get you. And talking about schools, I've decided to send you to boarding school, a place called Chipembi."

"What? Boarding school? Where? Why?"

"It's a very good school. I heard about it from Father Jones at the mission station. He highly recommended it and even helped me apply."

"You applied without telling me about it?"

"I knew this was no place for you. I could almost smell trouble brewing here whenever I came to visit. All that talk by Chenjerani and his friends, insults and cursing white people. Some white people may be bad, but so are some black people. But you can't accuse every ..."

"I don't want to go. I won't go!"

"Yes, you will. You have no choice."

"I ..."

"Tengani, come on, let's get your things," said Dora. "Your father is right. This is no place for you. I'm also thinking of going away. Maybe for a few weeks, maybe longer. I don't know."

That was how I ended up at Chipembi Girls School. But I swore that no matter what happened, I would not fall for the missionary charm the way my father obviously had, or the way some of the girls appeared to worship the ground on which the missionaries walked. As far as I was concerned, they were responsible for all our troubles. Chenjerani and his friends were right. If it weren't for the missionaries, explorers and colonialists like Cecil Rhodes would not have come to Africa. No missionary would pull wool over my eyes. They could not deceive me with their sweet smiles and religious talk. They could not pretend to mother me. Nobody could ever replace my mother . . . not my stepmother, and certainly not the missionaries. So when I responded "Amen," at the end of the Principal's prayer, it was a promise to myself, my mom and my brother that the war would continue. We would fight to the bitter end, until Freedom Day.

The problem was getting the girls organized. Chilufya and Likande tried to talk me out of it.

"You'll be the loser, Tengani," admonished Likande. "What will you do if they dismiss you from school? Where will you go?"

"What kind of job will you get without completing school? Nursemaid?" added Chilufya.

"A what? Why are you two so concerned about jobs? What you will do, where you will go, and so forth! Who cares about school in the face of exploitation? You're both nothing but Uncle Toms! You're the ones who will be the losers! When we get our independence, you can pack up and go with your missionary friends to England!" I walked away, leaving them staring at me with shocked and stunned expression on their faces.

But I paid for it later. They did not talk to me for a whole week. For seven whole days, they avoided me like a leper. They would giggle and whisper to each other when they saw me. My best friends were now my worst enemies. I felt miserable and betrayed. What had I really done wrong? Was it wrong to fight for freedom, justice and equality? Would they rather be ruled by Britain forever? Admittedly, I shouldn't have called them Uncle Toms, but was that reason enough to end our friendship?

Anyway, the feud dragged on, as Chilufya spent more and more time in Likande's dormitory to avoid encounters with me. I lay awake at night, thinking. I also wondered whether they were right. After all they were concerned about me and my future. Even if I wanted independence, I would still need to work, feed myself and buy clothes. I finally made peace with them. It wasn't easy and both sides had a lot of pride to swallow. But we did it.

Our friendship grew stronger with each passing year. Instead of trying to change each other, we learned to respect each other's differences. It wasn't easy, and although there were times when we still argued, our friendship flourished.

Academically, Likande and Chilufya were competitors, striving to be top of the class. The British system was like a pyramid. The base was broad, but the top, narrow. As each cohort moved from class to class, many fell by the wayside. Only the best went on to the top. I would probably have fallen by the wayside, if it had not been for Chilufya and Likande. They dragged me to their "study sessions," and we passed the exams that marked each hurdle, until we got to the final year.

I couldn't believe that I actually survived the gruelling years at the school and that we were about to sit the finals or "the biggie," as some girls called it. Relief at finishing was marked by trepidation and anxiety about what lay ahead. The idea of parting from my friends was foremost one hot October afternoon, as the three of us lay on a batik cloth under a huge fig tree, studying for our final exams.

The air was hot, muggy and humid, a sign that the rainy season was about to begin. The rainy months of November through April are my favourite. Many a year, rain has fallen during the month of October. I could almost feel the raindrops and smell the wet earth. I put aside the book I was reading and let my thoughts drift to the previous year, when we greeted the first raindrops with the Lozi song Likande taught us: "*Pula, pula, nela kapili, luche malaka*" (rain, rain, fall quickly so we can eat squash). We jumped up and down as we sang the song. But instead of "malaka," I sang "mango," as I don't care very much for squash. For me, the rainy season is a time for eating those delicious, juicy, yellow, sun-ripened mangoes. My mouth watered just thinking of them. I glanced at my friends, trying to catch their attention and remind them of the coming mango season, but their eyes were still glued to the books. Oh well, I would daydream a while longer.

But my thoughts again were of our coming crossroads. The time that would mark the end of our time together at Chipembi. After that, it would be each one for herself. I would be parting not only from two special friends, but from the two girls who had become like family to me. My father's house no longer felt like home for me. His life was wrapped up in that of his wife and three children. Nothing I did seemed right to any of them. At first, my father used to make the effort of listening to my side of things. Now, he took everything his wife said and her complaints about me as the gospel truth.

The last school holiday ended in a shouting match between Mandarena and I. As usual, she started bossing me around, telling me to do this and that. Her own children sat around doing nothing. When I pointed out that Nkwazi, who was then ten years old, could also help, Mandarena became angry and said I was a "spoilt girl." I said that she was the one spoiling her children. My father then shouted at me and said, "Don't be rude to your mother. Apologize to her!"

"She's not my mother, and never will be!" I screamed back.

So home was not really home for me. My brother was still languishing in prison. Where I would go after finishing school, was a problem. But first things first. I still had to sit for exams. Picking up geography book, I started reading about the rotation of the earth, why it is daytime in one part of the world when another part is night. Something about different seasons, and the very cold winters in the northern hemisphere and things like snow. What was snow, anyway? All I could recall was our geography teacher going on about how lucky we were to be "living in paradise." According to her, we were crazy for complaining about the weather. She said, "Here you are on this plateau four thousand feet above sea level, winters not too cold, summers not too hot. If Scotland were like this, I wouldn't have left!" She couldn't believe that sweaters were warm enough for our winters.

It was true that most of the year the weather was good and comfortable. But paradise or not, the heat that afternoon was really getting to me. I just couldn't concentrate. I switched to history. I opened the book on a chapter that read, "The Partition of Africa." I felt my hands tightening their hold over the page and my body felt tense. Anger seeped through my veins. What right did they have to sit around a table out there in Europe and divide our continent among themselves. They drew lines that cut across tribal and ethnic groups. My tribe, in the Eastern Province, was divided into two. One section remained in Northern Rhodesia (later Zambia), while the other went to Nyasaland (later Malawi). Many families found themselves belonging to two different countries.

While the big fish divided the continent on national lines ... this country for Britain, that for France, the other for Germany, and so forth, the white settlers and adventurers grabbed large tracts of land for themselves. A bottle of gin or whisky could buy a couple thousand acres of land. Others tempted the local chiefs with pieces of cloth. Still others used plain trickery.

One such story was a mineral prospector who convinced a chief to give him rights to "everything underground." At first the chief was bewildered. What on earth did the man want the underground for? Most people wanted land on which they could grow crops. The chief thought the man must be crazy, but all the same, he agreed to the man's request. It was only later, when his people were moved from their villages to leave their land for mining, that the chief realized he had been tricked.

But the day of reckoning was coming for all those exploiters. Freedom and independence were on the horizon. My duty, and that of everyone who wanted to help, was to redress the wrongs done to our ancestors. To fight for independence and get our land back. To pave the way for our future and hand over to posterity a land of milk and honey. Our leaders were already telling us that our country would be called Zambia, after the mighty Zambezi river. I would join the fight and help set my brother and all the freedom fighters free.

Yes, I would be part of the action. Right there, in the centre of it all, making history. I slightly moved my position on the batik cloth and leaned back against the fig tree. With my eyes closed, my mind drifted off ....

There I was on the platform, addressing a multitude of people. I could almost smell the sweat on their bodies as they leaned forward, straining to get close to me. My voice, clear and loud, shouted into the microphone. "Ladies and gentlemen, we've got to fight for independence now!"

"Independence now!" roared back the crowd. "Zambia, Zambia!"

"Zambia, Zambia!" they chanted.

Then I saw two hands waving across my face, and Chilufya was calling out, "Tengani, wake up! Wake up!"

"I'm not asleep."

"We were just saying that we should take a break and go back to my dorm, but you seemed asleep or far away from here," said Likande.

"I know, I've not really been here."

"Not been here? What do you mean?" asked Chilufya.

"Physically here, of course. But not mentally," I explained.

"You mean you've not been studying?" probed Likande.

"Not really, Likande. I've been thinking about more profound things."

"Such as?" asked Chilufya, cynically.

"Such as the future of this country. That is more important than reading all this colonial indoctrination and the irritating stuff about partition of Africa."

"Here we go again. Our devoted patriot! So what are you going do about it?" asked Likande, in a mocking and teasing voice.

"The question, Likande, is, what are you, Chilufya, me and everybody else going to do about it? Shall we let the British and other colonial powers continue to treat us like subhumans? To continue locking up innocent people like my brother? How would you feel, were your brother in prison now? I bet you wouldn't sit back, looking so smug and indifferent!"

"Well, not every Briton or European agrees with what these settlers have done. Our teachers are ..."

"To hell with our teachers, Likande! You've been so brainwashed that you no longer have a mind of your own. Don't think being a Head Girl gives you the right to tell others what to do all the time. You're nothing but a colonial mouthpiece!"

"How dare you talk to me like that! Is this what I get for being your friend?"

"Okay, girls," appealed Chilufya, "there's no need to get worked up over this. Tengani, I just want to make one point clear. Not all of us headed towards throwing stones against the British. We'll work for independence in our own way. I want to be a doctor so that I can help our people."

"And I would like to be ..."

"You, Likande, will be a nun, You'll pray for our souls!"

Likande glared at me for a moment, and then grabbed her books and marched off.

"Wait for me, Likande," called Chilufya, as she also picked up her books and the cloth and ran after her.

I watched as my friends walked away from me. There, again, my big mouth had done it. What was wrong with me? Why did I get so emotional and aggressive about things? On the other hand, why were they so blind and ignorant about what was going on? Surely, they were the ones who would benefit from our fight and struggle? They were pursuing self-centered careers – university and big money. I might even die fighting for my country! No, I was not the one who owed my friends an apology. They owed me one.

But the thought of cold treatment from them made me apologize before the day was over. I approached Likande as she was talking to two other girls.

"Likande, can I please talk to you ... I mean, when you're finished here."

"Oh, please go ahead, we're done. Bye, Likande, and thanks for your help," said one of them.

As soon as they were out of earshot, I said, "Likande, I'm terribly sorry. Please forgive me." The words sounded as if they were coming from someone else. It was hard. Really hard, especially as I still felt strongly about the issue.

"It's okay, Tengani. I was also to blame. I shouldn't have teased you. I wish I had your courage. I think you're better than most of us."

"Me? Me, better than you? Are you kidding? Please, don't start teasing me again."

"No, I'm serious. I think you are great."

"No, you're the great one."

"No, you are."

"You."

"You."

"Hey, what's all this?" Chilufya asked smiling, as she approached and noticed us pointing fingers at each other.

"I was just telling Tengani that she is great, and will one day make great a politician," said Likande.

"You know, Tengani, I should introduce you to my aunt, Mama Mulenga. She's a fanatic and is at every demo that's going on in Luanshya. She even goes to other towns to show her support," said Chilufya.

"I would love to meet her," I said.

"At least both of you seem to know what you want to be. A doctor and a politician. But what lies ahead for me? I would love to be ..."

"A nun?"

"Tengani! Don't start again," shouted Likande, as she moved towards me.

I ran into the back garden of her dormitory, calling out, "Catch me if you can!"

They both ran after me, quickening their pace, as we went into the fresh evening air.

Chapter Four

LIKANDE

I just couldn't get to sleep that night, at least, not until the very early hours of the morning. I lay there, my thoughts in a turmoil. I kept tossing and turning all night long. Ridiculous, really, when you think about it. But for me, the idea of looking back on my life had suddenly become a nightmare. It was as if I had finally come to the end and it was Judgement Day.

It's been fifteen years since I graduated from university. As expected, I passed with honours and I was ready to face the world. Even as I adorned myself with the graduation gown and cap, I could hear echoes from my childhood, "very bright," "she's a born leader." I was intoxicated with the energy of youth and high expectations for the future.

The question haunting me now was, what had I really accomplished? Had I done what I had set out to do? Had I fulfilled any of the expectations that my family, my teachers and other people had formed?

To find out a little about what those expectations were, let me take you back in time, to where it all began; to my childhood.

I was born of strict disciplinarian parents, the eldest of six children, four boys and two girls. There were strict and definite rules about manners and codes of behaviour in our family and like most children, we looked for opportunities to misbehave or get at our parents during their weakest moments, which was often when they had guests. My brothers Mbuye and Mwenda were particularly adept at this. They would ask for things from my parents when we had visitors, things they very well knew were not allowed. However, since my parents were very busy with their guests, they would nod their heads just to get rid of Mbuye or Mwenda. If I did the same, I would later be reminded that I was "older and should know better."

The same thing happened when we were given food. I was expected to eat whatever was placed before me although I hated certain things, especially spinach and cabbage. A small amount in my mouth normally ended with my cheeks bulging ominously, as if they would burst at any moment. Now I eat them with gusto and wonder whether their taste changed since my childhood.

But to get back to role modelling, my early school years were of showing "a good example." Whoever thinks that children whose parents are both teachers have an easy time, or that they act out in school, should have had my mother for a parent and teacher. In the classroom I got stiffer punishment if I misbehaved than was meted out to the other children. My disciplinarian Methodist mother was a firm believer in the motto, "Charity begins at home," which, of course, meant not only charity, but also discipline and punishment.

This really upset me and I often accused her of being unfair and very harsh. Her explanation was that she did not want other people to think that she was being soft with me, or that she was favouring me. She even tried to make it up to me and to show that she loved me.

Both my parents were supportive of us. When we did well, they complimented us; when we were upset, they comforted us and showed us that they loved us. While mother was the obvious disciplinarian, father was better at "damage control" and getting things back to normal as quickly as possible. He would explain the reason for the punishment and then soon afterwards move on to "fun time."

My father came from a large and rather easy-going family, whereas my mother came from a very strict one. Her parents were influenced by missionaries. Her father was a tribal chief and, as a leader, paved the way by sending his own daughters to school at a time when it was not heard of. He went a step further and sent them away to boarding school, "without chaperons or maids." My mother was sent to Chipembi Girls School. Grandfather was told by the missionaries that boarding school was the "done thing" by British upper classes, so he followed suit.

By the time I was born, boarding school had become the in thing for educated Africans. It was quite clear that I would follow in mom's footsteps and be sent away as soon as I was old enough. The day to go to Chipembi came four months before my twelfth birthday. The night before departure I was a bunch of nerves and hardly slept. It was a mixture of excitement and apprehension, a fear of the unknown, but anticipation as well. My mother tried to prepare me for what it would be like. She told me about the horrible teasing of new girls, but quickly added, "I'm sure things have changed by now. It can't be as bad as it was when I was there. The best thing to do is to show no fear."

So no matter how scared I felt, I told myself that I was not to show fear. When we got to the railway station and it was time to say goodbye to my mother, I held onto her as if I would never let go. She hugged me close, and as I looked up into her eyes, I could see tears shining through them. But she quickly fought them back and firmly removed my arms from around her. "Come on, Likande, it's time to go."

When I moved towards my father, he gently said, "I know how scared you must feel. I was also petrified when I first went to boarding school. Just remember that being new will soon pass and you'll get to know other girls. Boarding school can be an exciting experience, and you'll make long-lasting friendships."

Those words gave me the strength to board the train. But as it pulled away from Livingstone Station and the waving figures of my parents grew smaller and smaller, until they were no more, I bit my lip to prevent it from trembling. I'm now alone, I thought miserably. All alone.

"You're now a big girl," said my distant cousin, who had promised my parents that she would look after me. Actually, she had not really promised. The promise had been extracted from her by her mother and mine. Our mothers were supposedly cousins.

She sat down with a group of friends and they started chatting about their holidays. It was obvious that she didn't want a little nobody like me tagging along. After a few minutes she came over to me and said, "The fastest way to learn to swim is to jump into the water. You can't hang around me forever!" The thing to do is to show no fear, my mother's words kept turning in my mind ... show no fear ... show no fear ...

So up went my chin, and I embarked on a subtle study of the people in our compartment. In the seat opposite mine sat the "old timers," who seemed to be old buddies. They were discussing what had been happening in the school and who would be the prefects and house mothers this year. My glance swept towards the rest of the passengers, and the new girls stood out like bandaged, sore fingers. They looked lost, their faces sombre, downcast, or staring into nothingness. A few had their eyes glued onto the same pages of the books they were supposed to be reading. They seemed just as lost and uncertain as I was. The fact that there were other new girls did help somehow but it did not drive away the feeling of loneliness in that noisy and fast-moving train.

What I did, albeit for only a short while, was thinking about my family back in Livingstone. We were a close knit family. At that moment I would have given anything, all my worldly belongings, to be back home. This was the first time any of us had gone away from home. The next one to be sent to boarding school, most likely to Munali Boys School, would be ten-year-old Mbuye. He would be followed by Mwenda, who was eight. After him came six-year-old Sibeso, four-year-old Lubinda and finally my baby sister Nasilele, who was two years old. Even though to other people, especially Westerners, our family might seem large, it wasn't big by African standards.

I left for Chipembi in 1956 during the height of the struggle against the Federation of Rhodesia and Nyasaland. My parents however weren't active in politics. My father believed that the best way he could help our people was through education. He strongly opposed those who advocated the boycott of schools and who called them "enclaves of colonialism." Both my parents believed in education and in our family, there was no such thing as "I can't." My parents would often say, "Yes, you can do it," or "We know you can do better than that, so keep trying."

Apart from hard work and the usual expectations of discipline, we enjoyed weekend outings. One of my favourite spots was the Victoria Falls, which were known as Musi O Tunya, which means "The Smoke that Thunders." Indeed, the water sprays do look like smoke from a distance, and when one gets closer to the waterfalls, the air is filled with loud thundering noise. When we were very young, we actually believed that a monster lived in the seemingly bottomless depth of the falls, and that it was the one making the thundering noise. Our parents often diverted our attention by starting the "game of searching for the rainbow." We did this as we walked through the rain forest, cooling ourselves with water sprays from the falls. Whoever noticed the rainbow first would call out, "There it is! There!"

Our other treat was watching the traditional dancers, especially the Makishi dancers from the Northwestern Province. They wore masks and costumes representing animals like the zebra, lion, or elephant; and their movements as they danced imitated those of the animal they were playing.

From there we usually went to visit my uncle, a sculptor, who lived in Libuyu. I was fascinated by the way he turned a rough piece of wood into a beautiful carving of a person, an animal, or some other ornamental item. His main customers were tourists who came to see the falls.

"Hey, don't you want something to eat?" I almost jumped as the voice of my cousin suddenly interrupted my thoughts. I had been so carried away by my daydreaming that I'd completely forgotten about her.

"Where are we?" I asked foolishly, even though the sign at the railway station clearly read, MAZABUKA.

"Come on let's get down and stretch our legs."

I stood up and followed her. What a strange and unpredictable girl! Wasn't I supposed to learn how to swim by jumping into the river, even if that meant drowning? I thought I was nonexistent as far as she was concerned. She turned to me and said, "I,ve been watching you, and all you've done since we left Livingstone is sit like a statue, in the same spot, staring into space. We stopped at

Choma, but you seemed far away. It's been hours since we left Livingstone, and you've not bothered to talk to anyone."

Hours? Had time flown that fast? But how could she expect me to talk to complete strangers? Surely, she must recall what it was like to be a new girl and know no one. It was strange how people seemed to have such short memories.

"How much longer do we have to go?" I asked.

"After Mazabuka, the next station will be Kafue. Then we'll be in Lusaka, and after that we'll head for Chisamba."

"My mom told me that Chisamba is eighteen miles from Chipembi."

"Yes. Now, what would you like to eat? They're selling all kinds of things."

The platform was packed with students and other passengers bargaining for bananas, oranges, roasted peanuts and *vitumbuwa* (pancakes). I really didn't want to buy anything as I had no appetite, but to avoid another lecture from my cousin, I bought an orange and a few peanuts. Just as I was about to move away, my cousin snatched the bag of peanuts from my hand and gave it back to the vendor, saying to her, "No, not the peanuts. She wants a banana instead," and with that, she picked one and pushed it into my hand.

"Why did you do that?" I shouted. "I wanted those peanuts! I don't want the banana!"

"Well, that's too bad. No nuts. Not when you're sitting next to me. Sitting next to someone who's been eating peanuts is like being next to somebody who just ate onions or garlic. I hate the smell."

What a bully! What a self-centred and arrogant bully! Just you wait, you stupid fool, I thought angrily. You're mean, terrible and not at all like my cousins. As soon as I settle down, not only will you be a far-removed, distant cousin, but a long forgotten one.

Giving Namakao as nasty a glare as I could muster, I turned away from her. How different she was from the cousins I knew! The children of my mother's sisters and brothers, as well as those of my father's relatives. I loved going to visit them and my grandparents back in their villages. We saw more of my mother's relatives as it was easier, since grandpa's chieftaincy covered the area not too far from Livingstone. His village was within a stone's throw from the mighty Zambezi river. From its banks we could watch elephants grazing on nearby islands, while hippos and crocodiles lay basking in the sun, occasionally getting back into the water to cool themselves.

As soon as we arrived in the village, I would seek out my cousin Mbololwa, and off we would rush to the river. In the evening, as the large, orange-reddish sun was setting, it would be time to watch grandpa's herdsmen bringing back cattle from grazing. It was a large herd. Most of the cattle belonged to grandpa, but each one of his children also owned cattle, a few given to each at birth. By the time they were adults, they had multiplied. I recognized my mother's herd from the orange colour codes. The cattle were rounded up and moved into the *kraal* for the night. Early each morning after being milked, the animals were taken away to the fields to graze. They were often long gone by the time we woke up. We then settled down to breakfast, and every child was handed a cup of warm milk taken from the large urns in which the milk was boiled.

Thinking about my relatives brought a huge lump to my throat. When would I see them again? My parents, brothers and sister would now go visiting without me. I felt lonely and abandoned because I was going to a strange place. The figures of people around me suddenly appeared blurred, as my eyes filled with tears. I quickly wiped them off with the back of my hand. As I moved forward, someone pushed me and I staggered into the girl in front of me. She turned around and yelled, "*Puku*, watch where you're going!"

"I'm sorry, I didn't ..."

"Likande," said my cousin, "you don't have to apologise to that creep! Besides, she should know that there are many people trying to get back on this train. There's bound to be pushing or shoving."

"How dare you call me a creep?" demanded the girl, as she pushed me aside and confronted my cousin.

"How dare you call my sister *puku*?"

"Well, I didn't know she was your sister."

"Now you know I had better warn anybody else who threatens her that they'll have to deal with me first."

I just couldn't believe my ears! Sister, eh? My distant cousin was full of surprises! This was indeed a pleasant surprise. I took back my nasty thoughts about her as the benefits of being her "sister" soon became evident. As soon as we got back on the train I noticed a change in the altitude of the other girls towards me. They were more friendly, and the journey that had earlier seemed long and boring was now exciting. Someone even moved over from where they were sitting and said to my cousin, "Namakao, this is my younger sister, Tayana. Since they're both new, why don't they get to know each other?"

"Sure, why not?" smiled my cousin, as she gave me a conspiratorial wink. I moved over to make room for Tayana and we started talking. I did not feel alone and unwanted any more.

When we stopped at Lusaka, the capital city, an even greater number of girls boarded the train. There were also many boys from Munali Boys School who had come to see off their relatives or girlfriends. The presence of the boys appeared to attract the attention of the older girls. They giggled and nudged each other, parading up and down like peacocks. Since Munali was the famous elite school for African boys, the ultimate goal of any girl graduating from Chipembi was to marry someone who had been to Munali.

After that, we finally headed towards our destination. Chisamba was somewhat of an anticlimax after Lusaka. Tayana immediately made her feelings known. "Gee, so this is Chisamba! It's so small," she exclaimed.

"Didn't your sister tell you that it was a small place?" I asked.

"No. I didn't want to come, anyway. So I didn't want to ask her anything about this place. I would rather go to school in Livingstone."

"Oh, come on. You've nothing to worry about. You're lucky to have a sister, not like.. ."

"So are you. Anyway, what did your sister say about Chipembi?"

"My mother went to school there. She's thrilled to have me follow in her footsteps. I'll be the second generation."

"But your sister is already .. ."

"Look, we'd better go. Everyone is taking their stuff."

There, I nearly blew it. I almost gave away the secret. If being Namakao's sister would save me from being tortured and

44

tormented, then I had to watch what I said. It was worth keeping up the pretence.

When we got off the train, I kept as close to Namakao as I could. She appeared to enjoy the role of being my big sister. But this lasted only for a few days, as one of her friends disclosed to the others that I was just some cousin. I also found out that Namakao had quickly come to my rescue because the girl who pushed me was her arch rival. Apparently, Namakao never forgave the girl for "stealing her boyfriend." Anyway, by the time it was found out that we were not sisters, I was beginning to settle down to life at the school.

Although initially I missed my family, settling into the school routine wasn't hard for me. I soon made friends, and doing "the right thing" was second nature to me. Within a few weeks I was popular with teachers and many students. The only teacher I didn't get on well with was the maths teacher. I really didn't care much for mathematics. Since I was good at most other subjects, she assumed that I wasn't trying hard enough.

Her special student was Chilufya. She sat next to me in class and we hit it off from the start. As the weeks turned into months, it became evident that Chilufya and I were competing for top of the class. However, our academic rivalry was also drawing us towards each other like magnets instead of making us dislike one another. Chilufya worked out solutions to maths problems with an ease which I found fascinating. One day I said to her, "I don't know how you can like a subject like maths. It is so abstract and boring."

"No, it isn't boring or abstract. Mathematics is with us in our everyday life. Just think of simple tasks: your mum asks you to go and buy bread. You give the grocer a bill and he gives you back the change. Then you are peeling potatoes, carrots, or whatever, and she asks you to use only one half and put away the rest. What is abstract about that? That is everyday life. I could go on and on .. ."

"Well, don't go on. I just need your help on this."

"No problem. Algebra is simple. Here, I'll show you how to do it."

"You don't have to show her anything. She doesn't help you with history ... so why should you?"

It was that cheeky Tengani butting in. What was wrong with that girl? Why did she snap at people and make herself so obnoxious? She was rude to both teachers and students alike. She was the self-styled deliverer of our people from the yoke of the British. How could a twelve-year-old girl get so worked up about politics and our country's problems? Most of the girls avoided Tengani like a plague. After the incident over algebra, one of my friends said, "That girl is a pain in the ..."

"So full of herself!" remarked another.

"Don't get too involved with her, Likande. She is nothing but trouble," warned yet another girl.

But I did not keep away. Besides, how could I avoid seeing her when she was Chilufya's friend? Chilufya and I were fast becoming close friends. There was also more to it than that. Despite being diametrically opposed on most things, I was fascinated by Tengani. Here I was, the classic compromiser, always looking for the middle ground, not wanting to rock the boat. But there she was, the defiant girl, who didn't care what anybody said or thought of her. She seemed in charge and in control of her life. She had a vision of what lay ahead for her, and a mission in life. She would work towards the accomplishment of that mission, no matter what.

Yet I sensed that under all that bravado was a soft and vulnerable spot. I was already nicknamed "the nun," and was sometimes referred to as "Florence Nightingale" because of talking to girls who for some reason were isolated from others and were still having a hard time adjusting to boarding school. My relationship with Tengani therefore started with me feeling sorry for her, while I also secretly admired her courage. There was need in me to mother her. I wasn't the eldest of six kids for nothing! I was used to being a role model and to "mothering" my younger siblings. But Tengani didn't buy it. In fact, she became very angry when I once expressed how sorry I was to hear that her mother died when she was only eight.

"I don't need your sympathy!" she snapped.

After that, our relationship changed to one of interdependence. What I lacked, she had: self-confidence, guts and courage. What she lacked, I had: the capacity to bring calm to troubled waters, so to speak, and to find a compromise. My leadership qualities were also becoming evident. I was assigned supervisory roles by the teachers. In history classes, our teacher made us play-act important events. I was often chosen to play the part of the main character, such as Tshaka, King of the Zulu of Southern Africa; Marie Antionette of France; Catherine Howard, one of the eight wives of King Henry VIII of England; and so on. I loved dressing up in some historic costume, applying makeup, and putting myself in the position of the character I was playing and the period of the time.

But my leadership roles were not just limited to classroom sketches. During my third year at school, I was nominated a school prefect with ten other girls. Most were older than I was and in higher classes. We were responsible not only for ensuring that school rules were obeyed by students, but also for transmitting to the school authorities, grievances and recommendations from students. We were a kind of student government.

As our friendship blossomed with each passing year, Tengani grew more trusting of me, especially as I helped her get over situations that nearly led to her being dismissed from school. Both Chilufya and I constantly pleaded with her to keep her short temper in check. Sometimes she became angry and called us names, but often she listened to us. I think she realized that we cared about her and that our concern was genuine. She was also lucky that our Principal was a kind and motherly sort who kept giving her another chance.

Some of the teachers would have liked her sent back home. They were worried about Tengani's 'bad influence on others.' Besides, the political mood in the country was changing and could no longer be dismissed as the work of 'a few troublemakers.' The Nationalist Movement was gaining momentum and causing fear and trepidation in the white community.

Although most of the teachers sympathised with the problems of Africans and felt that their duty was to serve the people, there were others whose political sympathies lay with the settlers and the colonial government. These people believed that they had come to save Africans from paganism and ancestral worship, and that their salvation lay in Western civilization. They saw African nationalism not as progress, but as regression and a move back to 'bad customs'. For these, anything that was truly African and native, such as a dance and celebrations marking puberty, was considered evil and pagan. Being a true Christian meant adopting Western culture and even stopping the use of African names. There were, of course, those who resisted and refused to change their names, and insisted on being baptised into the Christian faith with their African names. But for many, especially the young, peer pressure was too strong, and they often adopted Western names and referred to their African names as "middle names."

This, of course, infuriated Tengani. She said such people were brainwashed by imperialists. Sometimes I wondered whether Chilufya and I would have stuck to our African names, if it weren't for Tengani's influence. How I admired her courage and being able to stand for what she believed in! How she seemed so sure of herself and where she was going in life! In contrast, I seemed like a sailor in a tiny boat in the middle of the ocean, drifting aimlessly.

Of course, my peers saw me as a role model – looking confident and delivering eloquent speeches at gatherings of students and teachers. Sure, I had mastered techniques of speech making as a member of the Debating Society. My rise to the top of the student body had been fast and smooth. By the time I was in my last year of schooling, I was Head Girl, an equivalent to President of the Student Government.

However, my external exposure and leadership qualities masked feelings of uncertainty and anxiety that were raging in my heart. I wasn't even sure what I would do after finishing school. Well, that's not really true. I wanted to be a social worker, but my parents were against it. They had spent years as teachers only to, as my mother put it, get stressed and burnt out. She warned me that social work would do the same to me. It seemed to me that they were trying to relive their lives through me and make the changes they wished they had made.

I was going to university because that was what was expected of me. But I had no idea what I would study once I got there. To make matters worse, I didn't have a choice about which university to go to.

Almost everybody from my school in those days went to the University of Rhodesia and Nyasaland, in Salisbury, Southern Rhodesia, now Harare, Zimbabwe. It was then a branch of the University of London. Nobody I knew wanted to go there. It was rumoured to be a hotbed for racists from South Africa. Students who had friends and relatives there said, "The settlers in the North are saints compared to those in the South." The only comfort for me was that at least Chilufya and I would be together.

This was the only university in the early 1960s for the three countries that formed the Federation: Northern Rhodesia (now Zambia), Southern Rhodesia (Zimbabwe) and Nyasaland (Malawi). It was also the only multi-racial educational institution in the region. Students who attended the university came from segregated schools and neighbourhoods. Children grew up in a kind of apartheid, never interacting with other races at social or academic levels until they went to the university. Apparently, the desegregated nature of the university was a result of the pressure and financial terms imposed by the British Government.

Presumably, the famous University of London would not have wished to be associated with an institution that discriminated against students on the basis of race.

As things turned out, I did not go to that university. Things took a sudden change a few months before my final exams, as a result of a casual conversation with one of the teachers. One afternoon I rushed back to the classroom, having forgotten one of my books. When I came out, I almost bumped into Jake and Kathy Dickson. He was our science teacher, while she taught physical education, or P.E., as it was popularly known. They were from the United States and seemed more friendly to the students, and much more informal than the British teachers. They encouraged us seniors to call them by their first names, something unheard of before. That really made us feel grown up and ready to face the world.

Anyway, as I came to a sudden halt after nearly knocking them over, Jake put out his hand to steady me and, noticing the book I was carrying, said, "Getting ready for those exams, eh?"

"Yes, sort of. But I've still got a million books to read!"

"Have you decided which college you want to go to?" asked Kathy.

"Do I have any choice?"

"Sorry, I keep forgetting that this is not back home," she said.

"Have you thought of going to college in the U.S.?" asked Jake.

"The United States of America?" I asked in an incredulous voice.

"Yes. Would you like to go there?"

I looked up into his face to see if he was teasing me, but he seemed serious. The United States? Me? It had never even crossed my mind! Not even in my dreams. It seemed so far away. Their stares suddenly made me realize that he was waiting for my answer.

"How can I go there?" I asked.

"By airplane, of course, Likande!" replied Jake, with a twinkle in his eyes.

"Aeroplane! Where on earth would I find money to buy a ticket for an aeroplane? Let alone money to pay fees for the university there? At least here it's free. The Government covers everything."

"I know. College kids here are lucky, in that sense. But if you want to go to the States, we can help you find a scholarship," said Jake, looking at his wife, who nodded in agreement.

"Yes, Likande," said Kathy, "I'm sure we could easily find financial aid for you. I've heard how smart you are!"

"Smart?" I asked, glancing at my school uniform.

"There I go again, me and my American English. I meant, intelligent, bright."

"Thank you. I really appreciate your offer to help me."

"Don't thank us yet," cautioned Jake, "we'll see what we can do."

As I walked away, I thought I would burst with excitement. I started humming to myself, but stopped when I heard Jake calling my name.

"Yes, Jake? What did you say?" I asked.

"You better start learning American English real quick. Airplane, not aeroplane!"

"Garbage cans, not dustbins!" shouted Kathy.

"What? Don't they speak real English in America?" I asked,

feeling somewhat confused. Both of them burst out laughing, as if it was the funniest thing they had ever heard.

A month after my discussion with the Dicksons, a bulky envelope arrived from Jake's sister. In it were application forms from Florida State University, located in a city called Tallahassee. The name sounded so strange that I couldn't believe it was in the United States. Somehow I had been expecting to go to a university in New York, Washington, California or Boston. These were more familiar places, from my geography and history lessons. Boston was the most recent in my mind, as we had just learnt about the American War of Independence and the Boston Tea Party.

Our history teacher also mentioned that the handsome and dynamic American President, John F. Kennedy, came from Boston. Little did I know then that I was heading for the United States during a time of civil upheaval and probably the most important phase in the history of the Civil Rights Movement. Nor could anyone imagine that the President who seemed to touch the hearts of so many people, not only in his country, but the world over, would be assassinated before the year ended. He was like a bud that is snapped before it blooms.

To get back to the bulky envelope from Tallahassee, it included a letter from Stephanie Dickson, Jake's sister. She said that she managed to obtain a scholarship from a group called "Friends of Africa." There were several conditions to the scholarship. One was that I had to sign a statement declaring that I would go back to my country upon completion of my studies. I laughed when I read it and said to Jake and Kathy, "Why on earth do they want me to sign this? Surely everybody returns to their country when they finish? Nothing will keep me from coming back here. Nothing!"

"Don't worry about it. They send this sort of thing to everybody," said Kathy.

Jake added, "You may not believe this, but there are students who try to stay on after they graduate. They don't want to go back for all kinds of reasons." He explained that some were scared to go back for political reasons, while others preferred to stay in the hope of finding better paying jobs.

Kathy glanced at the letter and said, "The other condition won't be difficult for you, either; You should manage to maintain good grades."

"Jake, your sister is very kind. I would like to write to her and thank her."

"She sure will be happy to hear from you. We've told her a lot of nice things about you."

"Don't worry about all these forms. We'll show you how to fill them," said Kathy.

"Why don't we first show her where Tallahassee is on the map? You must be wondering where it is," said Jake.

"Oh, yes, please. I would like that very much."

"The advantage of going there," said Kathy, "is that it has lovely weather ... not cold and no snow. Not at all like the North or Northeast."

After that, things became really hectic. There were letters to and from my parents, who were beside themselves with joy. They told their friends that I had been chosen to go to America. They made it sound as if I had won a national contest and that the award was to go to the United States. I received letters from my cousins, aunts and uncles, even from one of our neighbours. My brothers and sister sent me lists of things they wanted from the States. They seemed to think that I would just disappear without going home first. I wrote to them again, assuring them that I would see them before I left.

At school I was fussed over by both the teachers and the students, although there were snide remarks from one or two people as to why a girl as bright as you would go to a place no one has heard of. When I mentioned that I was going to Tallahassee, the reaction was, "Talla ... what? Where's that?" Someone even asked me whether it was in Russia! I told them what I had read in the brochures from Florida State University, especially the fact that Tallahassee was an American-Indian name. I also showed several people snapshots of Tallahassee in springtime, which Jake's sister sent me. It looked like a garden city I couldn't wait to get there!

However as the day drew nearer, I felt as if there was a heavy load in my heart. It was then that it dawned on me that I would be leaving Chipembi forever. The school had been like a second home for me. In fact, since I was twelve years old, I had spent more time there than I had spent with my own family. It was Chipembi and the large family within it that had seen me grow from an immature child to a grown young woman who was now going out into the world.

The last day was terribly emotional for me and my friends. Our eyes were perpetually wet and misty, and we kept dabbing at them, sniffing and blowing into the already soaked tissues. Tears poured down my face when the Principal handed me several awards and wished me a "good trip to the United States," and reminded me that I would be the "unofficial ambassador for this school and your country." What a huge responsibility! Would being a role model ever end?

That evening, after the celebrations and speeches were over, I invited Chilufya and Tengani to my dormitory. We camped on mattresses on the floor. Even the teacher on duty didn't seem to mind as she did not remind us of the rules. She chatted briefly with us and then left. We talked until the early hours of the morning. I still remember the night as if it were yesterday.

Just before we fell asleep, completely exhausted by the day's events, the long hours of talking and crying our hearts out, Chilufya said, "Likande, don't forget to write as soon as you get to the States."

"Of course, I'll write. As if I could forget you two!"

"I only wish you weren't going to the South. It's as bad as South Africa," said Tengani.

"Not according to what I've been told. Tallahassee is a very nice place."

Chilufya then said, "Tengani, I wouldn't worry about Likande. She'll probably be better off than I'll be at the University in Salisbury."

"You'll be fine, Chilufya," assured Tengani. "By this time next year we shall be free. Our lovely country will be the Republic of Zambia. Soon after that, the people in the South will also be free."

"And our dear Tengani will be one of the top officials, a Cabinet Minister, or something," I teased.

"Yes, Tengani," said Chilufya, "you'll probably be married to one of the prominent politicians."

"No. There's no marriage yet in the future plans. You, Chilufya, will probably marry a doctor and live happily ever after!" said Tengani.

I then said to the girls, "Since we are into reading the future, I'll look into mine. Yes ... I see him ... my Mr. Right. There he is in America, waiting for me. I'll probably quit college and ..."

"No!" cried Chilufya and Tengani, at the same time.

"Why not?" I asked.

"You've got to finish your degree," said Chilufya. "And don't you dare get married there," said Tengani.

"Gee, you both sound like my parents!" I remarked.

"Well, we're sort of like family, aren't we?" asked Tengani, and without waiting for an answer, went on to say, "I'll really miss you both. Please keep me posted about what you'll be doing. If you don't hear from me, it will be because I might be either in prison or worse, dead."

"Tengani, how morbid!" cried Chilufya.

"Only a short while ago, you told us that we would soon be free!" I pointed out.

"Okay, forget what I said just now. What's important is that we keep in touch, no matter what. Deal?" she asked.

"Deal!" we both responded.

Chapter Five

CHILUFYA

I

The years I spent at Chipembi School were exciting ones for me. I quickly settled into the routine of school life. My friendship with Tengani and Likande blossomed with each passing year. Academically I did well, even though at first they tried to place me in the French class for languages. It was a well-known fact that those who were not selected for Latin 'would not go to university.' When I asked my class teacher why I wasn't taking Latin, her only response was, "I really don't know, Chilufya. I don't know. But I can find out for you."

I was good at most subjects, and Likande and I were competitors, but I knew that I had problems pronouncing some words such as 'she' and 'he.' I tended to pronounce them as 'see' and 'ee,' respectively, as there are not that many words that have the letter 'h' in my own language.

One morning my English teacher made me repeat the sentence, 'He bought her some fresh fish' twenty times. At first I said, 'Ee bought er some fres fis.' Eventually, I managed to say it correctly. But I still couldn't understand why I had been placed in the French class. What did pronouncing English words correctly have to do with learning French? I decided to see the Principal about it.

Our Principal was a motherly sort of person who was easily approachable. She was a spinster missionary who seemed to believe that prayer and tea did wonders for those who erred from the straight and narrow way. Tengani spent a considerable time of our stay at school being 'invited for tea and prayer.'

One of the things the Principal had a knack for was remembering names. If she met you once, then your name was forever logged in her memory. When I went to see her, she remembered me from the afternoon Tengani and I were in the school orchard helping ourselves to oranges and guavas.

"Yes, Chilufya, what naughty things have you been up to now?"

"I came to see you about the French class, Miss Dudley," I said. "I would rather take Latin."

"Have you discussed this with your class teacher?"

"Yes, Miss Dudley, but .. ."

"But you would rather talk to mama here about it, is that it? First, tell me why you don't like French. It is a beautiful language. Latin is now a dead language. Why would you prefer a dead language to a live and kicking one?" she asked, smiling.

"I want to be a doctor," I answered. "They say Latin is better for going to the university, especially if I want to be a doc ... "

"Hah, hah. You want to be a doctor, eh? My dear child, I also want to go to the moon, but I can't. You've got to separate dreams from reality."

"Why can't I be a doctor? Why?" I asked angrily.

"There's no need to get all worked up about this. I'll see what I can do to change you to Latin. We'll first look at how well you've been doing in all the subjects. If I were you, I would stop dreaming about the impossible and plan to be either a teacher or secretary. Those are the kind of jobs available for African girls these days. Who knows, things might change!"

But I didn't care what everyone else wanted to do. All I knew was that I wanted to be a doctor. So I was thrilled when they moved me from French and I joined Likande in the Latin class.

When we left Chipembi, I headed straight to the University of Rhodesia and Nyasaland in Salisbury and enrolled in the School of Medicine. It was hard and intensive training which took a whole decade from beginning to the final qualification. Years of hard work in a country that was racially tense and politically charged was a bit like sitting on a time bomb and wondering whether at any moment it would explode.

I had only been there a year when things started deteriorating. Northern Rhodesia attained its independence on 24 October 1964 and became the Republic of Zambia. We held a huge party to celebrate the occasion. There were only a few Zambian students, but many well-wishers. However, there was a small band of right-wing, conservative students bent on disrupting our celebrations. They pelted the party-goers with tomatoes and eggs, much to the fury of our supporters and delighted glee of theirs.

After that, life for students from the North, especially from Zambia and Malawi, became difficult. The white-settler government was determined to prevent the spread of 'independence fever' from the North. They accused students from the North of being a bad influence on the others. Informers infiltrated the campus and accused students and professors who opposed government policy of being communists. The security agents dragged away ring leaders in the middle of the night to interrogate and harass them until they made confessions. When I went home for the holidays, my parents pleaded with me to leave the university.

"They'll arrest you, too, and throw you into prison," warned my mother.

"Yes, it is too dangerous for you to remain there," agreed my father.

"No," I said. "I can't leave now. The university has a good School of Medicine and excellent professors."

My father said, "Can't you see the danger you're in? That crazy minority government has made its Unilateral Declaration of Independence despite warnings from Britain and the whole world. They'll now stop at nothing. You'd better leave. We have our own university starting here."

"No, Dad," I said. "I would rather stay. The university in Salisbury is well established and will continue its affiliation with the University of London."

"Stay in Salisbury if you like," shouted my father, "but don't say we didn't warn you."

It was probably a silly decision on my part, but I insisted on going back. Besides, I had another special reason for staying; Sepho.

Sepho and I had been dating for several months now – that is, if you can call spending hours in a laboratory observing animal behaviour or testing chemicals, dating. But for us, it was as good as going to the movies. Sepho was also very worried about the situation in the country and about his family, who lived in a town called Bulawayo.

A number of his friends had quit college and left the country, some going for military training in Tanzania, Russia or Yugoslavia. They argued that if Britain could not help the Africans get back their land from the white settlers, then they would seek assistance elsewhere. Young men and women joined the liberation movement in large numbers and went to wage war against the minority regime from the neighbouring countries. One day, as Sepho and I were on lunch break, I said to him, "Don't you feel guilty about not going when most of your friends have left?"

"No," he answered. "I think I'll best serve my people by completing my training. We can't all be soldiers. What will happen after independence if everybody leaves school and college now?"

"You mean there'll be no doctors, teachers, and so on?"

"Right. What good is political independence, if you continue to rely on outsiders to treat your sick, teach your children, and build your bridges?"

"That is exactly what I used to tell my friend. She was a fanatic about fighting for independence. She even wanted to quit school so that she could join the freedom fighters."

"Well, I guess each person must decide for himself about these things," he said. "As for me, I certainly do not intend to drop out at this point. How is your friend doing in Zambia?"

"Very well," I said. "She has joined the Women's Brigade and wants to fight for better conditions for women."

"Hmmm. From political liberation to women's rights, eh? She won't be very popular with husbands and boyfriends."

I just smiled, remembering my last visit to Tengani's apartment in Lusaka. She had that look of 'mission unaccomplished.' She kept complaining that women were getting a raw deal and that, although they had equally fought for independence, men wanted them to continue with their traditional role in the kitchen.

"If we don't change things now while the political honeymoon is still on," she had said, "we'll be in real trouble. Even you will not be fully recognized as a doctor when you finish. Men will expect you to serve them coffee and tea."

Good old Tengani, I thought fondly. Still trying to fight battles for everyone else! Now that the British were no more, she had to find the next cause.

But she was right. When I finally started working as a junior doctor at the University Teaching Hospital in Lusaka, I discovered how difficult it was to be a female medical doctor. Not only were my male colleagues sceptical and condescending toward me, but patients felt they had a really good doctor only if it was a man. A Zambian female doctor was a rare commodity, and at first many patients called me 'nurse' or 'sister.'

I discussed my problems with Tengani and Likande. I was angry and frustrated at having spent so many years in training only to struggle at having to prove myself. I wrote to Sepho to encourage him to come and join me at the hospital, but he wrote back saying that his duty was 'with my people in Zimbabwe.' My heart sank as I read on: "I can't abandon my people now. In fact, you may not hear from me again because I am leaving for an undisclosed location to help our wounded comrades. If we are meant to meet again, we shall. In the meantime, pray for me and my country. Take care of yourself. Viva Freedom!"

I read the letter over and over... Undisclosed location? To help the wounded? Where on earth could that be? I wondered if he would be somewhere in Zambia. There were already rumours that some of the freedom fighters were operating from Zambia. There were even complaints that they were selling guns to criminals who were now staging armed robberies in the affluent suburbs. People were saying that Zambia used to be a peaceful country, but that people now lived in fear. Others wanted the Freedom Fighters sent away, as 'they have abused our hospitality.' Yet others argued that Zambia had a moral duty to help the African countries in Southern Africa who were still fighting racism and apartheid.

As the months progressed and I heard nothing from Sepho, I buried myself in my work. There was a lot to be done. It was becoming clear that more and more people were moving to the towns from the rural areas. Hospitals were becoming overcrowded, and facilities and resources were stretched to the limit. Far too many patients and too few beds. What worried many of the medical staff was that by abolishing fee-paying hospitals, the government had opened floodgates that would be difficult to control. For how long would the government bear the cost of free medical care for everybody? I felt that if the government let the people who could afford to pay for services pay for them, and then offered those services free to those who couldn't afford to pay, things would be better for everybody. But now we were expected to provide excellent medical care from dwindling resources and an increased caseload.

Some doctors found the situation so frustrating that they left to go into private practice, where there was more money and better working hours. Those of us who stayed found ourselves working double shifts and long hours for little pay. Some people asked me why I stayed on at the hospital. I think the main reason was that it was where I belonged. All my training had been paid for by the government, and I owed it to the people to work for them rather than abandon them to seek some lucrative private practice. Besides, despite all the problems, I grew to love attending to my patients and sharing their joy when they got better and were being discharged, as well as sharing their family's sorrow when modern technology failed to cure them.

With each passing year, I earned their respect and was recognized in my own right as a really good doctor. It no longer mattered that I was a woman; at least, not to my patients. They knew that I was by their side helping to combat the diseases that were ravaging their bodies, and in the process not only being their doctor, but also their counsellor and teacher.

One of my colleagues, Dr. Membe, was telling me how frustrated he felt when children he discharged from the hospital were readmitted a few months later for the same problems, such as malnutrition, diarrhoea, vomiting and dehydration. One day, as we were walking to the parking lot after another long day at the hospital, he said, "Whoever said Africa's main problems are poverty, ignorance and disease summed it all up. We need co-ordinated efforts to deal with all these problems and not just fight one thing at a time."

"I agree with you," I said. "What we need is public education, using every means at our disposal, including radio and television. Prevention is better than cure."

"I think part of the problem is this rush from the rural areas to the cities," he said. "People come here hoping for a better life, and what do they find? No jobs, no food for their children, nothing. I wish they would realize that city lights are not edible!"

"The fizzy drinks they keep feeding their infants on can't be good for them either," I said.

"No," he answered. "In fact, malnutrition sets in after babies are weaned and as soon as another pregnancy is underway. The weaned baby loses the mother's nutritious milk and instead survives on those artificially sweetened drinks."

I knew what he was talking about. It was now my fourth year at the hospital, and things seemed to be getting worse. After waving Dr. Membe goodbye, I walked towards my small, second-hand car, a Fiat 127. I prayed that it would start, as I had problems starting the engine that morning. It had taken a lot of pushing by children in my neighbourhood before the car started, and I could finally go to work. I now got inside but, as I had feared, nothing happened when I turned the key. I tried several times, but it only made a whining and groaning noise. I looked out for Dr. Membe, but unfortunately, he had already left.

I opened the bonnet of the car to check the oil and the battery. I knew virtually nothing about cars except how to drive them and occasionally check the obvious things, like the oil and water levels. Everything seemed all right. I went back inside and tried to start it again, but I was greeted by the same dreadful noise.

"Come on, you silly little car!" I yelled as I pushed my foot on the accelerator.

"Can I help you? It sounds like the electric connection."

I looked up into the face of a man who was leaning over my car. He was immaculately dressed in a suit and appeared to be a businessman. He had a bulging briefcase in one hand and gave the inside of my car a sweeping glance. He made me feel as though my car had done its work and was now ready to 'rest in peace' in some junk yard.

"Well ... er ..." I quickly muttered, "I would hate to bother you. I'll just walk over to the garage that repaired it last week. I thought they had fixed the problem, but they obviously didn't."

"Was it the same problem?"

"Yes, the same whining sound."

"Let's check it out. Open the bonnet, please."

I did as he instructed and then watched as he took off his jacket and walked over to a shiny Mercedes Benz parked close by. After putting his briefcase and jacket in the car, he walked back, rolling up the sleeves of his shirt, and then bent over the engine and started checking it.

"Try to start it again," he shouted.

I switched on the engine and for a moment it sounded as if it would start, but it gave out the same groaning noise.

"I think it needs to go to a garage. Let's go and get them to come and tow it," he suggested.

"I can't. I mean, I've got to find out first what all this will cost. I can't afford to pay any more money on this car. Two months ago I paid for repairs and again last week. And now this!"

His gaze swept me up and down, making me terribly self-conscious and embarrassed.

"What do you do?" he finally asked.

"Me? I am a doctor. Why?"

"Nothing. I just wondered."

"Well, I'm sure you know what miserable pittance we get as government doctors! I really can't pay for all these repairs. Sometimes I feel like taking it to the junk yard and leaving it there, but I can't afford to buy a new car either. So I'm stuck with this one."

"Look, a friend of mine runs a garage, and he will be happy to help."

"No thanks. I just can't ask a complete stranger to help me. I'll just go back to the garage that worked on ..."

"This friend owes me a favour. I also want to help you."

"Why?" I asked, suddenly suspicious.

"Why not? You're a doctor and one day, I may need help too. Come on, let's go before it gets dark."

I hesitated for a moment, but then shrugged my shoulders and followed him. I hoped I was not being stupid by following a complete stranger. He hadn't even told me his name. Lusaka was buzzing with news about the strangler named after the famous, or infamous, 'Boston Strangler.' Twenty-six women had already died at the hands of the strangler, and the number was rising every week. The strangler was getting more confident with each murder, and he had even resorted to leaving taunting notes for the police.

Rumour had it that the strangler was a well-to-do man who lured unsuspecting women to secluded locations and then strangled them. Some people said that he was a policeman, others said he was a soldier because he left no marks on his victims. Still others swore that he was a businessman. At first, most of his victims were prostitutes picked from hotels, nightclubs and bars. But his recent victims were ordinary girls and women, and even professional women like me, who were stranded by the roadside after their cars broke down.

I froze and just stared at him as he opened the door for me.

"Is anything wrong? You look as if you've seen a ghost!"

"I ... er ... It's just that I am not in the habit of going off like this with someone I don't even know. Most of the talk at the hospital has been about ... about ... this terrible news ... this ... er ..."

"The strangler? You think I'm the strangler?"

"I don't know! I'm sorry ... It's just ..."

"Please don't apologise. I can't blame you. Anyway, I should have properly introduced myself before encouraging you to come with me. My name is Zelani Chirwa. I can assure you that I'm no strangler or criminal of any kind. If you want more information ..."

"Mine is Chilufya. Dr. Chilufya Chabala."

"Nice to meet you Chilu… I mean Dr. Chabala."

I sank into the passenger seat beside him and leaned my head against the headrest.

"Mmm, this is luxury! What do you do, Mr. Chirwa?"

"Call me Zelani. This Mr. and Dr. stuff sounds too formal. I'm self-employed, a businessman."

"What kind of business?"

"All kinds. But mostly property, construction, and so on."

He is being rather vague, I thought, and I quickly sat up so that I could watch where we were going. If he tried to drive away from town I would jump out at a stop sign or traffic lights.

"What kind of property?" I persisted.

"I'll show you one of these days. Anyway, there's my friend's garage."

"Oh, I didn't realize it was so close," I said as I gave him a big smile, greatly relieved that he was no strangler.

When we got to the garage, he asked me to stay in the car as he went to talk to his friend. A few minutes later, he came out with the man and said, "Chilufya, meet my friend Mbesa. As I expected, he has agreed to have your car towed and repaired."

"No problem, ma'am. I'll send my men right away."

"How much will it cost?" I asked.

Mbesa glanced at Zelani and then, smiling, turned back to me and said, "Well, we can sort that one later after the car is fixed."

"I would rather have an idea now. Just an estimate if you can't tell me the exact amount."

"I'll tow it free. But you'll pay for the cost of the repair. I don't think it will be much, how about that?"

"Okay. Thank you very much."

Zelani drove me back to the hospital, and we were followed by the tow truck. I could have happily gone with the men in the truck, but he insisted on coming with me. When we got to the car park, he still waited and offered to take me home.

"Your car won't be done today. So let me take you home," he said.

"Oh, no. You've been more than helpful already. I'll go back with these people to the garage and then head home after filling out the necessary papers."

"Well, I'd better say goodbye then," he said.

"Bye, and thanks again," I replied.

After giving Mbesa my work telephone number and telling him how urgently I needed the car, I took a taxi home. Later that evening, as I got ready for bed, I smiled as I recalled how persistent Zelani had been at wanting to take me home. He seemed to be a man who was used to having his way. He probably would have stayed on for dinner had I given in to his offer. He might even be one of those married guys who cheat on their wives and try to have a good time whenever they can. I wonder whether he is actually married with children, I mused. He seemed to be somewhere in the mid-thirties, probably a couple of years older than I was. I was very old, according to my mother, who couldn't understand why I was not married yet.

"What excuse do you have now?" she often asked. "Before, you used to say you were still in training. Now you've trained yourself beyond the reach of any man who might want to marry you. You had better find yourself a husband before it's too late!"

"Oh, Ma! Please stop pestering me. I'll get married when I meet the right person."

"And when will that be? When you're sixty and too old to have any children?"

I now dreaded going home for visits and my mother's constant questions, such as "Chilufya, aren't there any men in Lusaka? What are you waiting for?" Well, maybe she was right. What indeed was I waiting for? For Sepho, who was still lost in his freedom war? I had not heard from him in ages, and there was no point even thinking about him. I suppose my problem was time. I just didn't seem to have time to socialize these days. My life was wrapped up in nothing but work, work, work. It was as if the long hours of work might help take away the misery and pain from those poor and miserable patients of mine, who had nothing, absolutely nothing. What a world! A few wealthy people like Zelani amidst the poor masses. How did he get so much money to dabble in all those businesses, property, retail and ... what? Oh, yes, construction. Well, I guess he must have worked hard for it. I hoped so, anyway, as he seemed to be quite a nice guy.

III

Before going to bed, I called my friend Marita to ask her for a ride into work the following morning. She worked as a sales representative for one of the private companies downtown. She was certainly in the right business. Marita was very friendly and sociable and could sweet-talk her way into anything.

Marita's sister was a pharmacist at the hospital, and through her we discovered that we lived in the same block of apartments. After that, she dropped in fairly regularly and became a friend, although I must admit we were poles apart in our social values and interests. I told her about my adventure with the businessman. She was surprised to hear that I did not let him drive me home. "Chilufya, how can you let such a big fish slip away? Being bashful in this day and age? I would have swooned over him!"

"He was kind of pushy and too slick," I answered. "That just threw me off."

"Well, if you don't want him, then I do. Don't forget that time is running out for you and me."

"What do you mean?" I asked.

"Biological clock time! You should know that. You're a medical doctor."

"So you're prepared to grab any man who comes along?" I asked.

"Not any man. A rich man, yes! Can you introduce me to him the next time you see him?" she asked.

"The next time I see him," I said. "Are you crazy? I might never see the man again."

But I was wrong. I recognized his voice when I was paged to the telephone around midday the following day. The operator said the caller told her it was a "matter of life and death." He thought it was very funny, but I wasn't amused and told him so.

"Okay, doctor; I won't do it again, but I had to talk to you."

"About what?" I asked.

"About going out to dinner tonight."

"Oh. Tonight?"

"Yes. What time should I pick you up and from where?"

What a cheeky, arrogant man! He seemed to take it for granted that I would go. It wasn't a request or invitation. Just a statement. I felt like telling him where to get off, but how could I be rude to him after all the help he had rendered me? Well, there was no harm in going. That would be a way of paying him back for his help. After that, no more. I didn't care what Marita ... safety in numbers? Wow! Why didn't I think of this earlier?

"Thanks for the invitation. I would love to come, but may I bring a friend?"

There was a moment's silence followed by a hesitant, "Well ... why not?"

"Thanks. There's no need for you to pick us up. Why don't we just meet where we'll have dinner? By the way, we can split the cost since my friend is coming."

"Don't worry about it. Let's meet at eight o'clock at the Ridgeway Hotel."

"Okay. See you later."

When I called Marita, she was beside herself with joy.

"You're a swell buddy, Chilufya. I'll do the same for you one day."

"Okay," I said. "My pleasure."

But as I stared at the telephone for a few minutes, I didn't feel at all happy. What bothered me was her cold, calculated manner. She hadn't met him, didn't know him, but she was prepared to grab him because of his wealth. I didn't want him to get hurt. I would talk to her on the way to dinner and advise her to cool it.

After work, I picked the car from the garage. Mbesa charged me very little. I couldn't believe the bill and told him so.

"It really was a minor problem. Besides, anyone who is Zelani's friend is my friend," he said.

I had suspected as much. I thanked him, but made a mental note not to go there again. I didn't want to feel perpetually indebted to Zelani, or he would really take advantage of me. First, it would be dinner; the next time, something else.

Marita arrived at seven thirty. I smelt her perfume even before opening the door. The strong scent drifted in through the open windows. When I let her in, she said, "Hi, I'm ready for this gorgeous man!"

"Good," I said matter-of-factly, "but please don't throw yourself at him."

"Hey, don't tell me you're jealous! Are you in love with him?"

"Of course not."

"Good. I wouldn't want to compete with a friend."

"Don't worry. You won't."

Yet I felt a heavy lump in my throat. I suddenly wished I was going alone, at least to check him out and decide whether I really didn't like him. But now it was too late. I couldn't compete with Marita, who earned huge commissions and a good salary. Sometimes I thought how ironic life was. Here I was, after years of training, unable to afford a new car. Why didn't I just pack it in and join private practice? Why did I have this guilt complex and the feeling that I owed everybody in the country my free training? Why weren't others bothered like me? After all, I was not the only one who had benefitted from the free educational system.

Most people did the required stint in government, and after they had met their "bond requirements" of a couple of years or so, they left for more lucrative careers. Now here was Marita who hadn't even gone to college. A quick course and 'training on the job,' and she was earning more money than I was. She had a brand new flashy car to show for it, while I spent time struggling to have my little second-hand car started. Marita wore the latest fashions and expensive perfumes. She was now dressed to kill, and I looked like Cinderella beside her. I suddenly wished I could call it off and just stay home. But how could I do that? What excuse would I give him? There was an added problem. I had no idea where he lived or how to contact him. Besides, there was Marita as well. I just couldn't go back on all these arrangements. There was no way out. I had to go.

Marita chatted all the way to the Ridgeway Hotel. She didn't even notice that I wasn't saying very much.

"I just can't wait to meet him!"

"I wouldn't be too excited if I were you," I warned. "He could be married for all I know."

"I don't think so," she said.

"What makes you so sure?" I asked. "We know nothing about him."

"Just a feeling. My instinct."

"Well, good luck."

I spotted him in the lounge when we arrived, and he stood up to meet us.

"Zelani, please meet my friend Marita," I said forcing myself to smile.

"Pleased to meet you," he said. "I'm greatly honoured to be dining with two lovely ladies."

Marita giggled and said, "I'm delighted to meet you."

When we sat down to dinner, she chatted and giggled all the time, while I seemed like someone who had lost her tongue. I rarely joined in the conversation, and I kept glancing at my watch praying that the evening would come to an end.

"Chilufya, you hardly touched your meal. Wasn't the chicken to your liking?" Zelani asked.

"It was delicious thanks. I think the portion was too much for me."

"She might get hungry again if we go out dancing, away from here to a nightclub," said Marita leaning over to Zelani and fluttering her eyelids at him. I felt so embarrassed that all I could do was stare at the napkin on my lap. I didn't want to look at him.

"Well, Chilufya, what do you want to do?" he asked.

"Me? I really have to go now as I have an early morning. I can take a taxi back. You two can go on to the nightclub."

"You don't have to take a taxi," offered Marita. "You can borrow my car. I'm sure Zelani won't mind giving me a lift."

"Er ... I just remembered that I also have a very early morning. So early to bed won't be a bad idea for me either."

I breathed a sigh of relief which did not escape Zelani's notice. His eyes met mine and sent my heart beating wildly. I quickly looked away and stood up.

"Come on, Marita. Let's go. Thank you, Zelani," I said.

"My pleasure. I hope we can do this again."

"Yes, and soon," declared Marita.

Zelani just smiled and accompanied us to the car. As soon as we got into the car, I started yelling at Marita.

"How could you humiliate yourself like that? Pushing yourself on him without shame?"

"Oh, come on Chilufya. You spent too many years at that mission school of yours. This is not the puritan age! Anyway, is this concern for me, or are you just jealous?"

"Jealous? Don't be ridiculous!"

But when she dropped me off and I finally went to bed, I started wondering whether she could be right. Surely it couldn't be. It was impossible. How could I love a man I had only just met? Besides, wasn't he supposed to be too slick and pushy for my liking? Why did I suddenly not want Marita to be with him? I tossed and turned and finally fell into an exhausted sleep in which I dreamed that he and Marita were getting married. People at the wedding kept pointing fingers at me and chanting, "You lost him. You lost him."

IV

I woke up red-eyed and wishing that I could sleep the whole day and not go to work. But I had to go to work after drinking two cups of strong coffee.

I was called to the telephone at ten o'clock. After rubbing my sleepy eyes and yawning into the telephone, I said, "Hello, this is Dr. Chaba ... "

"Good morning, doctor."

My heart started going boom, boom, boom, and my hands tightened their hold on the telephone.

"Chilufya, are you there?"

"Yes."

"Can we meet again this evening? Alone, please. No friends. Just you and me."

"Sure. Where?"

"At my place for dinner. How about seven o' clock? My address is ..." My hand shook as I wrote down the directions. I just couldn't believe my ears. Afterwards I briskly walked back. It was as if new life was breathed into my soul. I no longer felt sleepy. I couldn't wait for the evening.

When I left work I rushed to Cairo Road to buy myself a dress for the evening. I couldn't really spare the cash, but one can't go on in life worrying about things like that all the time. One needs a special treat once in a while. This was important for me, and I wanted to look my best.

The telephone rang as soon as I got home. I hope that's not him calling it off, I said to myself. Please, please let him not cancel our date.

I picked up the telephone and said, "Hello."

"Where have you been? I rang you several times, and you were not there." It was Marita. She wanted to know whether I had heard from Zelani.

"You mean he didn't contact you about last night or ask about me?"

I only hesitated a second or two before replying, "No."

"Oh, well, I guess that's that." And with that she hung up.

I felt kind of guilty for telling a lie, but not too guilty. Marita was so used to getting her own way that I didn't care. She changed boyfriends every few months and left broken hearts in the process. Her sister warned her several times about her risky behaviour, especially in the face of the terrible AIDS threat.

The disease was ravaging the population and taking away the cream of the nation. Young men and women were dying in their prime and at the peak of their careers. How many people out there were infected with HIV? How many more were being infected every day, especially with the polygamous habits of the new and affluent breed of macho guy? The more girlfriends a man had, the higher his social status. The old shame of infidelity and having illegitimate children had long disappeared. Some men even boasted of not knowing how many children they had fathered out there. Marita was trying to beat them at their own game. But at what price?

Anyway, this was my evening out. I wouldn't waste it by thinking about Marita or miserable things like AIDS. Of course, I would be careful and take precautions not to be rushed into anything I might regret later. I took out my new outfit and started getting ready.

When I dressed, I took another look at myself in the mirror. I felt good and liked the reflection that stared back at me. The dress had a shapely dropped waist, a flattering silhouette, a V-neckline, a buttoned bodice, and a pegged skirt in turquoise and white cotton/polyester. It was simple but elegant. Just right for an informal but special evening. The contrast against my ebony skin was superb. A pity I was going in my beat-up little Fiat. But, like a friend who knew how special the evening was to me, the little car behaved itself. One turn of the ignition key and the engine started and I took off like a space rocket. Whatever Mbesa's garage had done to it had produced wonders.

When I reached the affluent Kabulonga suburb, I started looking at the street names. I finally found his house in a secluded close. Wow! I thought, he sure does live in one of the posh areas of town. I again checked the number of the house just to make sure and then stopped at the gate. A security guard came to open the gate and gave my car suspicious scrutiny. I explained that I was Mr. Chirwa's guest. "Yes madam, he is expecting you," he finally said.

Zelani must have heard the car because he immediately came out. He wore a fawn safari suit. My heart skipped a beat when he rushed towards me with one hand outstretched. I went towards him and placed my hand in his, and the squeeze that he gave it sent a warm glow through my entire body. As I walked beside him to the house I said, "You have a lovely house and yard."

"Yup," he answered, "but it is far too big for me. I feel kind of lonely in it."

"Why did you get such a big place just for yourself?" I asked.

"Because of my wife and son."

I let go of his hand as if I had been struck by lightning. Wife and son? I should have known. How could an affluent-looking man like Zelani have remained unmarried?

"Where are they now?" I asked. "Gone out for a visit somewhere? Is that why you invited me here? Sneaking behind you wife's back for a quick .. ."

"Hey, wait a minute. Where do you think you're going? Come back here. Let me explain!"

But I was already heading back towards the car. He came running after me and grabbed me by the hand.

"I'm not married. I was, but I'm not anymore. I've been divorced over a year now. I'm terribly sorry. I should have said my ex-wife. I'm truly divorced. Do you want me to show you my divorce papers?"

"Of course not. Sorry. I shouldn't have reacted like that, but I couldn't help it. It's not my style to fool around with married men."

"It's okay. I understand. Things just didn't work out for me and Sepiwe. She went back to Lilongwe after our divorce."

"She's from Malawi?" I asked.

"Her dad is, but her mother is from the south. She obtained custody of our six-year-old son Tembo, claiming that I was too busy to look after him. Please come in. You can't just go off like that."

I followed him into the house. He ushered me into an enormous living room split into two levels. I gazed at the shiny wooden floors and the beautifully carved wooden panels along the walls. Above our heads, wooden beams criss-crossed each other to form a kind of ceiling. The room was tastefully furnished, with black leather furniture and several small Persian rugs. The lower level had a small bar in a corner stocked with drinks, and that part of the room was casually furnished with a couple of puffs, stools, a wooden bench-like fixture and several cushions. He led the way past the larger room to the bar and asked me what I wanted to drink. After telling him, I said,

"Gee, you do live in luxury. How on earth can you live like this when thousands of people are starving!"

"Are you accusing me of causing their starvation?"

"No. But we are all responsible for the rest of the people in this country. We've benefitted from free university education, so we should give something back."

"Speak for yourself. I've not been to any university."

"But ... I thought ..."

"Are you going to walk away again just because I don't have a degree?"

"Of course not."

"Good."

"How did you get all this?" I asked as he drew back the curtains to reveal large French windows that led to a porch overlooking a swimming pool.

"One doesn't need a degree to live comfortably. After completing school, I joined my brother who was in construction. At first he was just into the manufacturing of building materials and he was reluctant for me to join him, as things were really tough and his small company was on the brink of bankruptcy. But things started picking up when we started property prospecting, building apartments and renting them out. We moved to higher quality housing and then to offices. We are now on the road to big money."

"Your brother must be thrilled," I said, smiling at their obvious good fortune resulting from hard work. But Zelani's face seemed to cloud over, and his eyes shone with pain and unshed tears. I wondered what I had said to upset him.

"Zelani, I hope I didn't say anything to ..."

"It has nothing to do with you. My brother was killed by armed robbers. They tied up his wife and two children, ransacked the house and then shot him. I wish they'd taken everything and left him alive, but to kill him in cold blood. And he was such a kind and considerate man ... always worrying about his workers and never forgetting those early days of hard work. Sometimes I think God, if there is one, punishes those who are kind and good-natured. They die earlier. He was a better person than I am."

It was almost as if he was talking to himself. As if I wasn't there. I moved closer to him and hooked my arm in his. He turned to me and smiled.

"I'm sorry. I'm not being a good host. Come, let's go and eat." On the way to the dining room, I stopped by a large photo of a young boy who looked like Zelani.

"Is this your son? He is lovely."

"Yes, I miss him very much."

He briefly talked about his son and ex-wife during the meal and the problems they had had during their marriage. A flash of anger crossed his face when he related how he discovered that she had been unfaithful to him.

"She was a good-for-nothing gold digger!" he declared bitterly and immediately added, "The friend you brought last night reminded me of Sepiwe ... superficial and shallow."

"I'm sorry," I said.

"Don't be. I was just relieved that it was a woman and not a man. When you asked me if you could bring a friend, I thought you meant a boyfriend. I nearly said, 'No'."

After dinner we sat and listened to music. As the evening wore on, I found myself relaxing and kicking off my shoes. I curled up on the couch as he talked. Zelani moved closer to me and when I felt his lips nibbling my ear and moving down my neck and then up along the side towards my mouth, I thought I would faint with ecstasy. My lips parted and we explored each other, hungrily kissing each other as our bodies warmed to a point of explosion. When we finally separated to catch our breath, I lazily glanced at my watch and regrettably murmured, "Oh, gee I've got to go."

"Please stay. Don't go. You can sleep here," he pleaded.

"No. I'd better go. I'm on early morning duty tomorrow."

"Can you come again tomorrow evening?" he asked.

"No. You come to my place. Come and see how a struggling government doctor lives."

V

The following evening I prepared *nshima*, our national staple food, and chicken stew for dinner. We ate it by candlelight, sharing a bottle of white wine which Zelani had brought.

"There's no wine in the shops these days. In fact, one has to stand in long lines for almost everything. I don't have time to spend in long queues, so I eat very simply," I declared as he opened the bottle.

"Things are available, if you have contacts," he said. "What do you want? Wine? Say the word, and your patron angel will get it for you."

"No, thanks," I replied. "There's nothing that I can't survive without."

After we finished eating, Zelani leaned back and patted his stomach. "Mmm, that was delicious. The best *nshima* in the whole wide world!"

"I'll make us some coffee," I said as I stood up and started clearing the table. The telephone rang while I was in the kitchen.

"Please pick it up for me," I called out through the open door. Then I heard him talking to the caller.

"Me? Zelani. Her boyfriend. Would you like to talk to her? Okay, just a minute. Chilufya, it's for you."

When I picked up the telephone, I said, "Hello."

"You traitor! You double-crossing traitor!"

"Marita? Look, I can explain ..."

"Explain what? Why didn't you just tell me that you were in love with him instead of leading me on and making a fool of me?"

"Marita, can I call you later? I think you also need time to ... "

"Don't bother," she answered. "I don't want to talk to you ever again!" And with that she hung up on me. I stared at the telephone for a second or two before placing it down. How could I explain to her that I truly didn't know at first that I would fall for him? In any event, why was she making such a fuss over nothing? It wasn't as if I had snatched him from her. The problem with Marita was that she always wanted everything. She couldn't bear to be rejected by any man. She enjoyed doing the rejecting. Well, too bad. But this was now my man, and I would not let my evening be ruined by her. It just proved to me how fickle she was as a friend. So different from my real friends, Tengani and Likande. How I wished that they were there to share my new-found love! Tengani was away on a one-month leave in Chipata. I made a mental note to write to Likande over the weekend.

When I rejoined Zelani, I asked him as I handed him his coffee, "What have you been doing since your wife left?"

"I've been busy working. I just buried myself in work."

"No social life?"

"You mean dating? No. Once bitten, twice shy! You're my first date since my wife left."

"Really?"

"Well, I've gone out with groups of people. Friends also invite me to their homes for meals. There's often a single female around who is invited in case I 'hit it off with her,' as my well-meaning friends often tell me. But that really switches me off. I like hunting, not being hunted!"

"Mmm, so where have you been hunting lately?" I asked.

"Here. Right here."

He took a step towards me and with one hand, raised me to my feet and then swiftly crushed me against his body. The rhythmic pounding of our hearts filled the air between us. I was intoxicated with the tingling sensation that was sweeping through my entire body. We were both on fire. Red-hot and sizzling from the flames of passion and love.

"I want you now," he cried.

"I want you, too," I moaned, throwing all caution to the wind, and with it my long-held views against premarital sex so ingrained in me by my dear Methodist missionaries. I had even convinced Sepho about those virtues, and he had respected my decision, content to exchange kisses and stop when I gave the word. I was now thirty-three years old, but in terms of sexual experience I was a novice. And here I was now, aflame, there was no way this man could be made to wait. Neither could I.

We made love. It was the sweetest, most exciting love that could consume two human beings. It took us to soaring heights, propelling us far beyond the earth's axis into the timeless heavens of space. It was just he and I out there. Just the two of us. No one else. Not a soul. When it was over my small living room came into focus. My body trembled against his. He leaned his head against my breasts and whispered, "I can't believe it!" he said. "It was your first time!"

I just nodded. He stood up and before I knew what he was doing, he had lifted me and was saying, "This may be your first time, but it won't be the last. We'll have a zillion more."

We drifted into my bedroom and again took each other. We made love again and again. Countless times. It was as if the warm embers that had been lying dormant in my body were suddenly set ablaze. Hours later we fell asleep, utterly spent and exhausted.

I was awakened by the sound of the beep. His arms were still around me, and his chest rose and fell as he steadily breathed against my body. I quietly extricated myself from his arms and reached out for the beeper.

"Yes?"

"Dr. Chabala, you're needed in the emergency room. Please call immediately."

"Okay. I'll just have a quick shower and I'll be on my way."

I immediately jumped from the bed and rushed into the bathroom. Getting ready at supersonic speed was now second nature to me. I even managed to gulp down a cup of instant coffee that I made with hot tap water. It tasted like lukewarm medicine, but I just wanted to be wide awake and alert. The effects of the hectic night were now being felt by my body. Zelani was still fast asleep. I planted a kiss on his forehead and then gently shook him.

"Zelani, I've got to go."

"Go? Why, where?" he murmured sleepily yawning and stretching himself.

"To the hospital. They want me there. Please help yourself to breakfast when you get up. Lock and leave the key for me under that flower pot by the window."

"Okay. But I don't like this."

"What?"

"Your going off like that."

"Too bad, but it's my job."

VI

At first, my job didn't seem to be such a threat to him. I laughed it off whenever he said that he didn't like the amount of time I was spending at work or worrying about my patients. I just laughed. I laughed a lot in those early days. It was a whirlwind romance and we were both carried away.

"Let's get married in four weeks," he announced one evening.

"Four weeks? But we've only known each other for two months!"

"Two months, two days, who cares? I love you and you love me. What else matters?"

"Well, I guess it's okay, but I'll need time to get ready. I also want you to meet my parents. They've been looking forward to this for years. I want to show you off to them and they'll know that my waiting was worthwhile!"

His face lit up like a little boy's and he announced, "Let's go see them this weekend. Take time off. We'll go by plane."

"Plane? But that will cost too much money. Besides, I have to let them know first."

"Come on, it will be a nice surprise for them."

"Okay, as you wish." But I gave a silent prayer that the shock and excitement would not be too much for my mother. She was having problems with high blood pressure. On the other hand, the news might work wonders for her. She was overly concerned about my being an 'old spinster.'

As it turned out, my parents were thrilled at the news. When Zelani told them he would send a chauffeur to bring them to the wedding, they both beamed with delight. My father was so taken by Zelani's obvious importance and wealth that he kept addressing him as "*Emukwayi, Mwenfumu*, yes, Chief."

The next few weeks I was very busy getting my wedding dress and busily organizing everything. To my great surprise and despite the short notice, both Tengani and Likande said they would attend the wedding. Likande was the maid of honour, and Tengani was my chief bridesmaid. I couldn't have wished for anything more. It was like the good old days. We talked and giggled until late at night. They were surprised by the speedy marriage and bluntly asked me whether I was pregnant.

"No, I'm not. Hey, who's the doctor here? You or me?"

The wedding was big and was attended by many people, including top government officials and Zelani's business contacts. I also invited several people from the hospital – physicians, nurses, orderlies and even cleaners. The Cathedral of the Holy Cross was packed.

I would have preferred a small wedding at my parents' place, or else at the church which I often attended. The cathedral was mostly for Anglicans or Episcopalians, and neither Zelani nor I were members. But he convinced the priest that from then on we would be members. I was increasingly finding that my independence and self-confidence were slipping away as Zelani took control of things. He took charge, and all I did was follow. This was how he liked things to be. He was macho through and through. He ran our relationship as if it were a business venture with him at the helm. He organized everything – the wedding notices at the Boma, the district office that dealt with marriages, and the hotel where our reception would be held. I just followed along.

Our honeymoon was in Mombasa, and I loved every minute of it. Making love on the moonlit white sands of the East African beach late at night when the beaches were deserted. Swimming naked in the cool blue Indian Ocean, and then afterwards walking hand in hand back to the hotel. Going to bed and sleeping until the afternoon of the following day. One day after getting up around two o'clock in the afternoon, Zelani said, "I'll call room service for breakfast."

"Breakfast now?" I said. "Everybody must have had their lunch already!"

"Who cares if we have breakfast at two o' clock, lunch at four o'clock, and dinner at midnight? Absolutely no one. Besides, we're on our honeymoon, and the manager said we could ask him for anything."

It was indeed our honeymoon, so I sat back and relaxed. The weather was steaming hot. Unbearably hot and sticky. But I really didn't care. We went around Mombasa to explore and toured the old seaport built by the Portuguese during their heyday of explorations and trade with the Far East. Mombasa was one of the stopover ports along the East African coast, and the old fort was a mark of their fame and expansionism during the Fifteenth Century.

From Mombasa we flew to Nairobi, Kenya's capital city and tourist centre. We stayed for two days, browsing around the city which was full of tourists on their way to and from the famous safari tours. Our next stop was Lilongwe in Malawi. As we entered the Malawi air space I gazed at the picturesque mountains, the lush tea plantations and beautiful landscaped farmland. Lake Malawi, the country's waterline, was clear blue amidst the greenery, villages and towns along its side. Zelani had once mentioned that people in Malawi were very hardworking and that they made use of 'every bit of soil.' I could now see what he meant.

There was not doubt that the country was intensely farmed. "It's strange how Malawi is doing so well, and yet we had better resources than they had when our countries became independent," I said.

"The problem in Zambia is that everyone wants to rush to the cities, leaving behind beautiful land. I wish someone would remind our people that copper is not edible. It is really a shame to stand in long lines buying imported corn and mealie meal for *nshima*, when we could feed the whole of Africa if we worked as hard as these people here."

"Well, some of the problems have been due to bad rains and so on. We are not entirely to blame," I said.

"No. But we are also experts in looking for excuses for our failures."

My thoughts moved from that to our impending meeting with my stepson and Zelani's ex-wife. I was very nervous and prayed that we would get on well.

Zelani called his ex-wife as soon as we checked into the hotel in downtown Lilongwe. He arranged for her to bring Tembo to us. She arrived faster than I had expected. The arrangement was for her to drop him off and then come for him later in the day. He was a sweet little boy, and my heart went out to him. He seemed rather overwhelmed by two domineering parents. He was clearly caught in the middle.

As I tried to chat to Tembo and make him relax, Sepiwe's eyes swept me up and down, checking me out. She was slim and sophisticated and was dressed as if she was going to a business conference. I wondered whether that was to show off in my presence, or whether it was her usual way.

"Zelani told me that you are a medical doctor," she said, as we shook hands.

"Yes, I am."

"I hope you also took psychology and psychiatry because this man is crazy. He thinks it is a man's prerogative to fool around and ... "

"Sepiwe, I don't want you poisoning my wife's mind. Leave us alone!"

"I'm only speaking the truth. Forewarned is forearmed. Anyway, Chilufya, take care and don't let him bully you. He's the most possessive and jealous man on this planet."

Zelani grabbed her hand and firmly led her out of the door. "Bye-bye, Sepiwe. Don't bother to come for Tembo, I'll bring him.

His face was livid with anger. "The terrible witch!" he muttered. "I'll see my lawyer when we get back and arrange for my son to move in with us."

"Why don't you two go out for a walk," I suggested. "I think I'll lie down for a while."

"Good idea," Zelani said. "We'll walk for a while and then I'll take him shopping. We'll meet you for lunch."

"Okay. And don't rush back. You two must have a lot to catch up on."

I needed to be alone. I was still shaken by Sepiwe's outburst. In the end I brushed off her warnings as the muttering of a jealous woman. She probably wanted to go back to Zelani and was trying to spoil things for us. I felt much better and took my much-needed nap.

VII

Back in Lusaka, I got busy settling into my new house. I still couldn't bring myself to calling it my home. I was like a guest or a stranger, tiptoeing around the house. What a long way from my cosy little apartment! There, I would rush in and out, kicking off my shoes and walking barefoot when I was home. Zelani's home was another world. It was a bit like a military academy run by a general. He was the ultimate boss, and even the servants made that clear to me. There was a defined hierarchy: Zelani, the boss, followed by Sarafina, the housekeeper, who was the queen mother. Then came Kangwa, the cook, followed by Moono, the hefty, wrestler-like, security guard. There was a visible struggle for power among these three.

The outsider was the young gardener, Mwale. He took a liking to me as soon as I moved in, welcoming me with a bunch of freshly cut roses from the garden. The others saw me as a threat and intruder, one who would disturb their daily routines. In the house I felt like an unwanted prisoner, while in the garden outside I found peace and tranquillity. Mwale felt greatly honoured when I praised and admired his hibiscus, African violets and zinnias.

Conflicts with the cook and housekeeper came soon after I moved in. I walked into the kitchen one afternoon and asked Kangwa if he could make beef stew for dinner. He declined. "No beef stews on Fridays, Madam. Today is fish."

"Who says?" I yelled, getting really angry.

"I say. I'm Catholic. Bwana Zelani knows. He too now eats only fish on Fridays. If you want meat, you can find another cook. I can tell the Bwana that I can't stay."

"It's okay," I said. "We'll have the fish." There I was, again being led by the nose, even by people supposedly working for me!

But I shrugged off the incident. It was no big deal. After all, fish was better for the body than red meat. So why make a fuss about having fish on Fridays? I could ask him to prepare anything I wanted on the other evenings. I was also quite capable of preparing my own meals. I need not let Kangwa do all the cooking and dictate menus to us. Besides, Zelani seemed to enjoy my cooking. At least, he used to, back in my apartment.

My next problem was with Sarafina. She was responsible for the shiny floors in the house and the dust-free furniture. If she had her way, we would all take off our shoes before entering the house, leaving them in a line on the veranda. She was very upset one day when I kicked off my shoes and left them lying on the floor, the way I used to do in my little place.

"Look what you've done to my polished floor! It's now ruined!" Picking up the shoes and shoving them into my arms, she marched off in a huff. I thought to myself, "What the hell? Whose house is this anyway? Where do I fit into the scheme of things here?"

"Sarafina, come back here!" I yelled. "Right now!"

She sauntered back, defiance written all over her face. I said, "This is my house, and I'll no longer tolerate such an attitude. Do you hear me?" She looked surprised and nodded her head. "You may go now," I said, dismissing her with a wave of one hand.

After she left, I sank into the nearest chair. I was feeling tired, and I had a terrible headache. I wasn't used to having servants around, and the whole situation was beginning to get to me. I stood up to go and get some juice in the kitchen, but as soon as I opened the door, I rushed out again. I couldn't stand the smell of the fish that was cooking, and I almost threw up on 'Sarafina's' polished floor. I managed, though, to stagger into the nearest bathroom.

That evening I went to bed early. I told Zelani that all I wanted for supper was tea and a tomato sandwich. I also told him about the terrible attitude I was getting from servants. His reaction was that I was making a mountain out of a molehill and that he had never had any problems with them.

"I'll talk to all of them, but you've got to be firm. Stop treating them as if you're the one working for them. There's protocol in this house."

"So I've noticed, general," I said, laughing.

The fishy smell seemed to linger in the air during the weekend. Fish was not my favourite food, but never before had the smell made me so sick and ... Oh, no! I thought. Surely not? Not so soon. But my visit to the gynaecology clinic at the hospital the following day confirmed that I was indeed pregnant. I had been so busy with settling into the new house and rushing to and from work that it had not even crossed my mind that I had missed two periods.

"Yes, doctor. Positive. Congratulations," said Dr. Mistry, my good friend and colleague at the hospital.

I couldn't wait to see Zelani's face that evening. His efforts to get Tembo to come from Lilongwe and live with us had failed.

His ex-wife was making it really difficult for him. How thrilled he would be to learn that I was already pregnant and that we would have a baby of our very own!

Since both of us were working late that day, it wasn't until we were in bed that I got a chance to give him the news. He was indeed very pleased when I told him, but he added, "Now you can stop working."

"What?" I replied.

"Leave work, of course," he said. "Who will look after the baby?"

"I can find a nanny," I answered.

"I don't want my kid brought up by a nanny! You'll have to stop working and stay home." I was so shocked that all I could do was stare at him with my mouth wide open. I couldn't even manage a word. I was completely speechless. Turning away from me, he said, "Anyway, the baby is still months away, so let's not discuss it now," and a short while later he was fast asleep.

I felt like grabbing him by his shoulder and screaming at him. Did he realize what he just said? Did he think that I could throw away years and years of training just to stay at home and look after a baby? Of course, I would give the baby all the love and protection that it needed, but I couldn't give up my whole career to be a full-time wife and mother. Why, that would be like going back to my mother's life, something I had fought against since I was a child! No way would I give up working. I would work until I was incapacitated by illness or old age. I would do everything – be a medical doctor, a mother and a wife. I would show Zelani that it was possible to do it all.

My pregnancy was fairly smooth, so I worked until my eighth month. Zenai was born on a wet January morning. There was rain and thunderstorms the whole day. Zelani insisted on calling the baby Zenai after himself. He wished I had given him a boy.

"If it were a boy," he said wistfully, "I would have called him Zelani Jr."

Later, when I looked back on the day my baby was born, it was as if the continuous rain and thunderstorms were warnings of what lay ahead in my marriage.

Things came to head when the baby was two months old and I announced that I was going back to work. Sarafina, who had become very friendly and had pampered me throughout my pregnancy, brought her niece to help look after the baby. "I'll also be here madam, so don't worry," she assured me.

But Zelani was furious. He started yelling as soon as I told him. "So your work is more important than your baby, it that it?"

"That's not true! I can't take any more time. I've been away three months already, and the hospital is short-staffed. I just can't stay away."

"Well, you'll have to stay away. Put in your notice tomorrow and tell them you're not going back again."

"I'll do no such thing! I'm going back to work tomorrow," I said in a firm voice.

"You'll do as I say. You're my wife and the mother of my child. Besides, it's too risky for the baby and for me for you to continue working at that hospital."

"What do you mean?" I asked.

"You touch so many people there, some of whom may have AIDS. Who knows what you might catch there and bring home."

"Oh, come on. AIDS is not transmitted through touching someone. You should know that by now."

"Don't talk down to me! Just because you're a doctor doesn't give you the right to talk down to your husband!"

"I'm not ... "

"Shut up!" he yelled, and with that he stormed out of the house. He didn't get back until midnight. I could smell the alcohol on his breath as he staggered into the room.

It was the beginning of many long and lonely nights to come. When he found out that I did not resign from my job the following day, he went out again. I hardly saw him during the next few months. Whenever I came back home, he briefly appeared to change from work clothes to casual ones and then he was off.

Soon he started holding huge parties at home every weekend. We used to entertain before, and he often said, "Most business is made through social contacts." But the people who now came to the parties were those he met at the local bars. He no longer bothered to tell me who was coming or even when the party would be held.

A number of times I came from work and walked into a party that was already in progress. He tried to make me jealous by flirting with other women and telling them in my presence that he no longer loved me. As soon as his guests left, he would start yelling at me and being abusive. I couldn't believe he was the same man I had married. I finally realized that Sepiwe had been right after all, but thought I would stay on, at least for my child's sake. Is that how abused spouses get caught in the cycle of perpetual abuse? Because they believe that staying is for the children's sake?"

There were times I was tempted to quit my job in the hope of saving my marriage. I even took a lot of unpaid time off and started spending more time at home with the baby. But this didn't work. Zelani continued to be abusive, went out with whomever he pleased, and flaunted his women in my face. Poor Zenai. She didn't have a moment's peace.

All she heard from us were screaming and shouting matches. I was reminded about my own position one day when a woman who was badly beaten by her husband was brought to the emergency room. Her face was bruised and her eyes so swollen she could hardly see. At first she insisted that she had fallen on the stairs. Her mouth was also swollen and blood was oozing from her teeth. The husband who brought her in also told me that she had fallen.

Later, as I attended to the bruises, I talked to her alone. "I really don't think that all this resulted from a fall. Can you please tell me what happened?"

"Please don't call the police!" she pleaded. "He really loves me. He only does this to me when he is drunk. I always get better. We've been married ten years, and I can't leave him now. I have to stay for our children's sake."

I felt sick. Would this be me ten years from now? Finding excuses for Zelani? From verbal abuse he might graduate to physical abuse. What kind of home was I subjecting Zenai to? I thought a lot about that patient afterwards. It almost triggered me into leaving Zelani. But I put it off. I started looking for reasons why he had changed. Was it because I was more educated than he was? Was it because I had given him a daughter instead of a boy? Victims of abuse often end up blaming themselves for their problems, so did I. But the more I tried to be a better wife, the further he moved away. I felt like a runner whose finishing line was constantly being moved away every time she thought she had reached the end. I was not good enough, and whatever I did didn't please him.

He came home later and later each evening. There were also tell-tale signs of where he had been; lipstick on his shirts and the smell of perfume on his clothes. When I challenged him, he turned the tables on me, accusing me of not loving him and saying, "I'm not good enough for you. You're in love with one of the doctors at the hospital. That's why you rushed back to work." I was too shocked and astounded to even argue with him. Sepiwe's warnings echoed in my mind. I now realized what she meant.

As if things weren't bad enough, I started to receive unpleasant anonymous phone calls. They certainly added salt to my already painful wounds.

"Hi, doc," a voice said: "Isn't it strange that you treat patients but are unable to heal your own marriage?"

"Hello," I said. "Who is this?" But click went the phone. I stared at it for a moment, still holding it in my hand. It was the first of many to come. Whoever was calling knew the time I came home because the phone would ring as soon as I entered the house. Like someone in a trance, I moved towards it and picked up the receiver. Why didn't I just let it ring or let one of the servants pick it up? Was it because I was worried the caller might tell them something? That the doctor's husband was having an affair with someone else?

VIII

When a telegram arrived from Tengani saying that she was coming home from her diplomatic missions abroad for consultations regarding her reassignment, I was pleased. But also apprehensive. Happy and afraid. Afraid that she would find out how unhappy I was. I owed her and Likande many unanswered letters. My contacts with both had been through either brief and sporadic notes or Christmas cards. Zenai was almost three years old now. The last get-together for the three of us was during a party at my home soon after the wedding. As things got worse, I shielded Tengani, Likande and my family from my misery.

When I showed Zelani the telegram, he smiled and said, "Why don't we hold a dinner party for your dear friend?"

I agreed, but my heart sank. I knew the party would be full of his cronies and the young girls who were their escorts. I was now devoid of self-confidence. He said I was a bad mother, a bad wife, a bad doctor, bad everything. Nothing I did pleased him.

We were hardly seated at the dinner table on the evening of the party when Zelani announced to the twelve or so invited guests that if one fell sick, "The last place you should go to is the University Training Hospital. They employ useless doctors like my wife."

I immediately stood up and went into the kitchen, busying myself as though I was looking for something.

"Why do you put up with this?" asked Tengani after she had followed me into the kitchen.

"Oh, it's you. You scared me."

"Why, Chilufya?"

"Oh, he's not really bad. He doesn't mean what he says. I know that deep down he loves me." But the words sounded empty and hollow even to my ears. The image of my battered patient flashed before my eyes. But I closed it off.

"He sure has a strange way of showing it," Tengani was saying.

"Can't you ever take a joke?" I said, my voice rising in anger.

Why was I angry? At Tengani for touching a raw and painful spot? At me for being so stupid and foolish? Or Zelani for the misery he had caused me?

"Well, you can bottle it in your heart and burst out afterwards, or you can tell me about it later," Tengani said. And with that she went back into the dining room. I followed soon after.

The following morning, after Zelani left for work, I poured out my heart to her. I cried as if I would never stop.

"There, there. Stop crying," she said. "I'll go and make us a strong cup of tea."

Later, we took a picnic lunch at Munda Wanga, the zoo and botanical garden outside the city. I felt better after hours of talking to Tengani and pouring my heart out to her.

"Look, all I've done is bombard you with my problems. How about you? How have you been?" I asked.

"I'm tired of being away from home," she said. "I want them to find me a job here. But that shouldn't be a big problem. Not like yours, anyway. You've just convinced me that I shouldn't rush into any marriage."

"You haven't dated anyone since ... ?"

"No. And neither do I intend to!"

We both laughed. In fact, we laughed and cried a lot that afternoon. "Can you give me Likande's new address?" I asked as we walked back to the car. "I can't remember where I put her last letter."

"Sure. I've got it right here in my address book."

When we got back, Tengani would not stay because she didn't want to face Zelani again. She said, "You know me and my big mouth. I might say something that might make things worse for you. Besides, I really must leave for Chipata to see my father and my brother. I may not get on well with my stepmother, but my father is still my father."

"But it's already getting late," I replied. "You can't leave for Chipata now."

"Of course not," she said. "Just drop me off at the Intercontinental Hotel."

It was a week later that the last straw came, which pushed me into action. Zelani announced that he was going away to Kitwe on business for five days.

"I see," I said.

"I suppose you can't wait for me to leave," he said.

Silence. I said nothing. Absolutely nothing. What did he expect? That I would be heartbroken by his departure? That I would miss him terribly? When he saw no reaction, he said, "That will give you time to be with your doctor friends."

I saw red then. I yelled and screamed at him, bringing out foul language that I never knew my mouth was capable of. I also blatantly accused him of having an affair with his secretary.

"Your ex-wife was right. You're nothing but a heartless and double-crossing cheat!"

After several phone calls, I had finally recognized his secretary's voice although she tried to disguise it. One day I called her by name and threatened her with legal action if the phone calls didn't stop.

But one more came, the day after Zelani left. The caller said, "Doc, don't hung up on me. I'm just a friend warning you that they've gone to Kasaba Bay for a whole week!"

"They could be off to the moon for all I care!" I screamed and slammed the phone down.

My eyes caught the large photo of Zelani hanging on the wall just above where I was standing. The strange thing was that a kind of peace and relief descended over me. I felt no anger. No bitterness or hatred. Just relief.

"Goodbye, mister, and so long," I said aloud.

"Where are you going, Mommy?" asked my little daughter as she rushed towards me. I picked her up and swung her round and round in the air.

"You and I are moving from here, honey. I'll look for a place for us."

"Is Daddy coming, too?"

I slowly put her down and knelt beside her. "Zenai, Daddy and I can't live together anymore, so you're coming with Mommy."

"You're not friends anymore?"

"No. But he's still your Daddy."

"He yells at you a lot. Yell, yell, yell. I hear him all the time. But don't worry, Mommy, he can come and stay with us when he stops yelling at you. I told Towa that she's not my friend anymore."

"Oh, why?" I asked.

"Because she wouldn't let me play with her doll. She yelled and yelled at me. Just like Daddy."

"Well, I'm sure you'll be friends again. But we'd better begin packing. Come on."

"Towa will be my friend again. Just like you and Daddy."

I picked her up again and for a moment just squeezed her body against my bosom.

"I love you, sweetheart" I said, burying my face on her little neck.

My heart was choking with emotion and my eyes misty from unshed tears. How often did I tell myself that I was staying in the marriage for her sake? Here she was, fully aware that things weren't right.

My first reaction was to get away from Zelani, to leave town altogether and ask for a transfer to a hospital on the copperbelt. But leave my job, my work colleagues, my patients, and the friends I had made? No. I didn't want to do that. I loved Lusaka and had not lived on the copperbelt since I was young. Besides, I didn't want Zelani to think he had won and had actually chased me from town. I could just imagine him boasting about it. No. "I will fight him right here," I promised myself, gritting my teeth. "If he wants war, he'll have war!"

By the time he came back from his 'business trip,' I had moved out of the house and into an apartment that was just right for Zenai and me. Then one morning I drove into town in search of a lawyer. I knew nothing about lawyers. My choice was purely random: I saw a signpost and just walked in.

That was how I met Hambala Mainga. While the receptionist was telling me that all the lawyers were busy and that I would have to set up an appointment for another time, Hambala Mainga's scheduled client happened to call to reschedule another time.

"It's okay, I'll deal with this," he offered as he came in to get some papers, and turning to me he joked, "Looks like fate is telling us I've got to be your lawyer."

After relating to him everything and saying that I wanted a divorce as well as custody of our daughter, I warned him, "Zelani is an economic Goliath. So this could be a very bitter war."

"Don't worry, we'll be ready for him. From what you've told me, this shouldn't be much of a problem."

But what a bitter battle it was! At first he refused to grant me a divorce, claiming that he still loved me. I couldn't believe it. What kind of love could be so cruel and selfish? When that failed, he warned that he would fight tooth and nail for the custody of his daughter.

"You'll be sorry for this. Really sorry!" he yelled into the phone.

"Please don't call me again. You should address anything you have to say through my lawyer."

"That son of a ... "

I slammed the phone down. My knees were shaking and my palms were wet from perspiration. When will this nightmare end? I wondered miserably.

When we went back to court, he accused me of being a terrible wife and a mother unfit to be granted custody of his daughter. He even accused me of being unfaithful to him! He said I looked down on him because he'd never been to college. I couldn't believe that I was the one he was describing. I just couldn't recognize the person he was talking about.

Hambala challenged him to substantiate his accusations. Zelani stammered that he had no evidence to prove his allegations. Hambala then went for him. He put as much effort and energy into the case as if his own life depended on it. Even when I faltered and whispered to him to "just let him have what he wants, I can't stand this anymore," he wouldn't give up. He kept saying, "There's no going back now. We're in this till the end. We'll win."

Hambala was prepared to call Zelani's mistress as a witness.

Apparently, when Zelani found out that I had left the house and when be received notification of my petition for a divorce, he took his anger out on his secretary. He accused her of ruining our marriage and of 'harassing my wife.' He fired her immediately. Scorned and furious, she later called Hambala and told him she was 'prepared to talk and even be a witness against him.' I even felt sorry for him. Poor Zelani. He thought be could buy everybody and everything on his long and winding road from rags to riches. He used people like toys, discarding them when he no longer had use for them.

When he realized he couldn't use infidelity against me, he argued that I didn't have financial security and that was the reason he wanted me to keep the BMW – he didn't want his daughter 'being driven in some dangerous fourth-band car.'

He went through a long list of the property he owned – flats in Emmasdale, houses in Kabulonga and Chelston, construction companies, and what not. Just listening to the list made me yawn! Admittedly I couldn't offer Zenai the material wealth which her father could, but who said that love was synonymous with wealth? I would offer her the most important things I could give – love and emotional security. As far as I was concerned, that was better than the so-called huge mansion in Kabulonga, which was cold and devoid of love. It was a mere house as cold as the brick and mortar that kept it together. Therefore, I nearly laughed aloud when he said that he wanted custody of his daughter so that he could prepare for her eventual takeover of his companies. How many times had he said he wished I had given him a son so that he could replace Tembo, who was in Lilongwe?

Anyway, Hambala stood by me througbout the ordeal. He kept my spirits up when I was feeling down. The suspense and waiting were hard to bear, but he kept reassuring me that we had a better case than Zelani. He was right. When my divorce came through and I was granted custody of Zenai, with visitation rights for Zelani, I wept with joy. Rushing into Hambala's outstretched arms, I hugged him tightly as tears flowed down my face.

"I really don't know how to thank you for what you've done," I said.

"You can begin by coming to a celebration dinner with me at the Pamodzi Hotel," he said.

Later, during the meal at the hotel, he said, "What a blind fool your ex-husband was for losing someone as special as you. He must have been really crazy to treat you like that." He reached out across the table, and taking my hands into his, squeezed them slightly. I quickly pulled them away as if burnt by a hot iron. I didn't want to play with fire. Not now. Not again. Once bitten, twice shy.

"I love you, Chilufya. Truly love you."

"Please don't say that. Don't even mention the word. You did a superb job as my lawyer. But let's not spoil things now."

"I'm sorry. I guess it's too soon for you. But I mean it."

I don't know why, but I had a feeling that he truly meant it. Slowly but surely, we started dating. At first, I had a thousand excuses for not going out with him. But he wouldn't take no for an answer. If I said I had laundry to do, then he would turn up and help me with it, or he would clean the apartment while I did the laundry.

"I'm quite an expert at this. I did a lot of this when I was at Gray's Inn, in London, studying law."

One weekend he invited Zenai and me for lunch. We found him stir-frying assorted vegetables.

"Mmm, this looks colourful and appetizing," I remarked. "It's a Chinese special – Canton style."

"Where did you learn to cook Chinese!"

"In London. I shared a flat with a Chinese student from Canton. Next time I'll prepare chop suey or sweet and sour pork."

Next time? I didn't want to be rushed. I was like someone who had almost drowned and was still afraid of getting back into the water.

A divorce is like death. One doesn't get over it quickly. No matter how badly my marriage had turned out, I still grieved for it. I often wondered whether I was in some way to blame for its failure. There were days I woke up feeling very depressed. Nights when I shed tears for Zelani, Zenai and myself. For the lost years. The pain and suffering.

Hambala was patient. He just waited. He was there for me and my daughter. Compared to Zelani, he was like a calm and peaceful sea after a hurricane or turbulent ocean. Zenai immediately took to him. She had no doubts. A child's absolute trust. I was the one who was hesitant. Like someone who had been in a terrible accident and was learning to walk again. One step at a time, one step ...

"Mommy, when will you marry him? He loves you."

"Who, what?" I nearly jumped as Zenai, in her uncanny way, invaded my thoughts. It was now exactly a year since my divorce. The visits with her father were going well, and she often chattered about where they had been – to buy ice cream, to the zoo, to visit his friends, and so on. I had insisted that she be picked up and dropped off by his chauffeur, as I didn't want Zelani anywhere near my place.

"Mommy, Hambala loves you," she repeated.

"Now come here, young lady ... come this minute ..." and I started chasing her around the room. She shrieked with laughter, playing hide-and-seek behind the chairs.

"How do you know? Anyway, what does a four-year-old like you know about who loves who!"

"He told me."

"He what?"

"He said he loves you. But he's waiting until you're ready."

"And you, sweetheart, are you ready?" I asked, walking towards her and lifting her into my arms.

"For the wedding?"

"Yes."

"Oh, yes, Mommy! Yes. Can you do it tomorrow? Will the wedding be big? As big as the whole sky, with lots and lots of people? Can Daddy come, too? Can I ask him to come? Please, Ma ... "

"Well, let's wait and see, Zenai. We'll see."

Zenai was happy living in two worlds. Spending weekends at her father's place and weekdays with me. As our wedding plans got underway, she came from one of her visits looking very happy and excited. She announced that her father had taken her to see "our camping. I'll be manger when I grow up!"

"Company manager," I corrected.

"I told him about you and Hambala. I said I'll soon have two daddies."

"What did he say to that?"

"He said I have one real daddy. Hambala will be my stop daddy."

"Step daddy."

"If Daddy married again, I'll have two mummies and two daddies. Lucky me. Lucky girl!"

IX

Zenai was a flower girl at our wedding, together with Mutinta, Hambala's niece. She told Hambala and me to keep her dress in a special place so that she could wear it again when her daddy "finds his own sweetheart." Hambala and I looked at each other and burst out laughing. Zenai soon joined in the laughter, and the three of us laughed and laughed until we were clutching our ribs. I thought my sides would burst. Tears rolled down my cheeks. Tears of joy.

That was seven years ago. It's been seven happy and glorious years. Our son Mwinga was born a year after the wedding. Mwansa followed a year later. Hambala has not only been a loving father to our three children, but also a dear husband, friend and companion to me. We share everything. If one of the children is not feeling well, Hambala does not hesitate to offer to stay "and write reports here at home. You go, darling, since you have an emergency to attend to."

One day, as we sat relaxing in our verandah, a feeling of peace, quiet and contentment seemed to hang over us like a halo from heaven. "I love you, honey, and I love being with you, out here," I said, moving over to where he was sitting and kissing him tenderly.

"Mmm ... this is heaven," he whispered.

Our Spanish-style *hacienda* ranch is indeed like heaven. It takes my mind off the physical and mental suffering of my patients and the disinfectant and sterile smells of the hospital. It is a reminder that amidst all the illness and suffering, the hustles of life and the unending rat race, is nature's beauty and splendour. The sun shines, the birds twitter, stars twinkle and the moon lights the earth and the dark heavens when night falls.

I can't wait to get back to my home after a day's work at the hospital. Neither can Hambala. I often smile when I watch him quickly shedding off the business clothes befitting a lawyer and putting on his overalls, boots and a large sombrero over his head. Yesterday, as we both walked around in the garden, I remarked how large the cabbages and carrots were.

"That's the Tonga in me. We have green fingers. As you know,

Tongas are the lifeblood of this country. Where would this country be without the farmlands of Tonga people? Being half Tonga and half Lozi means I could either be a farmer or a fisherman," he boasted.

"Or a professor," I said. "Aren't Lozi people supposed to be brainy and intelligent?"

"Yes, of course. It's all the fish we eat ... come to think of it, what is your tribe famous for? Revolutions?"

I chased him round the vegetable garden, past the chicken runs and into the orchard. He hid behind a mango tree and then grabbed me around my waist, pinning me against his body. My arms went around his neck and we kissed and held each other tight.

I was home at last. Safe and secure. The brief marriage to Zelani that ended so painfully seemed like another world and another time. My real world was now, with my dear husband and children. I could almost see Hambala and me walking hand in hand into the future, watching our children grow. Together we will share happiness and any problems that might come our way.

Chapter Six

TENGANI

I

When I finished school at Chipembi, I went back to Chipata. At first, I was planning to take up Chilufya's invitation to go and meet her aunt, Mama Mulenga, who was a political activist in Luanshya. However, when I wrote to my father to inform him about my plans, he pleaded with me to go back home. I wondered why he suddenly wanted me back home, when things were still bad between me and my stepmother. However I decided to go when I received a letter from my brother saying that he was being released from prison. The release of political prisoners was top agenda in the discussions for independence.

My brother related how he and the other Freedom Fighters were beaten up when they were arrested and interrogated day and night, depriving them of sleep during the first week of detention. He said he had felt like a "sleep-walking zombie." He also feared that he might die in prison. He said to me, "I think what really saved us was the constant pressure that was being put on the government by our Party and the international community."

What I noticed was that his prison experience had given him a kind of maturity. He was more cautious and less impulsive. He was, of course, older as well. He also talked a lot about his friend Mwanza, whom he said, preferred being called "Che," short for Che Guevara, the Latin American freedom fighter. My brother said Che was trained in Moscow and was very disciplined, and that he told them revolutions which have undisciplined cadres don't succeed.

I realized that my brother's years in prison had not been wasted. I said to him, "I was expecting you to look terrible and haggard. But you look terrific!"

"Well, at first, things were hard. But conditions for political prisoners improved, as it became clear that it was only a matter of time before our country got its independence. Even prison wardens who used to harass us and taunt us about being the 'so-called freedom fighters' changed their attitude. They suddenly became friendly and even told us that they had all along believed in majority rule. What a joke! Anyway, we took advantage of their changed attitude and asked them to do things for us, including smuggling in some books and things to eat. They wouldn't bring in beer, though. Only things like chocolates. That's why I put on so much weight."

He told me that Che was arrested at the airport when he arrived from his training in Moscow. Apparently, someone tipped the police that he was on the way and which flight he was coming in on. They seized a lot of documents from his suitcases. What bothered my brother was that, although Che was also out of prison, it was rumoured that there were politicians in the Freedom Movement who were afraid of him and wanted to get rid of him. It seemed that some people had even been hoping that the colonial government might arrange to kill him while he was in prison. But it didn't. It would have been convenient to blame his death on imperialists and colonialists. But now be was out and posing a threat to other politicians who saw him as a danger and trouble-maker. Since his discharge from prison, Che had been widely quoted in the papers as planning to weed out neo-colonialists among our midst and to do away with the bourgeoisie, meaning all those who had trained in the West, in North America, Britain, or the rest of Europe.

I told my brother that I wanted to meet Che. He sounded like a terrific guy, a man I would really have loved to be involved with. My brother only shook his head. "Che is now a phantom ... an invisible man. I hear he is so afraid of being bumped off by his enemies that he rarely spends more than one night in anyone place. My feeling is that they will get him one of these days. If not his fellow politicians, then the CIA."

"The CIA? Who are they?" I asked, not fully comprehending what he was talking about.

"They are the American Central Intelligence Agency. You see, they don't want Russia moving into the vacuum that will be created when Britain pulls out of the country. They'll try and stop anybody like Che from getting into the new government. So the struggle will be between the CIA and the KGB, which is the Russian equivalent."

"But we don't want either of them! We can't gain our freedom only to lose it to the CIA or the KGB!"

"This is exactly what most Freedom Fighters are saying. They say we should be neutral, that we should be nonaligned, and not drawn into the fight; the Cold War between the West and East."

I listened attentively as my brother told me more about what was really going on in the political world. I realized then that I had a lot to learn about politics and that the issues were not just about gaining independence from Britain. They were about a lot more things. I looked at my brother with new respect. He definitely had not wasted his time during those many years in prison.

To celebrate my brother's release from prison, my father held a huge party in the village. He slaughtered a cow and three pigs and invited everybody in the village. There was drinking, dancing and singing all night long. Even my stepmother joined in the singing and dancing, as did my stepbrothers and sisters. It was as if we were a close-knit family.

A week after the party, I said to my brother, "What now? Are you just going to stay here and help Father?"

"Goodness, no! I just wanted to be with you and the old man for a while. You don't know what it's like to be cut off from your family for years. No visits. Nothing. You really begin to appreciate what it is to have a family. See how much effort Mandarena made for my party? She sweated for hours preparing meals, washing up and so on. Then she joined in the dancing and singing. She seemed genuinely pleased to see me back. I really felt touched."

"Mmm. So, what next?"

"Continue the fight, of course! Since you want to join politics, let's go where the action is! Let's leave before we overstay Mandarena's hospitality and her present good mood."

II

We went to the provincial town where my brother used to live before he was arrested and we registered with the new radical political party known as UNIP, the United National Independence Party. It was clearly spearheading the revolution and leading the country to independence. The party that had been fighting against the Federation and had laid most of the groundwork was called the ANC, the African National Congress. Young people were impatient with the ANC, accusing it of being too slow. The division and rivalry between the two parties became a generational one, with most older people supporting the ANC while the younger people followed UNIP. There were fights and violent acts between the two parties, and even tension among family members. Parents and their children constantly argued. Some children threatened to leave home while some parents threatened to have their children evicted.

The rivalry and violence between the political parties became so bad that some people died when petrol bombs were thrown through the windows of their homes, causing fatal explosions. Several months after our move to Chipata my brother Chenjerani received the sad news that Che had been killed by one such bomb. What was even more tragic was that he was killed at a time when the leader of the two political parties and all other groups were discussing the need to work together for the common good. Apparently, Che had even offered an olive branch of peace to everybody, including the bourgeoisie. He was tired of running and wanted to settle down. He was even planning to get married.

The letter which Chenjerani received from a friend stated that rumour had it that Che may have been killed by assassins hired by a jealous girlfriend; one he had left in order to marry someone else. However some people suspected that he was murdered by rival politicians who didn't trust him and were still afraid of him. There were others still who thought it was the CIA, because they didn't want him in power.

Another rumour had it that the KGB was responsible, as it was disappointed in him for trying to compromise with neo-colonialists and Western stooges. Some even accused the British and said that it was part of their ploy to prevent independence through divide and rule tactics. These people said that the British wanted to pour gasoline or petrol on the flames of dissent among the Africans.

Anyway, the truth was that no one really knew who killed Che except, of course, whoever committed the murder or was responsible for it. As for the move towards independence, the wind was clearly blowing in that direction. There was no way now of turning the clock backwards. The leaders of both parties closed ranks and told their followers to fight the enemy, not our own people.

I joined the Women's Brigade and became involved in organizing and mobilizing our women. Whenever politicians from Lusaka came to our province, we went round to people's houses early in the morning and also to the local markets, calling everybody to attend the meetings. We made life difficult for those who did not show up at the meetings. We organized boycotts of their goods if they had stalls at the market, or simply made them feel isolated and unwanted in our neighbourhood.

The long-awaited day finally came. We got our independence on 24 October 1964. When the British flag was lowered and our own Zambian flag was hoisted, the stadium reverberated with the shouting, shrieking and general jubilation that greeted our colourful emblem. The colours chosen for the flag were all important reminders of our heritage: black for the majority of people; red for the blood shed during the struggle; orange for copper, which was our export; and green for our natural resources. When the national anthem started playing and everybody started singing, "Stand and sing of Zambia, proud and free ... " tears rolled down my face. What joy, what jubilation. What a glorious day! How magnificent!

We were free, at last. Free. The singing and dancing spilt into the street where motorists honked their car horns and people waved thousands of little flags. The whole country was in celebration. Freedom was here at last. No more going around the country looking like beggars. No more watching our parents, brothers and sisters being humiliated. No more buying meat through back windows at the butcher's. We would go in through the door like anyone else. What euphoria! What expectations for the future!

Some of the politicians promised us that come 1970, every Zambian would have a decent breakfast every morning, shoes on their feet and a roof over their head. That was only six years away from independence day. I couldn't wait for 1970 to come! But there were a lot more things to be done before then. Changes to scrape the old colonial system came in fast. The Zambianization Programme was introduced to speed up the handing over of top-management positions to qualified Zambians. Offices were now run by Zambian secretaries who had to understudy foreign secretaries during the transition period.

Most of the settlers resented the swift changes and accused the new government of bringing in 'inexperienced and unqualified people.' But why were they complaining now and yet had been silent when jobs had been passed through the old boys colonial network? How many of those young, white, school drop-outs who had ended up as supervisors of African construction workers or labourers were really qualified or experienced? Well, Africans could not be deceived any more. As for those settlers who resented the changes, the writing was on the wall: "change your colonial attitudes, or leave." Some left but many more stayed to help rebuild our nation.

Those were the most exciting years of my life. We had a lot of hope for the future and deep trust in our leaders. I threw myself into the work of the Women's Brigade with all the energy and vigour I could muster. A year after independence, I moved to Lusaka, the centre of things, where all the action was. Every time I heard about the exciting and challenging "Development Plans" for the country, I said to myself, "Lusaka is where all these decisions are being made. What am I doing here?" So off I went to Lusaka.

The political honeymoon was still in full swing. The plan was to eradicate the three human scourges ... hunger, disease and ignorance. I was happy to throw in my lot with the women's group. After all, it was said that to educate a man is to educate an individual, but to educate a woman is to educate a whole nation. I was therefore at the centre of making history.

The opportunity for me to shine came one day after the woman I was assistant to, could not make it to a scheduled meeting and rally. I had to make a speech on her behalf. Instead of just reading the little note that she handed me, I added my own speech. It roused the crowd to a feverish pitch as I shouted out slogans, denounced the colonial government for our past ills, and demanded immediate and even faster changes in the country. The crowd roared with approval and chanted that it wanted "true freedom now!" My head was in the clouds and I was floating way up there.

When the next election for the Women's Committee was held, I vied and won with a resounding victory. I couldn't head the organization however, because I was relatively young and new and there were women who had fought against the Federation and colonialism for many years. However I was happy to be on the Committee.

I was also very pleased to see the swift changes that were taking place. After independence, the schools and health services that had been reserved for whites only were turned into fee-for-service institutions. Those who could afford the fees went there, and those who couldn't went to the free public schools and hospitals. By the early 1970s the fee-for-service system was scrapped altogether. The government no longer ran fee-for-service institutions. The idea was to prevent the now-widening gap between the haves and the have -nots, and to create a truly equal society based on the principle of socialism, or our own brand, known as 'humanism.' The principle of humanism placed man at the centre of things and everything else was secondary.

The ordinary folk were happy because it now meant that we would all be equal and everyone in the country was referred to as the common man.

However it was soon clear to some of us that things were not going according to our expectations and hopes. The political honeymoon was now truly over. Hypocrisy and double standards, the very things we had fought against, had set in. The very politicians who were at the forefront of demanding an end to government-run, fee-paying schools and hospitals were the first ones to abandon the use of the free services. They sent their children to the privately run, fee-paying schools and when they or members of families became sick, they didn't seek treatment at the free government hospitals. Instead they went to private hospitals run by mining companies or missionaries, and in some cases even abroad, to private clinics in Europe. England, our former coloniser was the most popular.

It was also to England that children, as young as eight years of age, were shipped to the elite boarding schools. So while we publicly criticized the imperialists and colonialists, our leadership and the *Apamwamba* were hobnobbing with our ex-colonial masters and their children at those special schools in England. Was this what we had fought for? Was this humanism? Was this true equality?

It would have been better if the fee-paying system had not been scrapped. At least, we would have been more honest about recognizing the different socio-economic groups. It was no use pretending that we were all equal when some were obviously more equal than others. It was also becoming clear to everybody that most people in our country were more common than the few elite. Looking back, I think that the end of our political honeymoon came in the early 1970s. Apart from a brief boom caused by the high copper prices, everything else heralded the trouble that was to come.

To begin with, our long-awaited promises never materialized. Nineteen hundred and seventy came and went and not every Zambian had shoes on his feet. Neither did every Zambian have a decent breakfast or a roof over their heads. Many of our people were living in ramshackles or cardboard dwellings in the already overcrowded shanty compounds, in the outskirts of the city. One could hardly call these a roof over one's head.

What bothered me, and other people as well, was the sudden watering down, so to speak, of what freedom really meant. We fought for free speech, freedom to organize ourselves, freedom to criticize when things went wrong, free expressions of our ideas, freedom of the press and so on. But now it seemed that freedom was not for everybody. The Party that closed ranks with us to form a united front in order to expedite independence, was now told, "join us or you're no more. We are now a one-Party state." Anyone who criticized the Party and its government was now a 'dissident.'

I felt disappointed and let down, as did many other people. The so-called free schools and free hospitals were now a mockery. I had celebrated their introduction with great joy and had fiercely argued with Likande and Chilufya, who believed that if the government had kept the fee-paying institutions, then public funds would have been used to run the free ones for those who could not afford to pay. Likande said to me, "If the government keeps these fee-paying places, then the free ones will also have better services. Look what has happened! No pencils in schools ... "

"No medicines in hospitals," chipped in Chilufya.

At first, I accused them of belonging to the elite class and wanting to hand down to the poor the trickle-down crumbs! But in the end I began to see their point. If the rich were left to pay for services, we certainly might have had extras to pay for the rest. As things stood, we were plodding along, mouthing socialist slogans, while our leaders were living better than most capitalists in America and Europe.

I got into constant arguments with people in the party over what I thought were the double standards and the hypocrisy. One day at our office meeting, I said, "I don't know about you people, but I'm beginning to hear rumblings among our people. They are tired of empty promises and nothing was being delivered. How can any of you stand at those rallies and tell people to tighten their belts, when they see you buying larger and larger belts to go around your affluent-looking waistlines?"

You should have seen the look on their faces! Some glared at me as if they could murder me with their looks. Others seemed downright ashamed of themselves and just stared at their feet, while still others mumbled excuses, such as that things could not change at once.

Someone even said, "Tengani, your problem is impatience. I want to remind you that Rome was not built in a day."

I felt like a trapped animal. Trapped in a system in which I was involved, but whose aims seemed to change according to the whims of a few selfish and self-centered people. I felt like resigning there and then, but decided against it. What good would that do? It was better to fight from within than from outside, as a dreaded dissident. At least within the Party there was still room for self-criticism and re-evaluation of programmes. Besides, there was something else that was bothering me – the status of women in the post-independence, new nation.

But my energies for pursuing that issue were temporarily diverted by other things. Soon after Chilufya and Zelani came back from their honeymoon, they held a huge dinner party. Zelani called it a "party to celebrate everything ... our wedding, the get-together with friends, the New Year ... everything."

The party was full of people, but my eyes and attention were on one man. Sifanu. Zelani briefly introduced him as 'one of our up-and-coming businessmen' and, turning to me, laughing said, "She's the fiery women's advocate. One of these days she'll be a persona non grata in my home ... unless she changes."

I didn't know whether to laugh or to take Zelani seriously, but since he was smiling, I assumed he was joking. Anyway, I shook Sifanu's hand, and he seemed to hold onto mine longer than was really necessary. "So you're a fiery type, eh? You're my kind then. I really love 'em hot and sizzling!"

Normally, I would have ignored such a blatant and flirtatious man. But when he started paying me so much attention and hovering on every word I uttered, I started liking him tremendously. By the end of the evening, I knew I was in love.

I hardly slept that night for thinking about him. I had never felt anything like it in my whole life. Was this love? Was this why everybody kept saying, "You'll know when it happens? You'll just know!" Well, I was in love and I knew it. But did he love me? That was what I wanted to know.

He soon made it clear through his actions that he wanted to spend as much time with me as I wanted to spend with him. My friends couldn't believe it. They were used to me talking, living and breathing politics. I was still involved in politics, but now I had time for other things. Sifanu took me to the movies. I couldn't remember when I had last been to the movies. He even took me fishing on a motor boat along the Kafue river. He loved the outdoors and he taught me how to appreciate nature.

"Life is not just about work, politics and business. It is also about relaxation," he said.

I started relaxing and enjoying life a bit more, taking things less seriously. At least, I did not have to perpetually worry about everything. My colleagues at work even started teasing me and telling me that I was smiling more. "You must be really in love," they said. I was indeed in love, but that didn't mean that I no longer cared about what was going on in my country. How could one shut one's eyes to the increasing problems and misery that our people were facing?

One day, as Sifanu and I were driving along Cairo Road, I said, "Look at that long line of women over there. They've probably been there since early morning, waiting for a bag of sugar, detergent, or cooking oil. Why are there so many shortages? Where have we gone wrong? What happened to all the hopes and expectations that we had after independence?"

His response was, "We could end those shortages by trading with South Africa, the way some of our pragmatic neighbours are doing. After all, even the arch enemies and greatest powers in the world, America and the Soviet Union, sell food to each other, despite their political differences. Why are we strangling ourselves and committing economic suicide in the name of idealogy?"

"Sifanu, is your balance sheet all you can think of? Making profit even if you have to trade with the devil?"

"There you go again! Like all these politicians, you think people will continue being content with slogans and ideological nonsense. You refuse to face the facts. This country is going downhill, and business is not to blame. You're to blame!"

"Me?"

"Not you personally. But all the politicians. Anyway, let's not argue about this. Why don't we just agree to disagree?"

III

Time seemed to fly. I pined for Sifanu when he was away on business and looked forward to our being together. One day while we were in his house, I said, "I can't believe that we've been dating for almost five months now."

"Five terrific months. Do you know what really drew me towards you?" he asked.

"Mmm? What?" I asked lazily as his lips nibbled at my ears, sending an incredible sensation through my body.

"It's your refreshingly direct and impulsive nature. Your frankness and your sincerity. Your eyes are so expressive when you feel strongly about something. They go teary when something upsets you, fiery like hot charcoal when you're angry, and sparkle like stars when you're happy. You're like an open book!"

No one had ever said that to me. No one. My heart felt as if it would burst with the love that was flowing inside me.

When we next met, he looked sad and preoccupied. I asked him what the problem was.

"I'm having problems with foreign exchange. The Bank of Zambia is putting more and more limits. If things continue at this rate, our small company will shut down. We need foreign exchange to buy inputs for the stuff we're manufacturing. I was wondering whether you could help me."

"Me? Help in what way? I'm no banker. I know nothing about foreign exchange or finances."

"But you know all those top people. After all, they are Party members and you have better access to them than I have."

"I don't think it would be right for me to ..."

"I don't mean that you should get me the foreign exchange. Just introduce me to them, and I'll do the rest."

"Okay. I don't see any problem with that."

So I started going with him to cocktails organized by the Party. I had actually stopped going there as a matter of principle. I couldn't understand how people at the top could dine and wine while the rest of the people starved and spent long hours in lines only to buy basics like meal mealie or salt. We were now like Marie Antoinette who, when told that the French peasants had no bread, asked why they couldn't eat cake. How out of touch with people who elected them can leaders be? How blinded by power can people be?

Anyway, for Sifanu's sake I thought I would go with him to hobnob with the *Apamwamba*. One thing about government and Party functions was that if you had the right contacts, you could attend anything that was going on, from simple parties for the ordinary, to the posh parties at Party headquarters or the Presidential palace. Sifanu was like a small boy following Santa Claus around. Attending parties was like a continuous Christmas for him.

One day, after we'd been going out for seven months, I called Sifanu and invited him for a meal at my place.

"I'm tired of going out to all these places and pretending that everything is alright. I feel like the hypocrite I've been accusing everybody of being."

"But those contact are beginning to pay now. I have managed some foreign exchange already. So we can't stop going."

"I don't know. I'll think about it. In any case, since you now know the people, you don't need me to take you around."

"Yes. I suppose you're right."

"Can you come for dinner tonight?"

"At your place?"

"Of course. I thought I already made that clear."

"I wasn't sure. Sounds great. What time?"

"Seven o'clock."

"Can you make it eight thirty? I'll be busy before that."

"Even better. That will give me more time to prepare. I'll make something really special."

"Can't wait!"

After work I rushed to Luburma Market to buy peanuts and pumpkin leaf. I was going to make him a delicious *ndiyo* to go with beef stew. When I had loaded all the things I had bought in a basket, including the tiny sun-dried *Kapenta* fish which I loved, I started walking back to my car. I was just about to cross the road to go where I had parked when I saw him. Sifanu had one arm around the shoulder of a pretty girl who seemed to be in her early twenties. He was so busy whispering into her ear while she laughed and giggled that he didn't even notice that I was right opposite them, across the street.

When he looked up and held out his hand to help her cross, they saw me. For a moment he hesitated, looking stunned and confused. But the girl tugged at his arm and they came towards me. The hand that was clutching the basket started shaking. I wanted to turn back and run away, but my feet stood rooted to the ground. I couldn't move an inch. I watched, panic-stricken, as they advanced. But when they got within touching distance of where I stood, he turned his face away. He completely avoided making eye contact with me.

I was seized by indescribable rage and fury. Anger fused with shame, and a terrible heartache. How I wanted to scream out in anguish!

I wanted to rush after Sifuna and smash his face into an unrecognizable pulp! But all I could do was stand there staring at the basket full of vegetables, ground peanuts, fish and fruit. With one mournful sound, I swung the basket and its contents into a huge garbage bin close by. A woman who was standing near me, with a baby strapped on her back, shouted, "Hey, lady, are you crazy or something ?"

She walked over to pick up the basket and its contents. I had a glimpse of her as she frantically waved the basket to me, but I furiously revved the engine of my car, then drove off at such a high speed that frightened pedestrians scuttled away. Angry motorists hurled insults at me, calling me a stupid driver and worse. But I didn't care. I don't think it would have mattered to me even if I had been stopped by a policeman. I was beyond the world of reason. I just wanted to end it all. My life seemed beset by problems, and there was no point in going on.

A car accident would be the best way of leaving this world. No one would know the truth. Committing suicide would be a cowardly act. Besides, Sifanu would be the ultimate winner. He might feel guilt-stricken for a time, and then relief would set in. He may have avoided my eyes today. But the day would come when he would have no choice but to face me.

When I got home, I threw myself on the bed and started wailing. I cried as if my heart would break. Hot, angry tears. After about two hours, I dragged my feet to the bathroom and splashed cold water on my face. The reflection that stared back at me from the bathroom cabinet mirror had teary, bloodshot, swollen eyes. After blowing my nose what seemed like countless times, I went to the kitchen to make myself a cup of coffee.

It was then I chided myself for throwing all that food away. It was a foolish and overemotional thing to do. Why stop eating because of a Casanova and double-crossing cheat! Why indeed even think of ending my life in an accident?

At eight thirty on the dot I heard a knock on the door. Surely he wouldn't dare! It couldn't be him. No way. He couldn't be so cheeky as to ...

"Tengani, it's me, Sifanu. I'm very sorry about this afternoon. Can I come in? I want to talk to you, to explain ..."

"Go away! I don't want to talk to you or ever see you again. Go away!"

"I just came to apologise."

"For what? For telling me lies?"

"Yes. I should have told you the truth. The girl you saw is my fiancee."

"Your what?"

I flung the door open and angrily faced him as he walked in. I no longer cared about my red swollen eyes. He looked very uncomfortable, and waving his hands in a pleading gesture, said, "I was planning to tell you this evening. I didn't want you to hear from other people, or the way you did this afternoon."

"In other words, you were pretending to love me while all the time you were seeing someone else."

"No. It wasn't like that. She has just come back from a year's diploma course in England. I knew I should have put a stop to our seeing each other, as you were getting too serious, and ..."

"So you were just using me, is that it? Using me to get the political contacts you wanted?"

"Oh, come on. We both were having fun. Besides, you and I could never really have made it. Marriage, I mean. It wouldn't have worked. We have nothing in common ... You're too ... too ...

independent. Too ... too ... er ... intimidating."

I was too shocked and speechless to react. I just stared at him as he mumbled on. Finally, the red switch in my brain came on and triggered me off. "Get out! Out, right now! I never, never want to see you or hear from you again!"

To say that I was heartbroken by Sifanu's deceit would be an understatement. I was completely devastated, and his cruel, parting words pierced my heart like a sharp knife. I had been so sure of his love for me! Didn't he say that I was "exciting, refreshingly honest and frank," and that I had "lovely, expressive eyes?" He was the first man who had ever brought out of me emotions I never knew lay dormant inside my body. I had laid out my body and soul to him. Sharing with him the most intimate thoughts and feelings. Feelings I had never expressed to another human being before.

There were very few people who really meant anything to me in this whole wide world: my brother, my two dear friends and, to a certain extent, my father. If fathers were bought in supermarkets, I wouldn't have bought mine. I had no choice in being his daughter, but I suppose I could have done worse. He loved me in his own way and I also cared for him in my own way. But it was a biological duty on both sides.

This was not so with my brother, or with Chilufya and Likande, who were like the sisters I never had. With Sifanu, my feelings had been different. Indescribable, and very different from anything I had felt for anyone before. And now he had abused the trust I had given him, callously tossing me away, like some used carpet.

I was now alone. All alone, laying my head on wet pillows, soaked by tears shed in the dead of night. I had no one I could talk to except Chilufya, who listened whenever she could, but she was so advanced in her pregnancy and so busy with her own marriage and work that I didn't want to overburden her with my problems. Likande was abroad and my brother was in Chipata. I had people I considered sort of friends at the office, but they were not friends in the real sense of the word.

IV

As if my world was not already upside down, more changes awaited me. One morning, as I was in the ladies' room, Mrs. Mudala, who was one of the "old timers" in the Party, said to me, "Tengani, I don't know whether to tell you this but it is rumoured that you're being sent away."

"What do you mean? A transfer? Who is sending me away and where to?"

I knew that there were constant reshuffles and there were also jokes about people being sent to Siberia or the remote districts of the country. I had become increasingly critical of the corruption, nepotism and general misconduct of certain top officials. However it wasn't the done thing to talk too much so it seemed that I was now paying for it, just at the time when I was planning to stand for the next general elections.

I suppose whoever was sending me away wanted to undermine my efforts. I would have to begin from scratch in a new and remote area, competing with people who were already well known there. Many people were getting frustrated and demoralized by what seemed to be illogical reshuffles and transfers. A person who spent years training for a profession such as medical doctor was suddenly promoted to head the Ministry of Transport. A qualified architect might find himself transferred to the Department of Fisheries, and so on. Now here I was, after working my guts out at the Party office, being moved away.

"Don't look so downcast. It isn't as if you're being sent to Siberia! I'm sure you'll love this. Besides, being away should help you get over your heartbreak. I'm sorry about what happened to you and your boyfriend."

"So where am I being sent, Mrs. Mudala? Please, tell me. Don't tantalize me like this."

"I promised my husband that I would not tell anyone until it's officially announced. So I'll only tell you if you swear that you won't react by rushing to discuss this in the office. That you'll not talk to anyone."

"Okay. I swear."

"On whom?"

"What do you mean?"

"On whom do you swear? It has to be someone really special to you. Someone deceased."

I stared at her. The last time anyone had demanded that I swear by my mother's grave was when I was nine years old. My friend had helped herself to several shortbread biscuits known as Eat Some More. I was the only witness to the 'crime,' and she was dead frightened of her sister-in-law, who demanded that she ask permission before getting anything from the food pantry. After I swore on my mother's grave, she gave me a biscuit. I nearly choked on it, and I could hardly sleep that night for fear that my mother might appear in my dreams and scold me for eating something stolen and for bringing up her name in vain.

There was a belief that angry ghosts could haunt someone who swore by their graves, especially when that someone had done something wrong. I finally fell asleep when out of sheer exhaustion I couldn't keep my eyes open anymore. It was with great relief that I woke up the following day, having slept soundly without nightmares or any sign of being haunted.

Mrs. Mudala was now asking me to do the same; to swear by my dear mother's grave. This time I had done nothing to be ashamed of and I would not invoke my mother's name. So I said to her, "Mrs. Mudala, either you tell me or you don't. The choice is yours. But knowing how rumours fly around this place, I'll be surprised if I don't hear about this before the day is over. What I don't understand is how your husband knows. Isn't he a civil servant, working for ..."

"Foreign affairs! So guess where you're going!"

"Abroad?"

"Yes! Just imagine! Isn't it wonderful?"

"Me? Abroad? Are you kidding?"

"It's true, Tengani. You're going abroad as a diplomat! Imagine all those diplomatic functions! CD number plates on your car, diplomatic immunity ... you lucky girl! As I may have told you before, we were abroad once. I loved every bit of our two years away. I even wanted us to stay longer. Our children were settled in their schools and even spoke French like natives. Kids learn languages very fast ..."

She went on and on, but I wasn't listening. I couldn't believe that I was going into the diplomatic field. Here was a perfect example of sending doctors to solve our transportation problems. Me, a diplomat?

I was hardly back at my desk when I was surrounded by colleagues, all asking me whether I had heard the top-secret news, concerning me. "You're off to New York," they whispered.

Aha, so it was New York! I had even forgotten to ask Mrs. Mudala where I was being posted, before I left the ladies' room.

Even before I could respond to all the questions and comments that were flooding me, I was summoned to the office of our overall boss. When I entered Mr. Mukwetu's office, he confirmed what I had already heard. Then I said, "I really don't want to go. I would like to be a candidate in the forthcoming elections."

He shifted his position on the chair and, diverting his gaze from me and talking as if he was addressing the window across, said, "I don't think you have any choice in the matter. The Party is like an army. Orders come from the top. Your duty is to obey, not ask questions or argue. You're like a soldier. You simply obey!"

"I thought our constitution says we're a democratic country. Since when did we become a military dictatorship?"

Mr. Mukwetu then faced me angrily and said "Tengani, has anyone ever told you that your mouth is your worst enemy? I'm now talking to you, not as your boss, but as one who thinks that you have the potential to go far in politics and the leadership of this country. But you've got to toe the line if you want to succeed. If you don't accept this assignment, which any of your colleagues here would give their right arm for, then the option will be Gwembe Valley for you. So take your pick. New York, or Gwembe Valley?"

Gwembe Valley? The joke in our office was that it was worse than Siberia. No one I knew had been there. The scenery was supposed to be good, although the place was very hot and humid. However, it was reported to be so rural that even years after independence, people there didn't know that the country had

117

changed its name to Zambia. They still referred to the monetary bills as *impondo* – the Sterling pounds, instead of the Zambian Kwacha. Going to Gwembe Valley at this stage in my political career, would be like opting for early retirement and oblivion! I would be history! Completely forgotten.

"Well, Tengani? I'm still waiting for your decision," said Mr. Mukwetu.

"New York."

"Good."

I hardly had time to put in a day's work, as people kept stopping at my desk with lists of things they wanted me to buy for them. They said they would pay me back in Kwacha. They all promised to deposit the money in my account, where I would find it when I returned. Some wanted Afro hair products, others, dresses, shirts, shoes . . . the list went on and on and it seemed endless.

Kandela, who shared an office with me, said, "Tengani, for me it's just one thing. A box of those mouth-watering chocolates. A taste of those again, and you'll have made me happy for the rest of my life!"

Kandela was huge and tall. He was always chewing something; gum, sweets, cakes, biscuits. All sorts of goodies came from his desk drawers the way papers, memoranda and pencils came from those of other office workers. He ate from the time he arrived at the office until it was time to go home. I often heard him call his wife to find out what was for dinner that evening. Sending him a box of chocolates would be like sending whisky to an alcoholic. He was addicted to food.

Most of those who asked me to get them things did not really want them for their own use. There was big business in contraband. The black market was full of imported goods that were brought in by people who went abroad; things bought cheaply and then sold at four or five times the original price. Often, such people left with a nearly empty suitcase, but returned with several overloaded suitcases and more stuff spilling out of equally heavy hand luggage.

Customs officials at Lusaka International Airport were renowned for being very strict and charging high import duty.

Those who were in the business of bringing all these items for resale had their contacts in the Customs Department. For a gift or two, these contacts could let through a passenger who was loaded with many suitcases, while they would detain another passenger with only one or two suitcases. The poor passenger would be interrogated, harassed and asked to produce receipts for all the clothing which he had bought prior to the last six months. If one failed to do so they would assume that everything in the suitcases was new, and they would charge full customs duty. Eventually one had either to pay the bribe or pay the high duty.

The secret, according to frequent travellers, was to know who the 'contacts' were. If a passenger tried to bribe the wrong people, meaning those who took their jobs seriously, then he or she could get into real trouble and possibly be arrested for attempting to corrupt and bribe a government official.

In many ways, one sympathised with people trying to make an extra buck through selling stuff. The economic situation was getting worse each year, and inflation and the devalued Kwacha were making it virtually impossible to exist on the low salaries most workers were getting. I could never understand how most families made it to the next pay day. Those who had extra income from the sale of contraband were the survivors in the system.

The problem was that a lot of office hours were taken up with buying and selling things like perfumes, watches, jewellery and even clothing. Since most of the state-run department stores were virtually empty or contained clothes which looked like uniforms, the demand for imported stuff sold on the black market was very high. Those who had relatives or friends in the diplomatic missions abroad were considered lucky because they could ask them to buy things for them. Those who actually got posted abroad were even luckier.

As news travelled fast that I was being sent to New York, I could see envy written on many of the faces that came by my desk to wish me well, or to ask for a favour or two... things I could get for them. Without sounding mean or rude, I explained that there was no way I could buy all the things that people wanted.

I said, "Even if you pay me in Kwacha, what good will that be to me? I shall need the money I'll earn there to pay rent, buy food and furnish my apartment." I planned to get a few presents for my family and friends, but I didn't want to join the business of buying and selling.

V

When I was finally seated on the plane and we were thousands of feet above the ground, I felt like a bird on its first long-distance flight. I could feel my horizons expanding and growing during the trip. Our first stop was Nairobi, then London, and from there, across the Atlantic to JFK International Airport in New York. I had never left Zambia, my country of birth before; my whole world had been centred there.

Everything now looked very large and incomprehensible. As if to get back to my real world, my thoughts went back to the week before, when I had gone to visit my family. I was touched by the bear-like hug my father gave me. I had not seen him show his true emotions towards me like that. Not since my mother's death had I felt genuine warmth from him. Chenjerani however was more direct and he didn't care that his eyes, like mine, shone with tears. When I drove away, I could still see his figure in the rearview mirror, waving at me.

The other emotional scene was at Lusaka International Airport, when Chilufya came to see me off. She looked huge, as if she were carrying twins or triplets.

"I wish I would be here to see your baby," I said, as I hugged and kissed her goodbye. "Both you and Likande will be mamas, while I continue to be an aunt to everyone's children."

"You'll be a mummy, too, one of these days. Wait till you meet the right person. I'll miss you, but in a way I'm glad you're going away – away from the heartache caused by Sifanu."

"Does one really run away from a heartache? Anyway, let's not discuss Sifanu. What I would like is for you to send me a photo of the baby as soon as he or she is born."

That had been the day before. Now the plane was getting ready to land. From my window seat, I could see the famous New York city, the metropolis which seemed to find a place in many magazines. I may never have been to New York before, but I could always recognize its skyscrapers from books and magazines. Those tall buildings, whose tops seemed to reach the blue skies. The other famous landmark was the Statue of Liberty, that symbol of freedom, which stood as though she was guarding her people from invaders.

The first few weeks following my arrival in New York were busy ones. Settling into my apartment in Manhattan, buying things I needed, going in and out of shops that seemed to be overflowing with merchandise and people. No wonder Zambians brought empty suitcases to such places in order to fill them up with anything they could buy. Here shortages were not known. The real problem was too much of everything.

What I also found baffling was the perpetual rush and the hustle and bustle of life. A throng of multitudes that seemed to be triggered by an invisible clock ordering them to rush, rush, rush. Even those who were walking were in a rush, weaving in and out of equally rushing traffic. Pedestrians walked at a much faster pace than our people back home.

What I found both intriguing and disturbing amidst the rush in this huge city were the static and empty stares of the 'outcasts,' the 'untouchables.' Those homeless men and women, junkies, drug addicts and alcoholics. The forgotten and ignored people in this land of plenty. No one stopped even to look at them, let alone talk to them. My heart went out to them and I felt a sudden longing for my homeland.

My thoughts went back to my village. Our rural areas might be poor in material things, but they were far richer in what really mattered – the human spirit. A person was judged not by the amount of money she had, but by the way she treated other human beings. If you were hurrying to another village or to do some errand, you slowed down when you passed someone on the road to exchange greetings. If she was from the same village, then the greetings took even longer: "How are you this morning?" was followed by, "How is the rest of the family?" and finally, "Is everything else well? The animals, and your crops this season?" After sharing information about the health or sickness in the family, and whether the rains had been just right, too little, or too much for the fields, then you would part. What indeed was this life, if so full of care, hustles and bustles, there was no time to stand and stare? No time to admire nature and no time to talk to other people?

At the office I started learning the basics of diplomatic life. The office was basically a representation to the United Nations comprising the Zambian Ambassador to the UN and a small staff. I learnt a lot about office procedure and the intricacies of the job from Noriya, who became a close friend. She had been at the mission for some years now and she knew her way around New York. She was the one who met me at the airport when I arrived and helped me settle in my apartment. Noriya took me round the shops and generally made things easier for me.

One day, as we sat down to lunch at the United Nations building, she said, "Well, Tengani, how are you finding New York so far?"

I told Noriya how closed in I felt amidst the tall buildings and skyscrapers, and how I longed for open space, for miles and miles of greenery and savanna grasslands. I also told her how I hated being on the thirtieth floor and that I didn't sleep well the first night for fear of a towering inferno. I was very worried about a fire breaking out while I was asleep. I said to her, "The first night I slept fully dressed, so that I would look decent when a rescue helicopter came to get me from that floor!"

"Oh, Tengani, the 'Towering Inferno' was just a movie. I wouldn't worry myself too much about that."

Then I told her how upset I was to see all those homeless people. I just couldn't believe that the most powerful nation on earth, and one of the wealthiest, could have people on its streets begging for food while the shops were overflowing. Every time I went into those stores, I felt like grabbing as many bags of apples as I could, in case they might be sold out the next time I went there.

Noriya said to me, "I know the feeling. That was what happened to me when I first arrived. Actually, I saw this aisle of canned food and I started loading it into my basket. It was only when I took a closer look and noticed the little signs of dogs and cats on them, that I realized the whole aisle was devoted to pet food! I quickly put them back on the shelf."

I burst out laughing when she related her story, and soon both of us were laughing our heads off.

"Hi, ladies, may I join in this fun and laughter? I need cheering up, I've had a hard morning."

It was Mwilwa from our office. We told him what we had been discussing, especially about the obvious disparities between the haves and the have-nots and the plight of the homeless. His reaction was, "I have no sympathy for the homeless and drug addicts. They deserve whatever has befallen them. They are just lazy. How can anyone be poor in this land of plenty and opportunity? After all, there are many stories of immigrants who came with only a few dollars and made millions through hard work and dedication!" I stared at him in disbelief. How could he accuse those desperate-looking people of being responsible for their problems?

Completely ignoring my incredulous stare, Mwilwa went on to say, "Don't tell anyone this, but my long-term plan is to settle here and make my fortune. I shall either seek political asylum or marry an American. I'm already working on acquiring an American accent!"

"Tengani, don't take him seriously," warned Noriya, "Mwilwa is the office buffoon."

"Everyone thinks so. But I'll surprise all of you one of these days. Anyway, Tengani, is there anything special you might wish to see in New York for which I might offer my services as an escort or tour guide?"

"I would love to go to Harlem! I can't come to New York and not see that special centre of African American culture, music and ... "

"Sorry, but that's one of those places I avoid like a plague! If I were you, I wouldn't go anywhere near it. If you think you'll meet Diana Ross or Aretha Franklin, or whoever your heroes and superstars were in the 1960s, you'll be grossly mistaken. More likely you'll be mugged, robbed, and worse, murdered!"

"Mwilwa, how can you say all these horrible things about a place you haven't even been to?" asked Noriya.

"I've read enough about the place to know that it's dangerous." Mwilwa was really getting on my nerves. I angrily said to him,

"Do you mean to tell me that people are dangerous because they are discriminated against by the rich and powerful? Surely, this society is to blame for what they've done to people of African stock! From what I've seen since I arrived here, it seems that slave trade never really ended. All it did was take on a new form. Instead of having blacks work on cotton plantations, they're now kept in those ghettos, far away from the white and affluent suburbs."

"Gee, Tengani, you do make long speeches," said Mwilwa. "One remark and you rattle on like a train without brakes! My advice to you is to cool it here. You're not a politician rousing the masses to rebellion. You are a diplomat. Here to promote good relations between nations. Being a diplomat means just that: diplomacy not war."

"Well, I don't know about you two, but I've a lot of work to do at the office," said Noriya, standing up and getting ready to leave.

I also followed her, and on the way out I said, "What an egocentric and irritating man!"

"I know. My heart sank when I saw him walk to our table. Mwilwa is okay, but only in small doses. Sometimes I think that if he were white and not black, he would have been a member of those neo-Nazi white racist groups."

I said, "Maybe whenever he looks in the mirror, the reflection he sees there is white, not black!" We both laughed at that and headed back to the office.

Later that afternoon, Mwilwa came to my office. I nodded him a greeting but continued to read the file in my hand, giving him a definite signal that I was too busy to chat. He obviously had a skin as thick as a mahogany tree, because he just pulled up a chair and started talking.

"Tengani, I hope you didn't take some of the things I said during lunch too seriously."

"Such as?"

"My joke about seeking political asylum here. It was only a joke, So don't report me back home or I'll be into real trouble."

"Me? Report you? Since when was I appointed Ambassador of this mission?"

"You may not be the Ambassador, but career diplomats are really scared of political appointees like you. There has been an increase in the number of Party people being planted in the embassies abroad. Rumour has it that they are spies, sent to check on us."

I was so shocked and angry that my hands started trembling and I had to place the file I had been holding on the desk to avoid him noticing. Was that why people in the office avoided me? Why they often stopped talking when I came into the room?

I suppose my vague title and dubious job descriptions didn't help matters. I was supposed to have special duties and help in several aspects of running the mission. Sometimes I went as an observer with anyone who was attending sessions at the General Assembly of the United Nations. At other times I joined those who were talking to investors and business people, trying to promote trade and investments for Zambia.

There were times when we addressed tourists, showing them brochures and pamphlets produced by the Zambia Tourist Board while at other times we answered questions from environmentalists. One irate woman once said, "I was shocked and disgusted by what I saw on TV last night. How can your country let poachers kill all those elephants just to get ivory?" We played down reports of top politicians and government officials being involved in the illicit trade.

I was a jack of all trades and a master of none. I was no career diplomat, and everyone knew it. However I was not here to apologise for being sent to New York. Neither Mwilwa nor anyone else had the right to question my presence there. I was working just as hard as they were and was keen to learn the ropes. Waving a finger at Mwilwa, I declared, "I'm no spy here. I have never been a spy for anyone, and I will never be. I'm here to do my job. The Party has the right to send whoever they wish. After all, this Party is also the present government! So if you'll excuse me, I have work to do. Your job seems to be that of being rude to people and annoying them."

"I'm sorry. I didn't mean to upset you. It's just that some people are being sent straight from their villages to London or New York, briefly stopping in Lusaka only to get their passports. They've never been anywhere near a city before. No training, and no experience. Their only qualification is that they have relatives in top government or Party positions. They can't even cross a busy road in a big city. You would think that cars were lions in the jungle the way they are terrified of them!"

"Mwilwa, why do you put down your own people? First it was the African American. Now it's our poor villagers. Who do you think you are?"

"Oh, my, aren't you oversensitive! You can't really take jokes, can you?"

"No. Not when the jokes are at the expense of poor people who can't even defend themselves."

"Well, I can see that warning look in your eyes. Let me leave before you throw something at me."

After that I kept him at a distance. I settled into the routine of work, diplomatic functions and parties, as well as getting to know some of the cultural and entertainment aspects of New York. Time seemed to fly at an incredible speed. Before I realized it, days, weeks, months and a whole year had gone by.

VI

I was now well into my second year in New York. While weekdays were spent mostly doing office-related duties, Noriya took me to various activities and functions around New York during the weekend. Harlem was on the top of my list, so we went there. I was a bit disappointed at the neglect and dilapidated state of many of the buildings. However that didn't take away the underlying cultural richness of the place. The next day at work, I even sought out Mwilwa to gloat over my tour of Harlem. I told him we were neither mugged, robbed, nor assaulted. All he could say was, "It's not Harlem per se. Even back home I avoid places like Mandevu and Kalingalinga."

I thought as much. He had an overinflated opinion of himself; thought he was too good for most mortals. He criticized African Americans but was a big fan of rap musicians, and even aped their hair styles. I often overheard him talking about the latest in electronic equipment and who was at the top in pop music.

Apart from Harlem, Noriya also took me to see the Statue of Liberty on Liberty Island, the Metropolitan Museum of Art, Central Park Zoo, Hayden Planetarium, Museum of the City of New York and Museum of National History. We also attended several concerts and performances on Broadway and at the Lincoln Centre. Noriya was really fond of museums and culture. By the end of my second year, we had been out literally every weekend visiting one museum or another or going to one concert or another. She spent money on art, museums and concerts the way some people spend it on clothes.

"I hope my next posting will be London, Paris or Vienna. I love those cultural centres of the world. There are times when I feel, deep down, that I was born on the wrong continent. This is no criticism of our beautiful continent. You know, I've been reading a book on reincarnation and I'm convinced that I was a European in my previous life. Probably a relative of Mozart or Bach! Or those famous Italian Renaissance artists and painters!"

We both burst out laughing. Later, we went to the Bronx Zoo to look at the animals and birds from all over the world.

I really enjoyed our outings, but I also found living in New York depressing and stressful. Amidst the sophistication, museums, concerts and so on, was an underlying malaise: the never-ending violence and senseless killings. Drug-related crimes, assaults, rapes, and homelessness seemed to make news headlines in dailies, radio and on TV. If I had based my perceptions of New York solely on what I obtained from the news media, I would probably never have left my apartment except to go to the corner grocery store and to the office.

Noriya did all the same show me another side although even the nicer, brighter side of the city, however, could not erase those

127

images of murder, kidnap, child abuse and neglect. I needed to get back to the sanity and tranquility of my country. Back to stopping and staring at nature and exchanging greetings with other humans, without rushing to destinations unknown ... to nothing.

When I talked to the Ambassador about my desire to go back home, he was surprised. He was used to people requesting extensions and pleading to stay in the Big Apple. He said I was due for some home leave, anyway, and I could therefore consult with the powers that be in Lusaka, which would be my best bet. Otherwise, I would have to await orders for the next move, like the rest. The Ambassador said we could never know whether we'll be recalled, sent to some other place, or have our stay extended. We had to play the waiting game, while the chess players were back home. We were the ones who got moved around on the chess board.

After much pleading, cajoling, and even angry and teary scenes at the Party headquarters, permission was finally granted that I could go back home. The weekend before I was due to leave, I went to Noriya's place for a cup of coffee.

"Tengani, it's been great being with you the last three years. I can't even believe that it's been that long since you arrived."

What with our trips to all those museums and other attractions, we hardly had any time just to sit and enjoy a cup of coffee. Even laundry had to be done at night because we were very busy during the day. Noriya took out her long list headed, "Museums and Activities of Interest in New York and the Surrounding Areas" of Westchester, Connecticut, Long Island, Brooklyn, New Jersey, the Bronx, Queens and Staten Island. The list had seventy six museums and activities of interest. I said, "Noriya. Surely you don't plan to see all these places. I feel as though we've been everywhere, and yet this list still has many more things to see."

"We could highlight a few more museums and go to see them. A kind of farewell for you. I'll pay. My goodbye present to you!"

"Thanks. But no thanks. Frankly, I think I've seen enough museums and zoos to last me a lifetime!"

Noriya looked at me as if I were the most backward and culturally ignorant person in the whole world. Peeping at me above her glasses, and looking more like a professor than a counsellor in a diplomatic mission, she asked, "Tengani, have you ever been to the Livingstone Museum?"

"Well, er ... no. Not yet. But I'll go when I get back home. I've been meaning to go but never got round to doing it."

"So you've not been to the Victoria Falls, too? Never seen one of the world's natural wonders, and right there in our own country?"

"No. Okay, I feel guilty about it, especially as I argued several times when I was at school about David Livingstone reportedly discovering them."

"I hope you'll make time to go there. I'll write to you to find out your impression. You'll really love the Falls!"

"Yes, Professor Noriya," I teased.

VII

When I got back to Zambia, both things and people looked as if they had been static from the time I left. In one sense it was as though I had never left. The shortages were still there, and the disparity between the "haves" and the "have-nots" seemed to have widened. People were into all kinds of money-making ventures. Drug dealing was even an issue, something hitherto foreign. That was certainly new, as were the increases in armed robberies and violent crimes. It seemed as though we were fast following the example of New York, the Big Apple. Trust us to pick up all the wrong things about foreign influence!

My greatest concern however was women and their status in the nation. Admittedly, some progress had been made. We had women Cabinet Ministers, women in the Party's central committee and women who were members of parliament and who had successfully competed against men in the national elections. There was some improvement in the working conditions of women, such as paid maternity leave for a couple of months. Nevertheless on the whole, the majority of women lagged far behind. Soon after returning from New York, I raised the issue at a staff meeting and I said it was not fair that women were still facing discrimination, when they too had fought for independence.

A month later, I was summoned into my boss's office and informed that I was being transferred from Lusaka to Kitwe, in the copperbelt.

"Why?" I asked. "Directives from the top."

"Does this have anything to do with my views about the status of women? Is this another attempt to get me away from the centre of government?"

My boss said, "Are you telling me that women's issues are only found here in Lusaka? Or are you just driven by your own ambitions and hunger for power?"

I walked away from the meeting and went back to my office. But when I cooled down, I realized that my boss was right. Like most politicians, I had fallen into the trap of wanting to be in the capital city because it was the "seat of government." Big cities were being developed while small towns and rural areas were being neglected. The problem of women was a national issue and I could fight for women in Kitwe, just as I could in Lusaka. So shrugging my shoulders, I said, aloud, "Okay, Kitwe, here I come."

Afterwards, I picked up the phone and called Chilufya. She was surprised and shocked to hear that I was again going away. "Why are they sending you away again? Someone obviously wants you out of the way."

"I'll be back when I've gained enough support to stand for the next elections. My fight then will not be in these offices, but in the National Parliament!"

"Good for you! Anyway, I'll miss you. Pity you're going just when I desperately need your support."

"Have you heard from Likande?"

"Yes. I just received a postcard from her. She sent it from Sao Paulo. They are in Brazil on a two-week vacation."

"Lucky Likande. I wish I were a thousand miles from here. Maybe I should have stayed in New York."

"Well, you can't have it both ways – build a political base and be away from the country."

"You're right. Anyway, do come and see me. Hop over when you come to Luanshya to see the old folks. Kitwe is very close to Luanshya."

"Okay."

My move to Kitwe went better than I had expected. In fact, the long drive from Lusaka gave me time to think about the position of women in our country. I realized that part of our economic problems was due to the fact that most of the work was being done by women, while most men were having a free ride on the national wagon. In the rural areas, it was women who did most of the work in the fields: planting, weeding, harvesting and then selling the produce. They also did most of the domestic work like fetching water at dawn, sweeping the houses, preparing meals and working in the fields.

Afterwards, it was time to fetch firewood. Where were their men? Some were at the local bars, drinking away the revenue from the sale of produce. Others were away in the cities looking for jobs. There were others who spent their days basking in the African sun while their wives, mothers, sisters, or aunts did all the work. How could a nation succeed, when its women did all the work and yet didn't reap the benefits? Since women did most of the agricultural work, the logical thing would be to give them support, such as credit facilities, incentives and general encouragement.

Unfortunately women were completely ignored. They were just women, second-class citizens, yet the whole country expected these same women to produce enough to feed the whole country. No wonder children continued to die from malnutrition! No wonder there was hunger and disease. They were overworked and nobody seemed to care.

VIII

I quickly settled into life in Kitwe, and as time went on I grew to like it there. I made friends with some of my colleagues at work while I got into inevitable conflicts with others, especially men who accused me of bringing women's lib ideas from abroad. One of them even suggested marriage, so that 'it would reduce the excessive energy which I possess.' Through the grapevine, news had already reached my new office that I was still suffering from a heartbreak and was bitter towards men in general. One or two men took it upon themselves to show me that not all men were terrible. I was continuously being asked why I was not married yet. If they really wanted to know, I would have given them an earful.

Take Sabina, a very good young woman married to another political activist. Apparently, their wedding had been the talk of the office because all the important local people had attended it. Her husband Kafupi was related to a very top-government official in the city, and the reception was held at the relative's residence. Sabina and Kafupi had been married three years when I moved to Kitwe. But they might as well have been married one hundred years! Sabina and I became good friends, and she often complained about the treatment she was getting from Kafupi.

One day, I met them in town when I went shopping. Anyone who didn't know them would never have guessed that they were married. Kafupi was walking a few paces ahead, while Sabina was struggling with a bag of shopping in one hand, baby in another and the two-year-old Mubanga clutching her skirt. Kafupi was sauntering as if he did not have a single care in the world.

"Hello, Sabina," I called out.

"Oh, hi, Tengani. How are you?" she asked, pausing to rest. "Fine. I see you're in a hurry and very busy."

"Yes, yes. I've got to rush. Kafupi is going to the football match, and he is ..."

"Come on, Sabina! Why are you chatting there when you know I'm in a rush! I promised Mwanga and Choba that I'll meet them at the stadium at three o'clock. It's already two forty-five."

"Sorry, Tengani, but I'd better go," said Sabina, looking embarrasssed. "Why don't you drop by next Saturday for a cup of tea?"

"Sure, I'll take you up on that."

I went the following Saturday afternoon. Kafupi and two friends were sitting on the porch, drinking beer. From the number of empty bottles on the small table and the floor, it looked as if they must have been at it for several hours. Their speech was slurred and their eyes bloodshot. The smell of beer on Kafupi's breath was heavy as he stood up and shouted a greeting to me. But he was so drunk that he could not stand straight or still. He swayed and then fell back onto his chair.

"Sabina, where are you?" he yelled. "Come on, woman, bring us some more beer!"

Sabina came running, and then she saw me and said rather sheepishly, "Oh, Tengani, hi. Please come in. I'm in the kitchen."

Scooping up a few empty bottles, she led the way. Back in the kitchen, two-year-old Mubanga was screaming his head off. Sabina turned to him and said, "Hush, Mubanga. Hush, here's a biscuit," and she handed him a cookie. But he threw it at her and wailed even louder. "Hush, you'll wake the baby up. Would you like ice cream instead?"

Mubanga nodded. Soon after that, he was happily digging a teaspoon into the small carton of ice cream. But just as Sabina placed a kettle on the stove for tea, the baby woke up and started crying. Sabina rushed to bring him to the kitchen. He was still crying as she rocked him and held him against her bosom.

"Hey, Sabina, can't you get those kids to shut up?" shouted Kafupi from the verandah. "Why can't you manage two small kids? How will you cope when we have six?"

Sabina's eyes filled up with tears, and she hastily turned her face away from me. "Tengani, what would you like? Coffee or tea?"

"You seem so busy, Sabina. I must have come at the wrong time. I'd better go."

"No, please don't go. Stay here and talk to me. I am cooking these men something to eat so they don't fill themselves with alcohol."

"They already look as if they've done nothing but drink all day," I said.

She moved closer to me, as if even the four walls might listen in on what she had to say. "Tengani, you may not believe this, but Kafupi was a very loving and considerate man when I met him. We were inseparable, and he used to take me everywhere ... discos, the club and even to play tennis with him. I didn't know how to play, but he taught me. But he changed soon after we got married."

"Why did he change?"

"It's those terrible friends of his, Mwanga and Choba. They both treat their wives like doormats, even going to functions without them, and hanging out with single women. When Kafupi took me out, they started teasing him. Now he says the club is not for married women! So I'm stuck here at home, doing chores and looking after the kids. He doesn't lift a finger to help. However he is not a violent man. I'm lucky so far. The day he hits me will be the day I leave him. I've already warned him that I won't let any man hit me, the way Choba beats his wife. I'm no orphan. My parents said, if I'm unhappy, I can always go back home. There are days when I feel, this is it, I won't go on like this anymore. But what will happen to my children if I go?"

Sabina was just one example of many women mistreated by their husbands. The plights of widows was another major problem. On one occasion, I attended the funeral of the husband of a woman working in our office. It was said that Chunga's husband was killed in a brawl over a woman who had been his mistress for many years. Apparently, the woman started seeing another man, and when the two men met at her house, a fight broke out which resulted in the death of Chunga's husband.

During the funeral, his relatives accused Chunga of having "caused our relative's death." I was baffled. How could they accuse Chunga of her husband's death? Surely, they should blame his mistress, or the man who killed him! An elderly woman who was sitting next to me said, "They blame her because if she had been a good wife to him, he wouldn't have looked for happiness outside marriage." My own opinion is that even if Chunga had been a model wife, they would still have found some way to blame her for her husband's death. Being a woman is a no-win situation!

People hid under the name of tradition to exploit women and harass widows. Poor Chunga was left with virtually nothing after her husband's relatives divided the family property among themselves. She had worked all her adult life and had in fact spent all her income on buying the little possessions they bad. His salary had gone to maintaining his mistress and her children. Chunga's five children were now left with nothing.

IX

There was a national debate about doing away with all these unjust practices. Women around the country called for a law to protect them against the greed of extended relatives who turned up at funerals to help themselves to property. One of the most vocal groups was the Women's Association, consisting of professional women working for the government, the private sector, or running their own businesses.

I was invited to several of their meetings, although I also turned up uninvited to some of them. They wanted close contact with women in politics. One such meeting I attended focused on the problem of AIDS, the deadly disease. Someone said that a close friend of hers had contracted the disease from her husband, who had been "running around with prostitutes." She described her friend as a very straight and honest person who believes in the sanctity of marriage. Now she's lying fatally ill in hospital because of a selfish and irresponsible husband.

Another person complained about what she called the macho syndrome in our society. She appealed to women to rise up and fight, or they would all have AIDS before this century was over. Someone else suggested a national drive for the use of condoms, but she was shouted down with cries of, "African men don't use condoms!" A lone voice yelled, "So what? Why should we die because of such men, who think only about themselves and their pleasure?"

In the end, they agreed that priority should be given to public education and public awareness of how the disease was spread. This would make people take precautionary measures including the use of condoms and refrain from macho tendencies of having many sexual partners.

I loved going to their meetings because I found them refreshing and lively. The group was like a small island in a patriarchal sea. It was stimulating to be with them. They were our elite women, the educated and wealthy ones. There were times I felt inadequate in their presence, regretting not having gone to university. How I wished I had worked hard at school and gone to college, like most of these women! Many of them were very bright and eloquent; their arguments logical and to the point. Although during the discussions things sometimes got out of hand, with people shouting out their opinions, order was quickly restored, and the summaries at the end covered a wide selection of opinions. When there was need for follow-up action, a vote was taken and the majority decision adopted.

The first time I was invited to speak to the members, I was very nervous. My mouth suddenly felt dry and my palms were wet from sweat. After coughing and desperately trying to clear my throat, I finally started talking, relaxing as I noticed their interest in what I was saying.

The second time I was invited to speak, I overheard someone say, "Another speech from those half-educated stone throwers!" I felt my blood boiling. I decided to really tell those snobs where to get off! I quickly made changes to my speech as people stood chatting in groups, waiting for the meeting to start.

In my speech, I dealt with snobs who seemed to have forgotten that if it weren't for the thousands of uneducated, peasant women who had put themselves at the forefront of the fight for independence, "none of you would be where you are today. You wouldn't be living in those mansions and driving your fancy Mercedes Benzes. You would be working as clerks or, if you were lucky, as assistants to some foreign expatriates. In those days, it didn't matter whether you had a Ph.D or not. What mattered was the colour of your skin. If you were black, you were nobody. A *Kaffir*! Don't you ever forget that you owe what you are to those very peasant women you look down on, the ones you ridicule as 'stone throwers.' They had the guts to use whatever weapons they could get, including stones, to fight for freedom and justice for you and me."

There was a moment's shocked silence, in which you could have heard a pin drop. My heart was beating so hard I thought everyone could hear it. But the moment's silence was followed by clapping that seemed to go on and on. Then everyone was on their feet, and the ovation was deafening. I finally raised my hand and gestured for them to sit down. After the Chairwoman called for order, I announced that I had two questions I wanted to ask them. "Okay, fire away. You have a captive audience."

I asked each one just to call out what her profession was. There were a few murmurs and raised eyebrows, but they responded. As I had expected, they represented the top of the professions: lawyers, professors, doctors, director of own company, general manager of another company, and so on. The cream of our womenfolk, floating up there in the national milk jar, while the rest were below.

Next, I asked them to tell me what their mother's professions were. You should have seen the number of heads that suddenly turned down! There was an awkward silence. Then the Chairlady led the way and announced that her mother was a retired teacher. Four other women followed, one with a mother who had been a nurse, another with a mother who had been a midwife, someone else whose mother had also been a teacher, and the fourth whose mother had been a nurse's aide. There was more silence and tension that made the air feel thick. It was broken by a woman who raised her hand and started talking.

"Tengani, I can't even find the appropriate words to express the gratitude and humility I feel, and I'm sure these other women must feel, too, at what you've done today ... "

She said that most of them had short memories, having forgotten their background and roots. She reminded them that they were really the first generation of successful women following the country's attainment of political independence. She appealed to them never to forget the fact that while they had been enjoying the "benefits of education at the university, our sisters and mothers were out there at the war zone, standing side by side with the men of this country. Tengani, you and our sisters in the political field sacrificed your own needs for the common good. We salute you, dear sister."

There was another standing ovation. As I acknowledged their ovation, and as tears shone in the eyes of each and every one of those thirty or so women in the packed room, I had this strange feeling that my mother's spirit was there beside me. It was as if she were telling me that she did not die in vain. She was a hero, like everyone else who had been a victim of the unjust colonial system.

"Mama, may your soul rest in peace," I prayed silently. This was the first time ever that I could bring myself to say those words.

After the meeting, everyone mingled for refreshments and several women sought me out to disclose their roots. It was a bit like being at a born-again Christian revival meeting. People bared their souls and spoke of the sacrifices their mothers or parents had made to enable them to go to school and to university. Someone confessed that she was caught up in this competition for material things. "We are the 'Me, Myself and I' generation, driven by the desire to have more things and to be better than anyone else." Some even made resolutions, even though it was no New Year's Eve, to devote some of their spare time to helping women and children in the shanty compounds.

I was rather sceptical and cynical about all these resolutions because I was convinced that once the guilt brought on by our meeting was over, all the good intentions would be gone. But the next time I met the President of the Association, she told me that one of the group's future projects was to deal with grassroot problems in the shanty compounds. Those with medical experience would help in projects dealing with malnutrition, while others would form a committee to help illiterate women learn how to read and write.

I was so pleased and excited by this news that I shared it with Sabina, Mwapona, Bwalya and Masiliso, from my office. I suggested closer cooperation between women's groups and encouraged them to attend the Women's Association meetings. Mwapona's reaction was, "I don't want to have anything to do with those women. They are snobs, full of themselves and their *apamwamba* life. They talk about clothes from London, Paris and New York. What their equally pompous husbands brought them from abroad, and so on."

Masiliso agreed and said, "I know someone in that Association. Her mother and mine are close friends, and we grew up together. But ever since she obtained her degree by correspondence and married one of these *apamwamba* men, I'm now too low for her. I've met her several times, but she looks through me. She pretends that she doesn't know me. The other day she was so close I could have touched her Benz at the crossing, but she turned her face away. I might as well have been an alien from Mars!"

Bwalya's remark was, "Their husbands are just as phony! I know a nurse who has been dating one of these *apamwamba*. But when you see him with his wife, you'd think they were the most loving and romantic couple in the world."

Sabina said, "At least they show respect for their wives. Not like our low-class husbands, who have more respect for their buddies and beer than for their wives!"

I appealed to them to try and work with other women, or no progress would be made. I said that we still had a long way to go before the status of women in the country really improved.

Masiliso said, "I'm sorry, Tengani, but I'm not going out there only to be humiliated. If they want to talk to me, they'll have to come to me. We may be poorer than they are, but we deserve some respect." The others agreed with Masiliso. They said they were prepared to have a discussion with the Women's Association, but the initiative for such a meeting would have to come from them.

It was clear that there were profound differences among the women's groups. It was a question of us and them, or the haves and the have-nots. Some of my colleagues also felt that I was trying to push everybody at too fast a pace. Bwalya told me that I didn't really understand the situation of women in the country. According to her, I was trying to "create a gender war here. But there isn't." Her argument was that, like most married couples the world over, those in Zambia had their ups and downs. She also pointed out that not all men in the United States and Europe helped their wives with chores at home. She said that even there, women did more than their fair share of work. They were still responsible for most of the child rearing, and they carried the double burden of working both at home and outside the home. She asked me, "If those women in the West are as free and liberated as we are told, why do they continue to fight for women's rights?"

"Yes, Tengani, we may still have a long way to go, but we're moving along," remarked Mwapona.

"I also agree," said Masiliso. "We're talking about having obtained independence only a few decades ago. You can't expect everything to change. One day at a time. Don't rush us or drive yourself too hard."

Looking back on that discussion, I must admit they had some valid points. We can't rush things. We should also take into account our own culture, but that doesn't mean that we should blindly follow tradition and customs. The good ones may stay, but the bad ones must go. As for the war to protect women's rights, I think it's a just war. It might take twenty years more, maybe a hundred or even a thousand years more, but it will continue until true freedom for both men and women in this country is achieved.

Having really reflected on how things have been in my life so far, I can't wait for my next meeting with Chilufya and Likande. The proposed reunion with our classmates should be really interesting. It might even turn out to be a good recruiting ground for women wishing to join this just war. Who knows how many of them have gone through bitter divorces, or have been widowed and left with nothing? I'm sure most will agree with me that this is no time to slow down. As the saying goes, *Aluta continua*. The struggle continues.

Chapter Seven

Likande

I

I arrived at Tallahassee Airport on a hot and humid August afternoon. The temperature was 100° Fahrenheit and the humidity 100%. As I disembarked from the plane, a gush of hot air hit my face. I felt a trickle of sweat run down my back, and my clothes were clinging to my body as if I were in a steam bath. Never in my whole life had I experienced such heat or humidity. Temporary relief came when we entered the air-conditioned terminal.

As I looked towards a crowd that had come to meet the arrivals, I saw two girls holding a small banner with my name on it. I walked towards them and introduced myself. One of them said,

"Welcome to Tallahassee. My name is Leopoldine, and I'm a graduate student. I'm from Senegal." She spoke with a heavy French accent. I suddenly wished I had learned French at school. It was such a musical and romantic-sounding language! The other girl also greeted me and said, "Mine is Asante. I'm from Kenya, and I'm a sophomore."

They then escorted me to get my luggage, and after putting everything in Leopoldine's car, we set off for Florida State University. On the way I remarked how hot it was. Leopoldine said that parts of West Africa were just as hot and humid, but Asante said that she had problems with the heat when she arrived.

"The part of Kenya I come from is not hot at all. In fact, people here were surprised that someone from Africa could complain about the heat. They don't understand that Africa is a huge continent with varied climates. They were even more surprised when I told them that there's snow on Mount Kenya."

"Well, Likande, apart from the heat, what do you think of Tallahassee?" asked Leopoldine.

"I haven't seen very much of it except a brief aerial view just before landing. It seemed like a fairly small town, although most of the city could have been hidden under all those trees. It also appeared to have many lakes and ponds."

"It is a small town," said Asante, "but lovely, especially in the spring, when everything is in bloom. It is really magnificent then!"

Much to my relief, they both left soon after helping me to check into my dormitory. I was too tired and jet-lagged to enjoy small-talk. Although it was afternoon in Tallahassee, my body was telling me that it was midnight back home. My family and friends must be fast asleep now, I thought. As soon as I was alone, I kicked off my shoes and just fell onto the bed. I drifted into a long, deep sleep.

I was woken up by a knock on the door. When my eyes flew open, I was confused for a moment by the strange room and the unfamiliar surroundings. Then I remembered where I was, and a glance at my watch showed the time as twelve o' clock. I had slept since the previous afternoon, right through the night and all morning! Several more knocks made me jump from the bed and open the door.

It was Asante, and she said, "Did I wake you up? Sorry if I did, but you have an orientation this afternoon, and I came by to remind you about it. I also thought we could have lunch together."

"Sure, I feel famished! I missed both supper and breakfast. But I need to take a shower and get changed. As you can see, I slept in my travelling clothes because I was too tired to change."

"Okay. I'll come back later then, say, in one hour?"

"Sure. I'll be ready."

When she came back, I had not only showered and changed into clean clothes, but I had even managed to unpack some of my clothes and to put them away or hang them in the closet. She took me to the Student Union cafeteria for lunch and then went with me to show me where the orientation for new students was being held.

Pointing to a spot on the campus map, she said, "We're here, and your dormitory is over there. I'm sure you'll know where places like the library are after your orientation. Please call me if you need any help."

That was how my first day at Florida State University began.

Asante lived up to her word to help me 'get sensed' and, she in fact, became quite a good friend. She took me shopping and showed me around Tallahassee. I didn't see much of Leopoldine as she was busy with her Master's thesis.

II

One day as we sat in a bus on our way to the shops, Asante said, "You won't believe this, but it is only recently that you and I could sit like this in the front seats of the bus. Blacks used to sit at the back. If the seats there were full, then they had to stand, even if there were empty seats in front."

"I'm shocked to hear this. I can't believe that such things happened here in America. So when did all this change?"

"I can't speak for the whole country, but here in Tallahassee, what triggered the change was a boycott of buses. It all started after two girls from Florida A&M, a mainly black university, took up some front seats and refused to go to the back. The driver refused to move unless they went to the back or got off the bus. They refused to leave the bus unless they were given back their money, so there was a deadlock."

"Yes, and then what happened?"

"I believe the driver called the police, and the end result was a huge organized boycott of buses by blacks and sympathizers. This led to changes and the end of discrimination, at least on things like buses. All the same there is still a lot of discrimination and racism out here."

"Gee, I wish I had not come. I didn't leave my country that is about to get independence, to come to more racism."

"Things are pretty tense at the moment, and there have been protest marches and demands for civil rights and justice for blacks and other minorities."

"I've not felt any discrimination since I arrived. Come to think about it, almost all the students I'm friendly with in my classes and at the dorm are white. So it can't be that all whites support discrimination."

"Of course not but most of them don't really care one way or the other. A racist group like the Ku Klux Klan takes this silence to mean consent. They have made life for blacks hell, especially here in the south."

"What do they do?"

"Burn crosses in front of houses of blacks. They have even killed some."

"Aren't they arrested?"

"Part of the problem is that the KKK, as they are popularly known, disguise themselves in long white robes with hoods that cover their faces. So it's difficult to tell who they really are. It could be your neighbour, or even your classmate, who knows?"

"Neighbours or classmates?"

"Look, I don't mean to scare you or make you paranoid. You just have to be careful and not get yourself into dangerous places."

"Like which ones?"

"Wandering away from the campus alone or even at the beach where these people stare at blacks as though they were aliens from another planet."

But venture to the beach I did, though not alone. I went with Judy McNeil, a girl I met at the laundromat the first week of my arrival. I was desperately trying to work out how to operate the washing machine but couldn't. I was in a new world of machines! Life back home was certainly much simpler. When clothes were dirty, all you did was handwash them and dry them outside in the sun. I normally washed mine in small quantities to avoid a huge laundry day. But Asante had pointed out the laundromat to me and simply told me that there were machines that did the washing and drying. Now here I was, with no idea how to use them!

Finally, I said to the girl who was near me, "How does this work?"

"Here, let me show you. You'll need coins, and you place them into this slot ... "

"Thank you very much."

"You're welcome. You seem to have a foreign accent, where are you from?"

"From Northern Rhodesia, but the name will soon change to Zambia, after we get our independence from Britain."

"Let's see, Northern Rhodesia ... isn't that just below the equator? In central-southern Africa?"

"Yes. Have you been to Africa?"

"No. But I would love to go. There are so many changes taking place there, I just can't keep up, especially with the new names of the newly-independent countries. I hope I'll remember which country is which when I finally go! My brother just came back from a safari in Kenya and loved every minute of it. He plans to go back."

As we introduced ourselves and chatted, we discovered that we were in the same dormitory and that Judy was also a freshman. She invited me for coffee later that day; and when I turned up, I met a friend of hers, who was visiting. It was then that Judy suggested we all go to the lake or to the beach.

"I discovered a secluded lake on the way to Wakulla Springs. It has crystal clear water. Why don't we go tomorrow afternoon?" asked Kim.

"How about it, Likande?" asked Judy.

"I don't think I can. Tomorrow is a very busy day for me. I have lectures morning and afternoon. But I'll come to the beach with you another day. I've never seen the ocean before. We only have rivers. My country is landlocked, in the hinterland of Africa."

"We'll take you one Saturday then," said Judy.

"A Saturday would be great," chipped in Kim. "We could go to St. George's Island."

"Oh yes," agreed Judy, "you'll love it there, Likande. The beaches have white sand, and it is just great."

On the day we went, I remembered Asante's warnings and said to Judy and Kim, "Are you sure it's all right for me to go with you? I'm told there's a lot of racism here, and people stare at blacks?"

"Who on earth told you that?" asked Judy. "I don't think there's racism here. In any case, if anyone bothers you, they'll have to deal with us as well. I can't stand such people!"

But Kim said, "Like everywhere, you may find people who are racist. You should just ignore them. Not every white is a racist."

"Why is there so much distrust among whites and blacks?" I asked.

"I understand that whites even move away from inner cities so as to avoid being with black people."

"That's not true," said Kim, "we've left because it is no longer safe there. Cities have been turned into ghettos of crime, muggings, murders and assaults. Who would want to stay in a place like that? Would you stay in a place where you felt insecure and threatened? Only the other day, I read that someone in New York was killed because he wouldn't let a gang of youths grab his jacket. How can people do such terrible things?"

Judy said, "Likande, there are a lot of whites who would like to make friends with black people. I, for one, would like to mend those bridges with the other side. It's a question of building trust in each other and working together."

We had a good time at St. George's Island, and I was glad I went.

As soon as we arrived I ran to the beach and just stood gazing, spellbound, at the enormous sea of water that seemed to stretch to the very edge of the world. It was so immense and it made me feel frightened. At first, I could not even bring myself to step into the water, as I was worried I might be carried away by the huge waves that kept flapping against the shore. Judy was concerned by my reluctance to get into the water.

"Likande, I thought you said you could swim?"

"Yes. But not in this! I meant in the river."

Kim let out a giggle and said, "Either you can swim, or you can't."

"Why don't you just keep to the edge here, where the water is only knee deep," suggested Judy.

Slowly, I edged my way into the water, wading my feet in it. The water was warmer than I expected. After splashing myself at the edge for a few minutes, I relaxed and I soon joined in the fun, rushing into the oncoming waves and screaming with delight as I felt wave after wave of water splashing against my body. We spent time lying in the sun, eating sweet and juicy watermelons, building sand castles and collecting shells. We left fairly late, after most people had long gone.

When I next saw Asante, I told her that I had no problems whatsoever at the beach and that I had a great time. I said, "Everyone was too busy doing their own thing to bother about who was black and what not."

I had gone to see her at the apartment she shared with some friends. I found her with two friends who were students at Florida A&M University. One of them introduced herself as Amy Jones and the other was Andrea Jackson.

When Asante explained that she had warned me about racism, Andrea said, "In many ways, I would rather sit next to a racist than those wishy-washy white liberals. At least a redneck will tell you what they really feel about things."

"I agree," said Amy. "Most of these so-called liberals are nothing but hypocrites. What amazes me is that when they see foreigners, they pretend to be nice to blacks. Why aren't they nice to us blacks in this country? Charity begins at home. Not thousands of miles away."

"Look, don't get me wrong," I said, "I didn't mean to imply that the racial problems aren't real. It's just that I believe in people. I don't make friends with someone on the basis of their colour."

"Me neither," said Asante. "I must confess, though, that when I arrived in Tallahassee, I expected black people to be more friendly to me than whites. But the opposite was the case."

"What do you mean?" asked Amy.

"Well, I just felt closed out by African Americans here. It was as if, as soon as people heard my accent, or if I mentioned that I was from Africa, they didn't want to know. It was only when I went to New York and Washington that I talked to black Americans who seemed to identify themselves with us. They actually wanted to know more about Kenya. It was as if they were interested in their roots."

"This is nonsense. Absolute nonsense!" shouted Amy, getting visibly upset. "I'm a Southerner, born and bred, and I don't agree with you. We may be cautious about strangers, yes. We may appear less outgoing and less warm, yes. If you knew our background and our history, you would understand why we close off outsiders, whether they be white or black ... ”

“So you agree with me,” declared Asante. “Why then are we arguing?”

“No. I don’t agree with you! Who was the one who first approached you when you came to that meeting for black students at Florida A&M? Who spearheaded the committee that organized the meeting to bring together black American students and international students of African origins? I was the one. So how can you accuse us of being .. .”

“Amy, please,” appealed Asante, “I didn’t mean it to sound the way it did. I’m very sorry.”

“You know, I’ve heard these complaints as well,” said Andrea. “In fact, my Nigerian boyfriend and I broke up after a terrible argument about this.”

“What happened?” I asked.

“He has this tendency to talk down to us black Americans. He keeps saying that it’s our fault that we’re getting a raw deal in this country.”

“Our fault?” cried Amy. “Why didn’t you tell me this before, I would not have invited him to my party!”

“He says we’re left behind because of our apathy and unwillingness to fight for our rights.”

“Did you tell him about the Freedom March, about the huge demonstrations and unrest all over the country?”

“Of course, he knows about all that. Anyway, I really got sick of him going on and on about us and how lazy we were and so on. He even said we are so ignorant that someone asked him whether in Africa people still live in trees! As if anyone could be so stupid. In the end, I told him that if things in his country were so good, why didn’t he pack up and go back there?”

“Good for you, Andrea,” said Amy.

“You know, I can believe his story about living in trees. Someone asked me whether my clothes were given to me at the airport when I arrived here. This person said that she watched a movie about the Maasai of Kenya in their scanty clothes. But, not all Maasai are like that. The old and traditional ones did oppose outside influence. That doesn't mean we all go around the country wearing next to nothing! Likande, that was why I didn't want to talk to your friend about game parks and animals."

"You mean Judy? Oh, she's not at all like that," I said.

III

Despite the racial tension and incidents of civil disobedience that marked my stay in the United States, and the terrible assassination of President John F. Kennedy in November 1963, my college years were both stimulating and fulfilling. The highlight was 1964. It was the year when the Civil Rights Act was passed, to protect the rights of blacks and other minorities in the United States. It was also a very special year for me, as it was the year my country obtained its independence from Britain, becoming the Republic of Zambia, on 24 October.

I deeply regretted not being there to share in all the excitement and celebrations. The letters I received from my family and from Tengani were all about the festivities that went on. It sounded as if the whole country was having a ball, and I was missing out. It was as if all the goodies would be gone by the time I got there; as if the celebrations would be long gone.

I held a party to mark the occasion, in a five-bedroomed house I was then sharing with Judy and three other students. We were a truly international group. The others were Monika from Germany, Maritza from Argentina and Pon from Thailand. Among us, we represented the continents of Africa, North America, Asia, Europe and Latin America. The party was a pot-luck dinner, and we invited friends and asked them to bring their own friends and contacts. Each person brought a special dish from their country or region. The result was a colourful and delicious international cuisine. After the meal we made room for dancing, and we danced all night long. It was indeed a memorable fiesta.

The following day I had many phone calls about how great the party had been. Amy Jones was the first to call, and she said to me, "Likande, that was the best interracial, intercultural party

I've ever been to. I really had fun. I also enjoyed talking to your friend Judy. In fact, we'll be meeting tomorrow at Florida A&M. She would like to look up some references at the library on black American history."

"I'm thrilled that you two got on well together," I said.

I was indeed very pleased that she and Judy hit it off. Through Amy, I had learnt something about black Americans, and I had visited her lovely family in Gainesville. They were a large and happy family and not at all cautious or less warm. I loved their constant laughter and the warmth and hospitality of Amy's mother, who was like 'Mother Earth.' Every time we went there, the house was full of extended relatives and friends. Even if they were eating, she would wave her hand to the latest arrival and invite them to join us. I loved her 'Southern specials,' grits and black-eyed peas, or 'baked beans' 'n pork, Southern style.'

At first, we hardly understood each other, as I couldn't catch her Southern drawl and she couldn't understand my Zambian accent. But we somehow worked things out and laughed our heads off. Sometimes, she even joked, "Who knows whether our great ancestor came from your part of the world? You might even be related to us!"

While I learnt something about black America, Judy took me to her home, where I saw a part of white, middle-class America. I also saw some of it at Jake's sister's home in Tallahassee, which I visited on several occasions, because she was my sponsor. With Stephanie, Jake's sister, it was a typical single person's existence, marked by rushing from one event to the next and eating fast foods.

Judy's home was in Newton, outside Boston, Massachusetts. I was invited to share with them the American holiday of Thanksgiving. Judy explained that it was the only truly American holiday, apart from the fourth of July which marked independence.

For Thanksgiving, we sat down to a huge meal of turkey and all the trimmings... roast potatoes, sweet potatoes, pumpkin pie, assorted vegetables, and then a dessert of apple pie and pecan pie. I could barely move after the meal! I met most of Judy's extended family, uncles, aunts and cousins. Her brother Bill even flew back from his business trip in Bangkok for the occasion. Judy said to me, "This is the one holiday all Americans celebrate, whether they be Jewish, Muslim, or whatever. Christmas is mostly for Christians, but this is for every American."

During the time we were there, she took me around the interesting spots in Boston. We went along the Freedom Trail, to the famous Quincy Market, the harbour site of the Boston Tea Party, then along Massachusetts Avenue to the famous universities of Harvard and MIT. After that, we went to the towns of Arlington, Lexington and Concord. She pointed out landmarks of the War of Independence against the British. When we stopped for lunch in Lexington, I said to Judy, "The British seemed to have bitten off more than they could chew!"

"Yes. There's a large Irish community here, and even now some people are very sensitive about it. My father still has relatives in Ireland, and whenever he reads about what is going on there, he blames the British."

"I thought the problem there is a religious one, between Irish Catholics and Protestants."

"It's not that simple. Anyway, see that painting over there?"

"Where it says Paul Revere?"

"Yes. He was a great hero. He rode on horseback to warn residents that the British were coming. Once a year, there's a parade along Massachusetts Avenue to re-enact the route he took. There are also many things named after him ... roads, bars and so on. Oh, here comes the menu, at last!"

"What do you recommend? Something light and not too filling. That huge meal your mum gave us should last me a week!"

"You must try our New England clam chowder. It is really delicious! Afterwards, we can order a piece of blueberry pie. That too, is finger-licking good!"

"Okay, sounds great. Now I know why you go on those crash diets whenever you come back to college!" I joked.

That was my first visit with Judy and her family. She invited me again to her home the following year, this time for Christmas. What I found interesting was that the festive meal for Christmas was exactly as the Thanksgiving one. Judy's mother remarked to me that having turkey on the last Thursday of November to celebrate Thanksgiving, and again on December 25 for Christmas, was a bit too much. She said, "When you add the turkey sandwiches from leftovers, you feel like never setting your eyes on another turkey again. But, come November, we are ready and looking forward to it!"

IV

In the meantime, my academic work at the university was going very well. I kept high grades, and most of my professors remarked how well I wrote. In many ways, it was thanks to my teachers at Chipembi and the British educational system, which had prepared me for hard work. Although my Form Six Higher School Certificate was equivalent to an American High School Diploma, my performance when I started at the university was at the level of a sophomore or a second-year undergraduate. For all intents and purposes, my last year at school had been preparing us for university. So it was with relative ease that I went through my college years. What I found strenuous was the sheer volume of work and the speed with which assignments had to be completed. I would have loved more time for deeper research and reading for some of the papers. But, alas, there wasn't enough time for that.

Time was flying at such speed that before I knew it, I was sitting for my exams; soon after which we were getting ready for graduation. I sent letters to my parents and to Chilufya and Tengani, informing them about the date and time of the Commencement Ceremony, as the graduation event was called. How I wished they could be there to share in my success! How I wished they could watch me walk to the podium to receive my degree! But it was wishful thinking. They were thousands of miles away, and not one of them could afford the fare to come and see me. But just letting them know made me feel better.

I woke up early on Graduation Day, the feeling of regret at my family and friends from home being unable to join me for the event that morning, replaced by a warm feeling. I sensed that wherever they were and whatever they were doing, they would take a moment to remember me in their thoughts, or even to say, "Likande should be at the graduating ceremony, around now."

When, a few hours later, the ceremony started, I was swept up in the general excitement and jubilation. My heart leapt when I heard my name. It was as if I was floating on air as I walked up the steps, all clad in my gown and cap denoting that I was now indeed a university graduate. There was clapping from the audience, but I also heard shouts of "Likande!" from my new, extended family and friends in Tallahassee. I waved a hand and smiled acknowledgement. I knew who they were. They were the special friends who had made my stay in the United States very interesting, and who had generously invited me into their homes and made me feel like family.

Later that evening, after the celebrations and parties were over, I said to Judy, "You and your family have been very kind. I feel guilty, though, for depriving you of your parents' exclusive attention this evening."

"Don't be silly! We wanted you to have dinner with us at the restaurant. So why should you feel guilty?"

"Well, you're their only daughter, and this was a special occasion for you."

"For you, as well, Likande. You've been like family to me. My only regret is that my only brother and sole sibling chose to be away in distant Hong Kong instead of coming to my graduation."

"He probably couldn't leave the business meetings to be here."

"I suppose so. By the way, my mom was thrilled with that carved wooden elephant you gave her."

"I'm glad she likes it. That was done by my uncle, who is a sculptor. I can't believe that this time next week I shall be back home, seeing my family, relatives and friends!"

"I'll really miss you, Likande. I don't even want to think about your leaving. I hate saying goodbye to people close to me."

"But you're coming to Africa, remember! So we won't say goodbye. As they say in Spanish, it will only be *hasta luego*."

"Until later, then, my friend. Until the next time," she said, as we flung our arms around each other and gave each other a warm and emotional hug.

V

It felt strange to be back home. There were so many changes! There was also a feeling of confidence and optimism about the future which had been lacking when I left. The political honeymoon was still there, following the attainment of independence and there were signs of 'Zambianization' everywhere. The affluent suburbs, which before had been occupied only by whites, were now full of 'top Zambians.' These were the local people who now held high positions in both the government and the private sector. The middle-class Africans were also growing in number, as more and more black people took over jobs that had previously been held by Europeans, as all whites or Caucasians were popularly known.

My first stopover was in Lusaka, since that was my logical destination from London. There I spent two days with Tengani and she took me around the city, showing me the sports clubs, hotels and other facilities which were now open to anyone who had money. They were no longer preserves of Europeans only. Independence and equality were finally and truly here.

I noticed similar changes when I went to stay with my parents in Livingstone. The first day I arrived, my mother said to me, "Remember how I used to pack a flask of drink and things for you kids to eat, when we used to go to the Falls? Well, now we can actually sit and eat at the restaurant! Anyone is welcome – blacks, whites, Indians, Chinese, Japanese, whoever! No one bothers you as long as you have the money to pay."

My father said, "It's the same for trains, butcheries and the lot. If anyone discriminates against you, all you have to do is report them and they will have their licence cancelled if found guilty. More often, they are driven out of business by organized boycotts against them."

To prove how changed things were, they took me to the Victoria Falls a few days later, and we stopped at the hotel for drinks. It was indeed full of people of all races. I even saw mixed couples who sounded like South Africans. As if reading my mind, my mother said, "Livingstone is now the boundary between a free and just society and the racist regimes down south. Even multi-racial couples come here to escape persecution in South Africa."

I was happy to be back home and to share in building a country that was open to anyone, no matter their race or tribal origin. I spent my time in Livingstone visiting relatives and looking up old friends, all of whom were still excited about independence and the changes it had brought. I also enjoyed my reunion with my sister and brothers when they came home for their school holidays. It was interesting to listen to what was going on in their schools, especially to get news about my old school. I asked my sister about my old teachers. When I first went to Tallahassee, I had written to some of them, but then as things became too hectic, I had stopped writing. Nasilele said, "They always ask after you. I wish Mum and Dad had sent me to another school. At Chipembi, I'm just your pale shadow. It's always, Likande was good at this and that. I love you, big sis, but I'm getting sick of hearing about all the good things you did! Why can't people accept me for what I am? I am Nasilele, not Likande!"

"I do accept you for what you are, little sister! I think you're great. At least, you seem much better at the sciences than I was," I said.

"You weren't good at maths or sciences?"

"Well, er ... I was so-so ... "

"Really? How come all those people at school keep saying that you were this great person who seemed good at everything? Are they trying to make me have an inferiority complex?"

"Now, now, Nasilele, why are you always so overdramatic about things?" teased my brother Mbuye.

I moved away as the two of them got into a heated argument. I went and joined my parents in the living room. My mother was busy knitting a sweater while my father was reading a newspaper. They both looked up when I entered, and my father said, "Likande, what are your plans about a job? There are many companies looking for workers in today's paper."

"Companies? Surely what she needs to do is to look for a job with the Ministry of Education. What else can she do with a B.A. degree but teach?" asked my mother.

"Why do you always butt in when a question is directed at someone else? Doesn't she have a mouth to speak for herself?" demanded my father. I had seen many changes since coming back from Tallahassee, but what had not changed was this type of dialogue between my parents! I watched them arguing but said nothing.

"Well?" asked my mother, turning to me.

"Well what?" I asked, getting impatient.

"What are you going to do, and when are you going to begin looking for work? My suggestion is that you apply for a teaching job here. Your father could even help you, as he knows people ..."

"No, thanks. I'll find my own job."

I made up my mind there and then not to work in Livingstone. I needed to find my own job and live my own life. I didn't go abroad and manage to attend college and finish my degree, only to come back to my mother's apron strings! I was now twenty-two years old and quite capable of looking after myself. It was great to be back home, but I needed space to work things out for myself. So that same day I sat down and wrote several applications. I only responded to jobs that were being advertised outside Livingstone. I focused on Lusaka, as the job market seemed particularly active there, and it also meant that I could be near Tengani. Chilufya was still at the university.

I went to several interviews, but in the end I selected the job offer of Lecturer at Evelyn Hone College of Further Education. My mother was very worried about my going alone to Lusaka.

"But Ma, I've been alone the past four years at the university, and thousands of miles away!"

"But I was hoping you would work nearer home. We've hardly seen you, and time flies so! First you were at boarding school, then college, and now you're off again!"

"That's why I've never really approved of boarding schools. You kind of miss out on seeing your kids grow," said my father.

"Now you're changing your tune, and yet you used to say, one made good friends at boarding school," said my mother.

There were times when I didn't know whether to laugh or take my parents seriously when they got into their arguments. It was a bit like a debating contest between them. Each one trying to be clever with words. But it was never a shouting match, and underneath it all lay caring and concern for each other. But they belonged to the generation and tradition where it was not the done thing to publicly show affection for each other.

Anyway, I assured both that boarding school had been an interesting experience, even though I had been upset at first about leaving home. But I was now an adult, and I had to work things out for myself. In the end my mother said, "Actually, it's not as though you'll be absolutely alone. You'll see your brothers, and your friends are there, too."

"Yes, in fact, even Nasilele can spend some of her school holidays at my place!" I said.

"Starting a new job and getting your own place is hard work," said my mother. "You must take good care of yourself, and don't hesitate to come back home if things don't work out."

"Yes, Ma. I will."

VI

I settled down to life in Lusaka fairly quickly. I taught history to adult students who had not completed high school, most of whom had jobs and were taking classes on a part-time basis. The college offered several courses for such students as well as for those seeking other skills, such as secretarial training and journalism.

Among the benefits of the job was housing. I had a two-bedroomed flat, not far from the college. Since history was my favourite subject, I quite liked teaching it, and my students also seemed to enjoy my classes. However, deep down, I felt that teaching was not really for me. It was as if I was blindly following my parents' footsteps. They were happy that I had chosen their profession. They no longer mentioned the stress and burn-out. Instead they told me that I had chosen a career that was very fulfilling and whose benefits were unquantifiable.

Maybe that was true. But after teaching for one year, I handed in my resignation.

My next job was with a private company that was involved in the importation and exportation of a wide range of goods: clothes, food, pharmaceutical products, construction materials. It seemed to have a finger in everything. Many companies were expanding, as the economy was booming, and there was great competition among them to hire graduates. Everyone wanted to hire college graduates, and they offered on the job training. It didn't matter what kind of degree one had. They promised high salaries and quick promotions to managerial positions, so I applied. It was indeed a graduate's market. Companies wanted to show the government that they were complying with the demands of quick Zambianization. Getting those with degrees was the fastest way to do it.

When I went for my interview, I was told that although I would begin as a Senior Buyer, after my training I would become the Assistant Purchasing Manager, and thereafter the prospects of being the Division Chief were very good. I couldn't wait to begin my job at Bwelani Industrial Company. From what I was promised, the sky seemed to be the limit!

The job kept me on my feet, continuously rushing from one meeting to another, carrying samples to customers, placing orders with suppliers abroad and chasing their progress. Bwelani was in the right business because, despite political independence, customers weren't interested in locally produced goods. The government's plans to substitute imports with local products wasn't yet in full swing. Many customers still believed that clothes or construction materials, and even food, were of better quality when they were from abroad. People were prepared to pay more for goods from overseas even if they were of the same material and quality as the local ones. Some of Bwelani's competitors resorted to placing labels pretending that the goods were made overseas when in fact they were locally produced. To run these imposters out of business, the Managing Director of Bwelani decided to launch an even more aggressive marketing policy.

He organized a reception for executives and up-and-coming young managers from Bwelani and its subsidiary companies. I attended in my new position as Assistant Purchasing Manager.

The reception was held at Mr. Bwelani's farmhouse just outside Lusaka. It was a huge farm stretching over six thousand acres of land. Someone said that he bought the land and the property on it for a song, as it was confiscated from an absentee landlord. There were people who had left the country and gone to places like South Africa to get away from a country that was now run by blacks. When they did not respond to ultimatums to come back and develop the land, their land was sold very cheaply. The problem was that people who benefitted from these cheap sales of property owned by absentee landlords were those in the know and with contacts.

At the party, before sitting down to listen to the new policy directives on aggressive marketing, we mingled with representatives from the various offices, chatting and helping ourselves to the lavish display of food and drinks that were laid out. Waiters from a catering organization in downtown Lusaka hurried around, serving guests with drinks. After chatting with several groups of people, mostly about the state of the market and which goods seemed to be in higher demand than others, I walked over to the large tables laden with assortments of various foods.

Waiters had brought around trays of spicy meatballs and samosa. My mouth was burning from the hot chili and spicy food and I went to look for something to neutralize the hot stuff. Something like a carrot, or celery. When I noticed a colourful vegetable platter, I reached out for a carrot, and there was a loud thud as my forehead banged into someone's head.

"Ouch!" I cried, as I touched my pounding head.

"I'm terribly sorry," said a young man who looked about my age, "here, let me have a look."

Without waiting for my response, he placed his hand on my forehead, running his fingers over the spot where his head had hit mine. He said, "No swelling. But to make sure, I'll ask one of the waiters for an ice pack, or just a piece of ice ... "

"No, please. I'll be okay. I feel fine, really," I said.

He then picked up celery and, after dipping it in a sauce, held it right on my mouth. I opened my mouth and took a bite, and our eyes met and held for what seemed like forever. It may have been only for a few seconds, but my heart started going wild and racing at an incredible speed. His eyes gazed into mine and held them with such intensity that I was like a pin being drawn towards a magnet. My eyelids automatically closed like shutters, but when my lips felt the cool celery, my mouth opened and took another bite. He was so close to me that I could feel his warm breath against my face. This is crazy, I thought. What on earth is happening to me?

Opening my eyes, and trying to shake off the sudden panic and embarrassment that I was now feeling, I said, "I'm really quite capable of feeding myself! It was my head, not my mouth, which you bumped into."

"Okay, why don't you feed me instead? I hit my mouth when we collided," he said, placing a hand over his mouth.

"I didn't notice anything," I said.

"Well, it's not too bad now. I was hoping you would reciprocate by feeding me, too."

"Okay, here you are," I said, placing a carrot in his hand. I could no longer trust my feelings about him and didn't want to be too close to him. I started backing away from the table and muttered as I slowly moved away, "Well, nice meeting you, Mr. Er ... er ..."

But he came towards me with his hand outstretched and said, "We didn't even introduce ourselves. My name is Musa Mufaya."

"Mine is Likande Nawa."

"Nice to ..." we both started, and then broke off, laughing.

He said. "There we go again. First, bumping our heads after reaching out for the same vegetable, even though there were many others. Now we're saying the same thing. Gee, do we think alike?"

All I could do was smile in a sheepish way, like a bashful damsel. Touching me on my shoulder, he said, "Come on, why don't we explore Mr. Bwelani's garden before the speeches start?" I nodded and followed him.

We went around the back of the house and then sat down on a wooden bench overlooking a large flower garden. I said to Musa, "I heard that Mr. Bwelani was planning to export flowers to Europe. I wonder whether this is the project?"

"Yes. Apparently, the white commercial farmer who used to own this farm had a thriving export business in flowers. He sent them to Europe during their winter and made a lot of money. Mr. Bwelani wants to try it out. He is accumulating more and more wealth. Isn't it strange that those who already have seem to get even more? I hope one of these days I'll make enough money to live in a posh place like this."

"One of these days? Or one of these decades?"

Musa laughed and said, "You're right. I'm being too ambitious. Anyway, how about you, Likande? What exactly do you do for the Bwelani Company?"

I told him what I was doing and also explained that I had a B.A. degree with a major in history from Florida State University. He was surprised that I should be working in business with a degree in history. But I added that I also had taken other subjects, including economics, psychology, political science and urban and regional planning. He almost choked on his drink, and between coughs and suppressed laughter said, "What a combination! I suppose anything goes in America, hey?"

"What do you mean?"

"You couldn't mix all those things in England. Either you choose business courses, sciences, or liberal arts. You don't crisscross from one field to another, historian cum business person, and so on."

"That's exactly what I loved about American education. It gives you a broad base and prepares you for the working world. If you don't like one field, you can easily pick another one. You don't have to tie yourself to one job for life!"

"We call that 'a jack of all trades and master on none.' English education is about specialization. The American education is about pretending to know something about everything!"

"Are you suggesting that I'm not qualified for what I'm doing?" I demanded, getting quite angry and upset.

"Oh, no. Not at all. I was just saying what people say ... "

"I don't really care who says what. Let's just drop the subject." I picked up my drink and started walking back to where the others were. He quickly followed me and said, "I hope you're not mad at me."

"No," I replied, without looking at him.

"Come on, the truth! Look, I'm sorry if I upset you. Am I forgiven?"

"Yes," I smiled, and when he took my hand, I didn't pull it away.

"There's a terrific movie showing downtown. May I take you there on Saturday evening?"

"I'm not sure," I answered hesitantly. "What is the movie?"

But before he could answer me, my boss came looking for me.

"Likande, come on, where's that package of materials I was going to show Mr. Bwelani?"

"I'll go and get it," I said, running to where I had left my bag and papers.

I didn't see Musa until the end of the event, when he came looking for me. We exchanged addresses and phone numbers, and then I went back home.

VII

Saturday evening was four days away, but to me it was like four years. I just couldn't get him out of my mind. People had to repeat statements several times because my mind was somewhere else. I almost called him to suggest that we go out before then, but I didn't want to sound too eager and pushy. I couldn't wait to tell Tengani! A phone call wouldn't do. I had to tell her in person. When I arrived at her place, I drifted inside with a quick waltz, beaming with excitement.

"Oh, Tengani, Tengani," I called out, as I danced around her living room.

"Hey, what's all this? Have you won a lottery?"

"Nope."

"It's your promotion? Have they promoted you, again?"

"Nope."

"Come on, I can't guess. Tell me."

"I'm in love with Musa!"

"Musa who? Who is he?"

I told her who he was and how we had met. But when I mentioned that for our first date we were going to a movie, she burst out laughing.

"What's funny?" I asked.

"Well, I guess, nothing. It's just that people who are in love seem to go somewhere special, like dinner at a hotel or something. But I'm very happy for you. Congratulations!"

"I can't wait to show him to you. He is tall and handsome! The most gorgeous man on this earth!"

"My, I've never seen you like this before. It sounds like love at first sight!"

"Yes, it is! I don't even care that we're only going to a movie. I would run like a flash even if he were taking me to the zoo! I simply adore him. I haven't slept well since we met."

The day before we were going out, I received a phone call from Musa as soon as I arrived at the office. He asked if we could go for dinner at the Intercontinental Hotel that evening.

"You mean, instead of the movie tomorrow?"

"In addition to that. Tomorrow sounds like a thousand years away!"

"To me, too," I said, no longer feeling bashful. I wanted to see him there and then.

"Terrific, then. I'll pick you up around eight o' clock, this evening."

As soon as it was five o'clock, I was out of the office. Luckily for me, Friday afternoons were not the busiest in the week, so I normally used the time to plan for the following week and make appointments with clients.

I rushed home and looked in the closet for something to wear. I tried several things on. Some looked "too business-like," I told myself, while others seemed "too casual." Finally, I settled on a white and black polka-dotted mini dress, with a triple-tiered skirt and short sleeves. It was simple but elegant, and fitted my slim body to perfection. I wore an ivory necklace with matching earrings and a bracelet. These were very special to me, because ivory jewellery was handed down the line from mother to first daughter, from generation to generation, dating back to my great-great-great on my mother's side. During my grandmother's time the gift was given at puberty, which was normally the age for marriage as well. But my mother got hers on her wedding day, when she was in her late teens. I received mine while I was in Tallahassee, when I turned twenty-one.

It was a special gift because my grandmother was of 'royal blood,' and only such people wore ivory in those days or could pass it on to their daughters. Even men of royal blood used to wear bangles around their wrists, but theirs were larger, normally plain and simply designed. Such jewellery was done by specially selected craftsmen who knew the specific emblems and totems of chiefs and their families. This was long before European merchants, with their automatic weapons, slaughtered herds of elephants to obtain ivory in large quantities and feed the markets abroad. After that, ivory could be bought by anyone and sold to anybody.

Even after independence, ivory could be bought from street vendors, from markets and from shops. Almost everyone had one item or another made of ivory. There was no respect or consideration for elephants, the way it used to be, when only the very old in a herd could be killed, or when those with young ones were left to tend their offspring, so as not to disturb nature.

Commercial greed later took over, and the amount of money ivory could fetch became the driving force. Only much later, with the move towards conservation, did human beings start worrying about the elephant population. But for me, the jewellery I owned was something special. A family heirloom, which I valued and respected because of its origin and its importance to my family. Deep down in my heart, I knew that this day was a special one for me, so I wore the jewellery. The last time I had worn the whole set was at my graduation.

I was ready when Musa arrived. When I opened the door for him, he gave me a look that sent my heart pumping at a high speed. "You look wonderful. You look so gorgeous, I wish I could just be alone with you and not have to share you with the whole world."

I felt the same. I wanted us just to be together, at my place or his. But I wanted everything to be done just right. For some reason ... maybe it was the jewellery I was wearing ... my grandmother's words seemed to echo from a distance. When I became of age, she said to me, I'm glad you're going on with school. I wish I had the same opportunity when I was your age. Instead, I married young.

But even then, I made your grandfather wait. It doesn't do to rush towards men. Let them wait. In the end, they'll appreciate you."

Grandma was a chief's daughter and believed in style and protocol. Apparently, when Grandpa turned up with his entourage to meet the chief's daughter, whom he was supposed to marry, she took her time before going to see him. He was the eldest son of another chief, and the plan was to cement the improved relations between the two chiefs and their tribes through marriage between the two.

Grandma's advice, to 'make your man wait for you,' echoed in my head, but hers and mine are different worlds. What did she know of real love? Love that struck one's heart in a flash, like lightning? Hers was an arranged marriage, and Grandpa had been chosen for her. Admittedly, she grew to love him after they got married, but that was not the same as seeing someone for the first time and the heart leaping out in ecstasy. In the end, Grandma, I thought to myself, you made Grandpa wait because you were not in love then. You really didn't know such love, had not felt it, and were not sure about what you were letting yourself into. I know how I feel, and this is the man for me. But I'll do as you say, Grandma. I'll give myself time to know him better.

Turning towards Musa, I said, "I didn't dress up like this for an evening at home! So, come on, let's go."

He took me to the Makumbi Room at the Intercontinental Hotel. There was a dinner dance, and visiting performers and a musician from Europe. Musa and I danced to every tune that was played. As he took me in his arms for a slow waltz, I leaned my head on his shoulders and, closing my eyes, drifted into heaven. Our hearts beat in unison, and he squeezed me so tight, I thought I would faint from breathlessness.

When it was over, we went out to the car and then just sat inside and embraced, covering each other with kisses. He kept whispering, "I love you, I love you, dearest Likande."

VIII

When we began our dating and passionate romance, we couldn't see each other as frequently as we wished because Musa's job carried him outside town several times a month. We were also both very busy during the week. But when we met, it was like a long time had elapsed, and we had to make up and catch up on what we had missed. Several months later, as we squeezed a quick lunch into our busy schedules, he leaned over and whispered, "I love you. Will you marry me?"

"I didn't hear what you said," I said, although my heart was going "Boom, boom," at such a fast pace that I thought I would die from the excitement!

"I love you. Will you marry me?" he shouted, and heads in the restaurant turned towards our table. As if only he and I were in that room, my voice rang out, loud and clear, "Yes, I'll marry you."

There was an instant, spontaneous clapping from the other people in the restaurant, and the manager raised a glass to toast our future happiness.

When Tengani heard the news, she insisted on throwing an engagement party for us at her apartment. I was thrilled. But my parents were furious when I informed them about the engagement. I gasped in disbelief when I read the letter from my mother.

" ... you've got to follow tradition. You just can't announce that you're getting engaged. Who is Musa anyway? What sort of family does he come from? His father, uncle, or guardian will have to come here to meet your father and your uncles to discuss the bride price."

Bride price? I couldn't believe it! I wrote an angry letter to my mother telling her I was not for sale and that there would be no bride price for me! Her response was, either we did as tradition demanded, or we could go ahead and get married "in your own way. But don't expect to see us at your wedding." She added a postscript to the letter in which she said, just because I had been to America didn't mean that I should forsake our traditions. My mother knew how to get me. In fact, any time someone accused me of looking down on my background because I had been to America, I backed down. It was emotional blackmail, but it worked. I wanted my parents to share in my happiness. I wanted them to be at my wedding. So I gave in.

Musa told me it didn't bother him to have to pay a cow as my bride price. "You're priceless as far as I'm concerned. But let's just do it to keep them quiet," he said.

Musa went to meet my father and some relatives with a group of male relatives. Apparently, Musa was reminded by my relatives that he got off "lightly, in view of the fact that Likande has royal blood in her, and she is very educated."

Anyway, after the negotiations were over, we got busy preparing for the wedding, which was held in Livingstone. Friends, colleagues from work, relatives from Musa's side and mine, took the journey to Livingstone for the wedding. Chilufya took time off from college, and she and Tengani were my bride's maids. It was one of our rare reunions as 'The Three Musketeers,' and we had a lot to catch up on.

My mother, who heard us whispering most of the night, finally knocked on the door and said that I would be a "red-eyed bride, if you don't get enough sleep!" But we still managed a few more whispers before we finally fell asleep.

Chilufya said, "You've made it, as usual, Likande. The first to be married."

"The next one will be Chilufya, of course," said Tengani.

"Me? Are you kidding? I can't even dream of that before finishing my training. By then both of you will have tasted life, while mine will only be beginning!"

"I hope by life, you don't mean marriage," said Tengani. "Even those who aren't married, or have decided on careers, have life you know!"

"Oh, you know what I mean, Tengani. But like a politician, you play with words."

"Hey, girls," I said, "don't tell me we're back at school and arguing again! We're now adults, so no fighting, please!"

We all laughed, and then Tengani said, "Here we go again, the nun! I wonder what I'll call you after you're married tomorrow? I can't very well tease you as the nun anymore."

"How about saying Mrs. Likande Mufaya!" I said.

"Wow!" they both shouted, and we all laughed again.

As I drifted off to sleep, I felt happy and content. I wished my other friend, Judy, had made it to my wedding, but I had just received a postcard from her to say that she was in Jakarta, Indonesia. A telegram from her was read at the wedding and in it she wished Musa and me a happy married life.

The wedding was huge. My parents were well known in Livingstone among the teaching community. Since my maternal grandparents' home was also fairly close, almost everybody from the village turned up for the wedding. Musa and I used our salaries to pay for the wedding, and my mother had one of her cows slaughtered to raise more money. We were married in the small Methodist church in which I was baptised as a baby. It was packed, and the heat inside was unbearable. But who cared? This was a special day for me, and what mattered was standing next to the man I loved and repeating vows of marriage, as the minister instructed. Outside the church a throng of people waited for us to come out, and then there was ululation and dancing as the church ceremony ended.

We then went off to a hotel in downtown Livingstone, where the reception was held. When the band started playing, Musa stood up and immediately swept me onto the floor to begin dancing. We were followed by the bridal party, and soon everybody was on their feet in the typical African fashion. Dancing in Africa knows no age, and so the floor was full of people ... the old, the young, teenagers, everybody just stayed on their feet, tune after tune and number after number. Drink and food flowed as guests gobbled every tiny bit, including teeny-weeny bits of wedding cake, which had to be cut in minute pieces for it to go around to everyone.

After the reception we got into our car and headed to Botswana for a week's honeymoon. What we needed was a quiet week to be together and enjoy each other's company. We checked into a small hotel in Francistown and relaxed. The weeks preceding the wedding had been hectic for both of us, and we needed to be in top shape before getting back to our jobs and the usual rush and hustle.

One night, as I lay in Musa's arms, he said, "I want to treasure every bit of this, before the babies start arriving. Then you won't have any time for me."

"What do you mean?"

"It seems to me that as soon as a woman bears a child, she becomes so wrapped up in the baby that she forgets the romantic side of marriage."

Waving a finger at him, I said, "Hey, have you been hiding something from me? Were you married before? How do you know all these things?"

"Silly you," he said, holding me closer, "of course not! Never been married before. You're my first, and I'll love you forever and ever, until eternity. Unless, of course, you get sick of me!"

I snuggled even closer against him, until I could hear his heart beating against mine. Then I murmured, "We don't have to have a baby yet. There's lots of time for that. I'm now completely and surely yours. As we promised the other day, to hold and keep you, bla, bla,"

"For richer and poorer," added Musa.

I told Musa that what I wanted was to continue working for a while and then have a baby later, after two or three years. "That suits me fine," he said. "I love children, but we've got to enjoy being together before tying ourselves down. Besides, you too have a career and your own ambitions to fulfill. Children can wait. For now, it's only you and me."

"Anything you say, sugar," I said, kissing him tenderly on the mouth.

"Mmm, I love it when you call me that," he said, as his lips started nibbling my ears, moving down the side of my face and then across towards my mouth.

IX

When we returned from our honeymoon, we got back into our busy work schedules. Three months later, Musa was promoted to be General Manager of Bwelani's latest subsidiary company, a kind of engineering and manufacturing enterprise. He was a Mechanical Engineer by profession, having trained at Leeds University in Yorkshire, England. We were thrilled at his promotion. It not only meant more money, but a move to a company-owned house. In time we would buy our own property, but we would allow ourselves enough time to save money for the deposit on a mortgage. The company house was a large, colonial-style one in Rhodes Park, with a spacious, screened verandah, ideal for sitting out in the summer evenings without being bothered by mosquitoes. Life seemed good to us, and we were so happy that the months seemed to zoom by.

In my scheme of things, the only thing that seemed lacking in fulfillment was my job. I worked hard and it paid well, but it still left me with an empty feeling inside. Was this really what I was meant to be doing? I couldn't imagine myself going on like that for years and years and then receiving a pension at the end.

One evening after getting back from a dinner celebrating our first wedding anniversary, I said to Musa, "I wish I could find another job. I'm beginning to get sick of rushing around chasing bucks! Money, money, money, and what good does that do really?"

"It helps buy things like houses, remember? We could live on my salary. But what will you do? Just sit at home?"

"No. Not just sit at home. I could ... could .... "

"Could what?"

"Could have a baby. It's now a year, and we can ... "

"So that's the real problem? I thought you wanted to build your career and so on?"

"Yes, I did."

"Well, what has changed then? No, don't tell me. I think I know. Your mother has been counting fingers since we got married and wondering why there's no baby. Knowing you, you're giving in to pressure."

"It's not just my mom. Your mother asked me if I needed to see a herbalist to help me conceive. She assumed, of course, that I was infertile!"

"You mean, my mother's been bugging you about having a baby? Why didn't you tell me?"

"Well, I didn't want to bother you. You've been so busy ... "

"Bother me? Busy? I'm your husband, for heaven's sake! You come first. Not my job. Not my relatives. If you want a baby, we'll have one. But don't let your mother or mine pressure us into having babies if we're not yet ready for them."

"I want a baby, I want us to have one."

"Okay, sweetheart. Okay. Why don't we begin now ... "

I became pregnant as soon as I went off the pill. I was thrilled when my doctor confirmed it. When I told Musa the good news, he was so happy that he took me in his arms and started leading me into a dance on our living room floor. It was too early for a baby to move inside, but I could almost feel it jumping up and down inside me, as though sensing the excitement awaiting its arrival.

I continued working, but my job was a real drag by then. I felt guilty about the enormous profits the company was making at the expense of poor people. I now agreed with some of Tengani's concerns about the rich growing richer and the poor poorer.

There was another thing I thought was true, and that was that we women were getting a raw deal in everything. The euphoria and political honeymoon that had brought quick changes were now over.

The situation was like stale food after a huge party. It was now clear that I was stuck at the position of Assistant Purchasing Manager. A man who had just completed his training had been appointed head of our division. He kept asking me to update him on who our suppliers were and what he was supposed to do. We soon found out that he was Mr. Bwelani's prospective son-in-law. He was bossy and difficult to work for. He even had the audacity to ask me to make him a cup of coffee because his secretary had to take her baby to the doctor. My response was, "And what happened to your own hands?"

It seemed I was no longer Assistant Purchasing Manager, but his own personal assistant to order around. When I told Musa this, he cautioned me to be careful about what I said, as it might affect his own position. For the first time since our marriage, I really lost my temper and accused him of being a "typical African male chauvinist!"

He was shocked and taken aback by my outburst. My accusation was, of course, unfair, as he was one of the most considerate and caring husbands any woman could have wished for. But I was angry and miserable, and he took the bulk of my fury. He didn't respond. He just quietly said that he had work to do and would see me later. Afterwards, I felt awful and guilty. I apologised as soon as he walked in, and put my arms around him. He tickled my belly and said, "Hey, I can't really reach you. Not with this between us!"

We laughed, and then he added, "At first, I was hurt and angry by what you said. But afterwards, I put it to your condition. Apparently, some women become very touchy and can be as vicious as tigers when they are pregnant."

"Are you calling me a tiger, mister?" I demanded, and then tried to chase him around the house. But I was so big that all I could do was wobble around. When I sat down to rest, the baby moved and Musa noticed the bulge on my side. He immediately rushed over and put his arms around me.

He said, "I'm sorry your job is not going well. If you want to leave it, just go ahead."

But I thought leaving at that time would be a foolish thing to do. We had a baby on the way, and we still had plans of buying our own home. Instead I gritted my teeth and tried to be as nice as I could to my new boss, without grovelling in front of him. Once he realized that I was an asset to the department, and that it would help him if we were friendly to each other instead of being enemies, his attitude towards me began to change. One day, he said to me, "I'll miss you when you go on maternity leave. I hope it won't be too long, otherwise I'll be lost without you."

Talking to Kellie, a colleague and friend with the Bwelani group of companies, also helped me deal with the problem. One day, we were discussing the stress and frustrations of our jobs and how we were lagging behind men in promotions and benefits. She told me that at one point she had thought of resigning, but decided against it. She said that since she started doing volunteer work with low-income families in the shanty compounds, she had found a new sense of purpose and fulfillment. Like me, the money-making ventures of the company were beginning to get to her, "but the pay is good and they also help guarantee mortgages. So I had better stick around. At least, in my own time, I can do what I like, which is helping other people."

I suddenly realized that that was what I could do, too. It was exactly what I wanted to do. So I went with Kellie to the next meeting she attended, organized by the Red Cross. There, I met several professional people who spent some of their time, especially over the weekend, working on projects to help with the poor. I immediately signed up to join, but could not actively participate as the baby was due any time now.

X

Dinayi was born early one morning, after hours and hours of labour. Musa told me later that he almost died from worry and anxiety. Apparently, he kept pacing up and down the corridor and would not go away even when the nurses appealed to him to go and sleep for a while, with a promise that they would wake him up as soon as there was any news.

Finally, after heaving, pushing, groaning and moaning on my part, and wondering whether I would ever see daylight again, out came the baby. Despite the long ordeal, she was a healthy and lovely infant.

Later, when I was back in the ward, Musa beamed with pleasure. He was bubbling with excitement and joy and he kept saying, "She's like a photocopy of you, darling. Simply gorgeous! But there's a bit of me there, as well! There's no doubt about it, she's the most gorgeous baby in the whole world!"

Smiling fondly at him, I said, "I suppose all parents think that their baby is the most beautiful infant in the world!"

"Gosh, I can't believe that I'm a daddy! Likande, you and I are parents! Can you believe that?"

"I know. I can't believe it, either. It feels great, strange and scary, as well. I'm filled with wonder and awe."

"But we'll be together to watch her grow and help each other," he said, leaning over and planting a kiss on my cheek.

A few days later, when we were discharged from the hospital, Musa fussed over me and the baby like a mother hen. My mother and his, who arrived to see the baby, kept laughing and giggling just watching him. He held the baby as if she were an egg that might break! He reluctantly went to work and said, "I hate leaving you alone. I wish I could take a few days off, but we're very busy now, and there are so many meetings."

"But I'm not alone," I protested, "I haven't even put into practice what I learnt about washing babies. Your mother and mine have already divided chores between them, including giving the baby a bath!"

"Well, she's kind of special. The first grandchild for both."

I stayed at home to take care of the baby for three months, the first two being paid leave and the last one unpaid leave. My mother had stayed for two weeks, while my mother-in-law had spent a whole month with us. She also found me a nanny to help care for the baby.

A few days before I was due to return to my job, Musa said, "It's a pity you're going back to work. I've been looking forward to coming home to delicious meals cooked by my wife. Can't you just quit? I'm sure we'll manage. Besides, it will be better for the baby."

"I wish I could stay, but there's no way I can. The secretary from our office called me to give me a schedule of my appointments for next week. It seems they can't wait for me to get back!"

"I suppose their gain is my loss."

"Why do you say that?"

"I'm losing a wife. She's now back to being a rushed, career woman, with both of us staggering home tired. Too tired to sleep well, or make love!"

"Oh, come on. You're not losing a wife. You now have three in one; a wife, mother and career woman!"

"You're right. I must learn to count my blessings. I'm a lucky man."

"I'm the lucky woman for having a husband like you."

"There's Dinayi crying. I'll go and pick her up."

"No, don't," I said, restraining him by the hand. "I was just reading a book that said a baby shouldn't be picked up every time she or he cries, as that baby will get very spoilt."

"Throw that book away! There's no way I'll ignore my daughter when she cries."

I smilingly shrugged my shoulders and said to myself, "There goes my wasted reading time!"

But I thanked my lucky star and God for a wonderful husband, a happy married life, a healthy baby and all the good things that had been showered on us.

Little did I know then that my luck was running out. Tragedy struck early one morning when my baby was exactly five months old. I had only been back at work for two months. I went to bed feeling tired, but did not sleep well as for some reason the baby kept crying most of the night. Since Musa was leaving around five o' clock in the morning to go to a meeting on the copperbelt, I was the one who kept waking up to attend to the baby. I finally fell into an exhausted sleep, and I only faintly felt a peck on my cheek from Musa. He mumbled something about getting started as it was "a long drive. Darling, give the baby a kiss from me when she wakes up. I don't want to wake her as she has hardly slept."

"Mmm," I murmured, and covered my head with a sheet to get back to sleep.

But my husband never made it to the meeting. I was later told that his car slammed into a trailer that was parked dangerously around the curve of the Great North Road, the main highway from Lusaka to the copperbelt. I was woken up within an hour of his departure. Mr. Bwelani and a group of other officials, who had been going to the same meeting, were the first ones at the scene of the accident.

"I'm very sorry, Likande," said Mr. Bwelani, "I know this is a hard time for you. If there's anything I can do to help .. ."

I just stared at him, too shocked to move or say anything. I was clad in my nightie and had thrown a gown over it when the persistent knocking woke me up. I stood in the doorway, shivering like a leaf. My teeth were chattering as though I were standing in snow with nothing on. I was cold to the bone. Dead? Musa? My Musa, dead? As if the word 'dead' had finally registered in my brain, I let out a piercing scream of anguish and fell down in a heap, bending myself into a fetal-like position as if to close that terrible word off. No, no! Oh God, no! I cried over and over again. Surely it couldn't be. It was not true. There was no way he could die, just like that. Why, oh God, why? What did I do wrong? Why me, oh God? Why?

At first I was too numb to cry. I just stared at everyone with a blank expression. There, but not really there. Vaguely seeing those around me, and yet not really seeing them. I felt hands lifting me up and someone murmuring, "She's in great shock. She's still shivering." Someone called the housekeeper and the nanny, who had rushed from their dwelling at the back of the house and were now in the kitchen talking in hushed tones.

"Take the Dona to her room to change," said Mr. Bwelani. Suddenly realizing that I was still wearing a thin nightie and a dressing gown, I drew them closer around me, as if to look more respectable.

News travels fast in Lusaka, so there was soon a stream of people coming and going. Our close friends started making phone calls to our families to notify them, and later that day my parents arrived from Livingstone. Musa's parents were driven over by his brother from Choma, where they lived. The continuous flow of people and the wailing and weeping had finally registered the fact that he was indeed gone. Dead. Never to be seen again. Never to touch, hold, kiss, or to be just in each other's arms, the way we used to. I cried buckets and buckets of tears. It was as though the flood gates had been opened and let loose, and nothing in this world could make the tears stop flowing.

I went through the motions of the funeral but I was like a robot, just being led here and there. Physically, I was there; but mentally and emotionally, I was in a deep, dark tunnel of anguish and pain. There was a deep, open wound in my heart and in the core of my very existence. Its oozing could not be stopped by a Band-Aid. No medicine could heal such pain and anguish. Nothing could. Not my parents. Not our church minister. Not even my two best friends and long-time buddies, Tengani and Chilufya, who were constantly by my side, offering comfort and support. I was alone. I felt let down by everything, especially by God. How could a loving and caring God let such cruel things happen? Poor Musa, snatched away at such a young and tender age! Just when his career was at its peak? Just as he poised like a bird to flap his wings and fly away into the skies, to realize his career dreams and ambitions?

What unfulfilled plans! He didn't even have time to buy a home for his family! What dashed plans, what thwarted hopes! How he loved every minute he spent with his daughter, scooping her in his arms as soon as he got back from work and bouncing her up and down in the air until she was shrieking with laughter! Poor baby, she only had a brief glimpse of her adorable and loving daddy. Was that why she cried so much that night? Was it premonition? She was normally a good sleeper, and she had even stopped waking up for a feed at night. But that evening she was restless and kept waking up and crying. I once heard that babies have extra perceptions, an extra sense that is lacking in adults.

I was tormented by questions and thoughts of, "If only ... " If only he had waited another hour before leaving. It would have been lighter then, and he would have seen the truck. If only the truck driver had left parking lights on. If only he had not parked around that curve. If only I had woken up and had a chance to hold my husband in my arms and at least kiss him farewell. Normally, we slept with an arm around each other, feeling each other's presence throughout the night as we turned and dreamed. But not that night. I was so busy waking up to tend to the baby, who I feared might be developing a fever, that I barely paid attention to Musa. He also wanted to sleep, as he was getting up early. If only ... if only ...

I don't know how I went through the months following the funeral. I got up, went to work and buried myself in my job. But I was slipping more and more into loneliness and depression. The nights were worse. It was when I had nothing to do but try and go to sleep. How I wished I could just sleep and never wake up! Is that how people end up committing suicide? I had never before felt the need to leave this miserable world and just go away. But now I did.

My mother came to visit me four months after Musa's death. She heard me sobbing one night, and she came to my bedroom. Instead of offering me her shoulder to cry on, the way she had done often when I was upset, she started yelling at me, tears streaming down her face. "Likande, you've got to pull yourself together! You have a baby to think about, not just yourself. You hardly touch that baby, or spend time with her. All you are doing is wallowing in self pity and being selfish. That baby needs you! You're now the only parent she's got."

My mom walked out, leaving me sobbing. She didn't understand or know how I felt! How could she? No one really could, I moaned. I fell into an exhausted and restless sleep. She apologised the following morning. "I'm sorry, dear. I feel for you, and I do understand. After all, you're my own flesh and blood! But you've got to think about the baby. She needs you now, even more than before."

I heard her, but nothing really sank into my brain. It was only one evening, three months later, that her words really struck home. I was standing by the bathroom cabinet with a bottle of sleeping tablets in my hand, when the echo of her words rang out loud and clear in my mind. I had not used a single tablet of the pills thai my doctor had prescribed for me, and now I was looking at them. The thought of taking a number of them suddenly crossed my mind. I was now on the doorstep of death. All I had to do was empty the bottle into my mouth and wash them down with a glass of water, and the door would open. I would be gone forever.

It was at that point that my mother's warning rang in my mind. What on earth was I doing to my baby? Had I brought her into this world only to abandon her and leave her an orphan? I suddenly saw the writing on the wall. If I killed myself, not only would I leave my baby alone, but if there was a life after death, neither she nor Musa would ever forgive me when we finally met in the other world.

Musa had died in an accident. His wish had been to live a full life and to look after his family. I was still alive and had responsibilities to fulfill, especially to our daughter. I was now a mother and father to her. My duty was to show her what loving parents she had. Her dad may be dead and gone, but his spirit of love and joy would live on. He was a happy and caring man who greatly enjoyed life. It was the quality of life that he led on this earth that was important, not the number of years he spent here. It was as if a stream of light had finally broken through a crack in the dark tunnel and was beckoning me to follow it into the fresh air and sunshine outside.

Emptying the bottle of pills into the toilet and flushing them away, I went and picked my daughter up from her crib and just held her in my arms, rocking her against my bosom. She smiled in her sleep, and then her little hand rested on my shoulder. "I'm very sorry, baby," I whispered, "I didn't mean to abandon you. Mommy loves you and will look after you. Daddy loved you very much."

Without me, she would never know what her daddy was like, as a father to her or as my husband. I was the one who had to talk to her about him. The one to take care of her and watch her grow. There was a lot to do, and life had to go on.

Life went on for Dinayi and me. I suddenly realized that she had grown so much during the months I had been wrapped up in my own bereavement. Her first birthday had just come and gone, while I was too deep in my world of grief even to notice. She had gone through several developmental milestones, but I had left her completely in the hands of the nanny and the housekeeper. Briefly giving her a peck on the cheek when I came from work, I would then bury myself in more work or simply retire to my room to dwell on my misery. Now I could enjoy her company. I could play with her and spend more time with her.

I started taking her around with me and was happy to watch her grow and do all the things babies do. I was now determined not to miss out on any of the things she was learning to do. I couldn't recover what I had already lost, but I could make up on what still lay ahead.

Things did not change overnight. Recovery from bereavement is a long process. Like physical wounds, a scab over the injury develops over time, but the bruises are left. Healing is slow, and only time is a healer of such wounds. Time, which was there long before we were even made into humans, knows how to heal the wounds deep inside us. It is the best, natural healer. It also helps us see things in their right perspective. It teaches us that life must go on. That healing doesn't mean forgetting or betrayal. The special memories we hold for the departed ones, can remain there in one section of our memory, in the way a computer stores materials on its hard disc. Each piece of information is stored in its own special place, to be retrieved through memory and remembrance.

XI

For four years after Musa's death, my life revolved around my job and my daughter. Dinayi was an energetic happy child. She was very active and curious and had a sleek of stubbornness. Whenever I watched her drawing or playing with toys, she had a look of concentration and a slight frown on her forehead that reminded me so much of Musa. I no longer cried when the similarity struck me although I still had a twinge of regret that he wasn't there to watch her grow. A smile would cross my face every time I imagined what his reaction might have been if he were there. I could almost see him kneeling down to help her with a puzzle, or taking her for a ride in the car. My memories of him were now focusing on the zeal and joy with which he always saw life, rather than on the sudden accident that took his life. A kind of peace settled over my restless and bereaved mind and it was as if he were close to us and telling us that life must go on.

It then occurred to me that in four years I had not taken time off for a vacation. I always told everybody to "go ahead and take your holiday, I'll be around to man the Ship." The truth was I just could not bring myself to face a vacation without Musa. But now I thought I owed myself and Dinayi one. It would give us some time together without a nanny or a housekeeper.

One evening, as I read a bedtime story to her, she kept referring to the sea as "river, river." I told her that it was an ocean and that I would take her to see it.

"Let's go now, Mummy. I want to go, right now! I want to see the ocean."

The following day I went to the Zambia Airways office and booked flights to Mauritius. I took a three-week vacation just to be with my daughter. She was beside herself with excitement as I told my nanny and the housekeeper to take their well deserved time off and spend it with their relatives. They often had a few days off here and there, during Christmas, but not so many days at once, and certainly not both of them at the same time.

It was easy to lock up the apartment and just leave. I had good neighbours, most of whom worked in our group of companies. How relieved I was that I had not quit my job, despite not really enjoying it! It paid me well and there were other benefits, such as a generous bonus. I had also finally been promoted to Group Purchasing Manager, a job that came with a higher salary and a company car. I now had my own car and a company car as well. To ensure that my daughter was not left with nothing should I also die suddenly, I was in the process of negotiating a mortgage on a house I had seen in a suburb called Woodlands. Bwelani Company had already agreed to guarantee my mortgage. I now wanted only what was best for my child.

During our vacation in Mauritius, we rented a chalet by the sea. The place had several self-catering chalets run by a French couple, who also owned a restaurant where residents could eat or just sit around to chat. They served delicious sea food which I really enjoyed since fortunately, I had learnt to eat sea food during my college days in Tallahassee.

At first, my typically Zambian daughter, who was used to eating only fresh river fish, screamed when she saw a crab and a shrimp. She grabbed me by the hand and shouted that the waiter had placed "horrible insects on that lady's table!" I had talked to her about the sea, but had forgotten to prepare her for the delicacies that come from it. When I ordered shrimps, she said to me:

"Mummy I will pour Dettol into your mouth, if you eat them. That will really kill the horrible insects!" Dettol is a disinfectant popularly used in Zambia, but certainly not for pouring into anybody's mouth!

Anyway, Dinayi and I had fun splashing in the sea, building sand castles, and taking rides into town to shop or look around. Three weeks was a rather long time to spend on such a small island. By the second week we had been to most tourist places. But the ocean was a never-ending attraction and we spent hours on the beach, watching people come and go and just lying on towels on the white sands.

The water was a clear blue and a few yards into the sea from the beach, and one could see all kinds of fish swimming in the ocean.

During our stay, Dinayi made friends with children whose families were staying in the chalets. Some spoke English, while others only spoke either French, Dutch, German or Chinese. The island was a meeting ground for people from all over the world. In fact the population itself was a mixture of European, Indian, African, Chinese and other races. It was like the biblical Tower of Babel, with people of all races who spoke several different languages. Once again, I wished that I had learnt French at school, instead of Latin.

During our last week, we spent even more time at the beach. I usually took a novel and a couple of magazines to read because Dinayi was now so independent and into her own friends that my attempts at helping her with sand castles were no longer welcome. One afternoon, a girl her age, with blond hair and hazel eyes, came and asked me if she could play with Dinayi. I asked where her mother was, and all she could say was "gone." Gone? Did her mother leave her alone to play at the beach? I looked around to see if her parents were on the beach, but no one seemed to recognize her. Then I heard a man calling, "Amanda, Amanda, where are you?"

"Here, Daddy. I'm here!"

A tall, lean man in his mid-thirties came running from one of the chalets, and when he got to where Amanda was, he angrily waved a finger at her and said, "I've told you before not to wander off without telling me where you're going. Never do that again, do you hear?"

"No, Daddy, put me down! I want to build a sand castle."

"You're coming with Daddy," he said firmly, "because you've not promised that you'll never wander off again without my permission."

"Please, Daddy, please. I promise."

He put her down, and she rushed back to continue playing with Dinayi.

He came over to me and said, "Gosh, children! Is that your daughter? She looks like you."

Smiling, I said, "Yes. She and your daughter seem to have hit it off quite well."

"I'm sorry about what happened just now, but I was very worried about her. One minute she was near me, playing with her dolls, and the next minute she was gone. Well, I suppose that's not really true. I was reading a paper and must have dozed off, and when I woke up, she had slipped away."

He looked tired and worn out and as he spoke, he kept pushing a lock of auburn hair back from his forehead. He had longish hair, in the Beatles' fashion of the 1960s. His eyes were the same as his daughter's, although her complexion was much paler than his. He seemed robust and with a slight tan, as though he spent a lot of time outdoors.

We both watched as the kids played, and then I stood up and joined them in building their castle. However I was there only for a couple of minutes when Dinayi shouted, "Mummy, don't put so much sand there! Leave me and my friend to do it."

"You should say, my friend and I, Dinayi. Not me and my friend," I corrected. Shrugging my shoulders, I walked back to my towel.

Amanda's dad said, "Sounds like my five-year-old daughter! These children know it all, hey?"

"Dinayi is only four, but she sounds like a ten-year-old going on sixteen!" I said, laughing.

When I sat down, he said, "By the way, my name is David Scott." I shook his hand and said, "Mine is Likande Mufaya."

Then he said, "I've been trying to place your accent ... are you by any chance from Zambia?"

"Yes," I said, surprised. "How did you know? Have you been there?"

"No. But we're on our way there. I've just accepted a job as Advisor to the Ministry of Education. I believe they are in the process of carrying on some educational reforms."

"Did they send you a few tapes as well, so that you could listen to our accent?" I asked, casually.

He laughed and said, "No. I spent a lot of time at the Zambian Embassy in London and was dealing with Zambian officials there. What confused me about your accent however is the slight twang that sounds American."

"Really? I was there only for college. I can't believe that I could have picked up an American accent."

"It's not just your accent, but usage of words. For example, you just mentioned 'college'; we often say 'university', and I'm sure most Zambians would say the same."

"Well, I suppose you're right. It never occurred to me before."

"I could be wrong, of course. I need to listen to more Zambians speak before I make sweeping statements about a Zambian accent. Is your husband here with you? I would love to meet him."

"No. If you'll excuse me, I have to go now," I said, and started putting my book, towel and other things together, ready to leave. I then turned to Dinayi and shouted, "Come on, Dinayi, we've got to go now. We've been here for hours!"

"No. I don't want to come! I'm playing with my friend."

"Dinayi, you'll come now. This very minute."

"Why, Mummy, why?" she pleaded, as she tugged at my shorts in an attempt to detain me.

"Look, we'll be here a while longer. Why don't you leave her to play and I can bring her later. Where are you staying?" asked David.

"Oh, well, forget it. I'll just stay, I guess."

I spread the towel down again and, sitting down, immediately started reading. That should do it, I thought. No more small talk!

"So you're here alone, with your daughter?" he asked.

I couldn't believe it! Weren't the British supposed to be cold and reserved? He had a posh English accent and had obviously gone to one of those posh public schools! I still could not understand why they referred to those elite schools as public, instead of private. Only a small percentage of people in England could afford to go to such schools. Someone once said to me that the main difference between America and Britain is that in the United States you can tell where people come from by regional accents. Their accents will tell you whether they are from the South, from New York or from California. But for the British, someone's accent, and the way he speaks, denote class. It will tell you whether they've been to public schools and to universities like Oxford or Cambridge.

Those who belong to this privileged class only have to open their mouths and say a few words and doors to top jobs, to exclusive clubs, or to obtaining credit are opened to them without any problems. Such people speak the same way whether they were originally from London, Liverpool, or Birmingham. They belong to the same socioeconomic class. They are members of the upper classes who hobnob with princes and dukes at the posh schools. This man David seemed to belong to this class. We had so many "Brits" in our country, that even we locals could recognize who was who on their chart of social classes.

I pretended not to have heard what he asked me and continued staring at the same page, without reading. He seemed unbothered or unperturbed by my attitude all the same. Instead, he said, "if you're a single parent or you are here alone, there's nothing to feel ashamed of. I understand ... "

"What do you know or understand?" I asked, almost shaking with anger. "And what makes you think that there is, or should be, any shame in being a single parent? There are many reasons why people are single parents. Some choose to be, others become single parents because their parenthood wasn't planned, still others are single parents because ... er ... due to ... to ... death, or divorce!"

"That's what I was trying to say, but you never gave me a chance."

"Okay. It's now your chance. But first, it's my turn to ask you a few questions. Is it only you and your daughter who are here? Or has your wife gone ... er ... downtown, to the shops?"

"I wish to God that were true," he replied, almost to himself. The smile and twinkle disappeared from his eyes. They now looked forlorn, as if a dark cloud had descended over them. They were transformed to a dark, greenish-brown colour that was hard to read. He seemed lost to another world. After a pause, in which he had withdrawn to his inner self and where I somehow sensed he was better left alone, he quietly said, "My wife died of breast cancer two years ago. Amanda was three years old."

"Oh, God! I'm sorry. Truly sorry ... I feel awful."

"Please, don't. How could you have known?"

But I still felt terrible. How mean I must have sounded! Here was someone just trying to be friendly, and I blew up and snapped at him without bothering first to find out more about him.

"Please, don't worry about it. I'll feel more upset if you show pity and sympathy towards me or Amanda. The last thing people who are bereaved want is pity. Understanding, yes, but not pity."

Oh, gee, are you telling me! Don't I know that? I thought, as I recalled how well-meaning people seemed to read the wrong signs. Overwhelming you with pity and words of sympathy, when all you need is to be left alone. Then disappearing and leaving you when you want company and friendship, when all you need is someone to be there, just to sit and be near, even if they don't have much to say.

"By the way, what did you say your name was?" asked David, breaking into my thoughts.

"Likande Mufaya."

"Likande," he repeated, "a very beautiful name, sort of musical. What does it mean?"

I smiled, but said nothing.

"No meaning? Such a pretty name?"

"Gosh, are you curious!"

"That comes from being in education, always searching for knowledge and information. Well?"

"News."

"News?"

"My name ... it means news, message, notices, et cetera."

"Were your parents journalists?"

"Nope. I really don't know the origin. It was an aunt's name. Maybe one of our ancestors carried messages from place to place. Who knows? I'll have to ask my father one of these days."

"Is the name from your father's side?"

"Yes. It's also very unlikely that on my mother's side any ancestor would have been a messenger."

"Why not?"

"Nothing. No reason. Just a thought."

"Well, I'm very pleased to meet you, News Mufaya. And what's the news from Zambia, News?"

I heard my voice ringing out in laughter. I hadn't laughed so much in a long time. He made a funny face and, putting on a kind of German accent, said, "News, what did I say that was so funny?"

I burst out laughing again, and soon we were both laughing and laughing until I felt tears on the side of my face. Still laughing, David said, "Well, I'm glad I made you laugh. I was beginning to wonder whether anything makes you laugh! You're a very beautiful and attractive woman. But there's haunting sadness in those brown, almost teary eyes."

"Hey, what are you? A psychoanalyst or what? Are you in the habit of playing therapist to everyone you meet?"

"No. Not everyone. But my father used to say I was like an anthropologist or archaeologist, always digging and digging into people's histories and their past."

"You must step on people's toes and hurt their corns sometimes!"

"Sometimes. Although that is not my intention. Did I just step on yours?"

"We're in the same boat, so to speak. I'm a widow."

For the first time in four years, I spoke about Musa's death and how it affected me. The anguish and pain, the anger, the sense of betrayal. I just poured out my heart to this stranger from England and he just listened, not once interrupting or babbling on, the way he had before. His eyes never left my face. He just sat there, giving me undivided attention, except for an occasional glance at the two children playing. I talked and talked to this kindred spirit, who seemed to understand and feel what I had gone through.

I ended my long story with an emphatic, "One thing I know for sure is that I shall never get married again. Never!"

"Neither will I," he agreed, "my life now is my daughter and I. My mother and other relatives tried to persuade me to leave Amanda with them, but I refused. We'll stick together. I'm all she's got now, and she's all I have."

He then proceeded to talk about his wife. The pain and suffering, and the help and support they received from a local hospice. He said she was in her twenties when they diagnosed the cancer. As he spoke, tears shone in his eyes.

"I loved her so much. She was so bright and intelligent. She had been looking forward to being a mother. But poor Nancy, they found the cancer soon after Amanda was born. After that, it was in and out of hospitals, chemotherapy and hair loss. She had beautiful, long, blonde hair, exactly like Amanda's and that same pale skin, through which you can see every vein ... "

He had difficulty continuing as tears filled his eyes. I wanted to say something, to tell him that he need not say more if he didn't feel like it but I had a feeling he wanted to. Like me, he had found someone to talk to. Someone who understood. Fighting back tears, he continued. I just sat and listened.

Finally, he straightened up his shoulders and said, "Enough of this morbid conversation! You haven't answered my question yet."

"What question?"

"About Zambia. What it's like over there. My wife loved Africa. She had travelled to many African countries before I met her. She loved it so much that she almost married an African, but when she went to England she met me. We got married a few months later, but she never stopped talking about Africa. Her exact words were, "It grows on you". I thought I would bring Amanda to this place her mother loved so much. Who knows? She might decide to come back when she grows up."

"Mmm, who knows? In regard to Zambia, I'll only tell you a few basics. You can find out the rest when you get there. It's better that you make up your own mind rather than be influenced by my perceptions."

After that we spent a lot of time together, either watching the girls play on the beach while we talked, or joining the kids in splashing in the water. David loved scuba diving and went off with the Mauritius Diving Club for some underwater diving. He arranged for a babysitter through the hotel, in spite of my offer to babysit Amanda. However, Amanda would drag the babysitter to where Dinayi and I were so that she could play with Dinayi.

The babysitter, a French girl, seemed impatient with Amanda for preferring the company of a little African girl instead of the other white girls on the beach. But Amanda's stubborn streak came through. She firmly said, "No. I want to play here, with my friend."

Soon it was time for Dinayi and I to leave. David and his daughter had a week more. The day before we left, David said, "It was a real pleasure meeting you Likande. I don't know where I'll be in Lusaka, but if you give me your phone number, I'll ring you."

I gave him my office number although I did not really expect him to follow it up. He would be busy with the new job, settling in and meeting new friends and I would also be busy with my own life. He had been good company from a therapeutic angle, and it had been great talking to a kindred spirit. I felt rejuvenated and ready to face the busy work life again. He and I seemed to feel alike in very many things, including not wanting to get married again. I wasn't alone after all! Most of my friends were trying to match me off with any divorcee or widower they heard about. They kept saying that it was "unnatural to go on like that. You must think of marrying again – for Dinayi's sake."

As if I could marry anyone for my child's sake! If I got married again, which was out of the question, it would be to someone I really cared about.

XII

Back in Zambia I got down to my busy schedule, and it was as if the vacation had been a long time ago. I had been back a month or so when one morning, as I was about to rush to a meeting, my secretary said there was a Mr. Scott on the phone who wanted to talk to me. I said to her, "Please just take a message, it must be a client ... no, wait, did you say Scott?"

"Yes. He says his name is David Scott."

"I'll take it. Put it through," I said, and rushed back into my office. "Hello," I called into the phone.

"Hello, Likande. It's David Scott, remember me? Mauritius?"

"Of course," I replied, but the truth was he had really not been on mind for weeks. I did think of him and Amanda soon after we came back, but not afterwards. Not that I had forgotten. He had just not been in my mind, or a part of my daily life. But it was nice to hear from him.

"David, how are you and Amanda? How are things? How do you like Zambia so far? Are you in a hotel, or have they found you a house?"

"My, the number of questions! I see we've switched roles. You're the archaeologist, digging and digging . . . What was your first question?"

"I can't remember but I'm glad you called."

"I was planning to ring you earlier, but settling into a new place takes time. I also had to enroll Amanda in school. Look, I was wondering if you and Dinayi could come to our place for lunch."

"Thanks, David. But I should be the one to invite you first, this being my home. I'm planning a house-warming party in two weeks. My mortgage has come through, and we're moving into our new house this weekend. Would you like to come? Both of you?"

"Oh, yes, we would love that very much."

My friends couldn't believe their ears when I told them about the party. They had seen the house, but they had not expected any house warming party. They were now so used to my turning down any social event that they had not even suggested a party for my move. I invited several people, including some from my office. I even wore a new dress for the occasion.

As soon as Chilufya came in, she exclaimed, "Oh, Likande, you look like your old self! Actually, you seem different since you came back from Mauritius. The sea air and breeze did wonders for you! Musa would be thrilled to see you like this. It would hurt him if he thought you would spend the rest of your life grieving for him."

"Don't let your romantic ideas run away with you. I'm not off onto some new romance or anything like that."

But that was what everyone who came to the party thought. They started calling David my boyfriend. Who could blame them? We hardly left each other's side and seemed wrapped up in each other, while my nanny looked after our two children in another room.

After the party, we didn't call each other for three weeks. Each one of us was afraid of the feelings that were developing for the other. But as though drawn to each other by an invisible hand of fate, we met again at a party thrown by someone neither of us knew. I went because someone at my office was selling tickets for a fundraising event to help the poor in Chawama Shanty Compound.

I was going to donate some money, but the women persuaded me to go to the party, so I went.

When I saw David, my heart started doing flip-flops and pumping wildly. I couldn't believe what was happening to me! What was wrong with me? Then I felt something like a sharp knife pierce my heart when I saw a tall, blonde woman place her arm possessively on his shoulder. I felt panic gripping me, and I was about to retrace my steps and walk out when he looked up and saw me. His face lit up, and with a dazzling smile he came towards me. The woman with him seemed taken aback, but followed him. "Hello, Likande. Good to see you!" he said, taking my hand and giving it a squeeze. I thought everyone around us could hear my heart beating, Boom, boom. The woman with him sharply glanced at my hand still locked in his. David quickly let go of my hand and said, "Carol. Please meet a friend of mine, Likande Mufaya."

"How do you do," she said coldly, ignoring my hand put forward in greeting. We stood staring at each other, critically checking each other out, furtive glances, up and down. The tension between us was thick in the air, but we both wore polite masks. Her eyes were a deep blue that now seemed as cold as ice, even though she bared her teeth in a pretentious smile.

"David, come and meet some of my friends," she crooned, leading him away. I sighed and looked for some familiar faces. But my heart was heavy. Was she his girlfriend? Was he in love with her? A voice within me reprimanded me with: what business is it of yours, anyway? Why are you turning a brief encounter on a vacation beach, thousands of miles away, into something serious? He had only been friendly. Talking to you because you happened to be there. And his phone call? That look in his eyes that sent my heart going wild? Did he feel the same for me?

Food was being served, so I joined the line for the self-help buffet. But I hardly touched my meal. Nor did I really listen to the hostess' speech about the projects the group was sponsoring in the shanty compounds. After that, dance music started. From the corner of my eye, I saw David and the blond woman dancing. When the next one started playing, I went to join the hostess in the kitchen and asked her whether I could help clean up. Then I felt a hand on my shoulder, and that deep voice with the superb English accent said, "Likande, here you are! I was afraid you'd left. Come on, I'd like a dance with you."

I didn't hesitate even for a second. I grabbed the outstretched hand and we skipped onto the dance floor. We danced and danced as though we'd been partners somewhere before, in another world, another life. We swung sideways, he pulled me towards him, pushed me away, lifted me into the air, and then we bounced on our knees, bending lower and lower until our knees were just above the ground. We made up steps as we went along. It was as if we had practised the steps before. People around us stopped dancing to watch us, clapping to the rhythm of the music. Afterwards, there were shouts of "Encore, encore!"

The next one was a slow waltz, and I floated into David's arms as though I belonged there. As his strong arms went around my thin, slim waist, I leaned against him and closed my eyes. I was in heaven, in those never-ending, nebulous skies. But a tap on my shoulder brought me, with a thud, down to earth. It was Carol. With a smile that didn't match her cold and angry eyes, she said, "Well, well! May I break this cosy dance? I've been forgotten all evening, except for one dance!"

"Of course. Please go ahead," I stammered, and then moved away. I went outside for some cool, fresh air, and just to calm my quick pulse and my hot face. I sat for a few minutes on the patio.

Someone said, "You are a terrific dancer, as is your partner." "Thanks," I said, and then walked away into the garden. I needed to be alone, to sort out my jumbled thoughts. I couldn't believe that it was I who had let myself go wild in that room. I couldn't remember ever dancing like that. Not even with Musa. Never. It was as if David and the music had taken possession of me and transformed me into someone I didn't know existed inside me. I had to leave before I ended up doing something I might regret the following morning. I was like someone who had taken an intoxicating drink and didn't know what exactly she had drunk. I never drank alcohol. The only drink I had taken was orange juice. But my head felt light and my heart was singing. I went back into the room and, without even saying goodbye to anybody, slipped away.

I found it hard to concentrate on my work the following day.

Several times, I glanced at the phone and asked myself, should I call him? But a war of different voices was raging within. Why do you want to call? Just to thank him for a lovely evening. Come on, is that the only reason? What are you trying to do? Can't you see that there's someone else in his life? In the end, the voice of reason prevailed, and I forced myself to work until it was time to go home.

Later that evening, after putting Dinayi to bed, I made myself a cup of tea and then sat down to watch TV. But my thoughts were far away, and I switched it off and put on some music. Then I heard several knocks on the door.

"Yes? Who is it?" I asked, wondering who could be visiting at that time of night.

"It's David."

My heart started its wild beat! Boom, boom, it went. I quickly glanced at my faded jeans, wishing that I hadn't changed from my two piece suit which looked chic and appropriate. But a two-piece suit at home? Well, I could have pretended that I had just come in from work and I was working late or something. But it was too late to change now. I wish he had told me he was coming, I thought.

"Likande, are you going to open the door for me?"

"Yes. Sure. Please come in," I mumbled, as I opened the door.

Without giving him a chance to say anything, I rattled on, "I was going to call you today, to thank you for a lovely evening. I really enjoyed it. I'm sorry for monopolizing you and leaving Carol out."

"I came to talk to you about that. I tried to look for you afterwards, but you'd already left. I thought of ringing you, or calling you, as they say in America, but I thought it might be better to see you in person."

He seemed very nervous and uneasy. Was he trying to break the news to me in a gentle way? Warning me not to take him seriously? That he was in love with Carol? My heart suddenly felt like heavy metal. But I would save him the embarrassment. He need not know how heartbroken I was. Putting on a brave face, I said, "Look, David. You needn't worry about last night. Of course, I didn't take you seriously. You don't have to feel guilty about me. So if you'll excuse me, I have things to do now .. ."

He stared at me in disbelief and shock. His eyes searched mine, probing and willing them to reveal the truth, but I turned my face away and then moved to open the door and let him out. But he blocked my way and shouted, "I'm not leaving until you look me in the eye and tell me to my face that you don't care about me. That I mean nothing to you. So last night meant nothing to you? Answer me, Likande!"

I continued to look away. The tears I had been desperately trying to hold back now poured down my face.

"Look at me!" he yelled again.

I swung around and faced him, neither caring about my tears, nor ashamed about crying. I was seething with anger. "Why do you want to know, anyway? To boost your ego? So that you can boast to the world that you're being chased by two women?"

He grabbed me by the arm and pulled me towards him, and with one hand under my chin, tilted my face upwards so that I was facing him. Then his lips came crushing against mine in a long, deep, sweet kiss that sent shivers down my spine. We were both on fire, moaning, "I love you, I love you," over and over. When we stopped to catch our breath, I timidly asked, "What about Carol?"

"What about her, my love?" he asked, trying to take me again in his arms.

But I gently pushed him away and said, "Look, David, I wasn't born yesterday. Last night, she gave me a look that clearly warned me to keep away from you."

"I was afraid that was what you thought. That was why I wanted to explain the situation to you."

"You mean, there's nothing between you and Carol?"

"No. Nothing. Her boyfriend broke off with her, and she was trying to get him back by making him jealous. That was why she invited me to that party."

"Really?"

"Well, she also wanted me to date a friend of hers, but I wasn't interested. She couldn't believe that my choice was you, instead of Melissa, who is white.

I was silent for a moment. I had completely forgotten about the implications of David and me loving each other. What he said brought me down to earth with a painful bang. I slowly said, "She's probably right, David. This won't work. It just can't."

"Anything can work if we want it to," he insisted.

"The best thing is for us not to get too involved," I cautioned. But David wouldn't hear of it. He firmly said, "No. I won't accept it! Do you think it was a coincidence that we met the way we did? There were many people on that beach, but something was drawing you and me together. The children were only a medium through which we were brought together."

"You look so serious!" I said, but my heart was singing.

Was I the same person who had sworn never to love anyone again? Many times, when I had emphatically said that I would never love anyone again, or get married a second time, Chilufya had cautioned, "Likande, never say never. You don't know what the future holds, or what plans God has for you."

How right she was!

XIII

David and I were married a year later. We wanted to prepare not only ourselves, but the children as well. However as the months ticked away, both of them became very impatient. They couldn't wait for the occasion.

"Are we moving to Amanda's house, mummy?" asked Dinayi several times.

"Yes, honey, yes."

"Oh, I wish it were today. Please marry him today, mummy. Please!"

David was going through the same pressure from Amanda. She hated it when we had to part after an outing together. One day, she angrily said to her father, "One whole year? Why?"

But no sooner was the wedding over than resentment and competition between them set in. We couldn't even go away on a honeymoon, as both refused to be left with relatives or friends. They kept saying, "Why can't we come on your honeymoon?

Why?" So there was no honeymoon for us. We spent the day after our wedding with the two children, feeding ducks at a local zoo!

It was the beginning of a rough road that lay ahead. They fought over everything, from who would sit where at the dining table, to who would be the first to use the bathroom before going to bed, whose toothbrush would hang where, and so on. Many times we heard them shouting at each other.

"This is my house! Why don't you go back to yours?" Amanda would scream.

"I don't care if it's your house. I hate your house, and I hate you!" Dinayi would shout back.

The children's fights started affecting our own relationship. Any time David and I tried to spend a few minutes together, or tried to discuss things, Dinayi or Amanda swiftly came to separate us. If it was Amanda, she wanted "daddy" to help her with something or other. If it was Danayi, she would firmy lead me by the hand to go and "see something."

We realized that they were feeling insecure; that each of them had lost a parent through death and therefore wished to hold onto the remaining parent. Both David and I had spent the last years as widowed individuals, giving our children undivided attention. Now they felt threatened. But it wasn't just the fighting that worried us. We had somehow forgotten that we were not living on an island with just the four of us. David and I didn't care what the world thought of our relationship. We loved each other, and that was all that mattered. But for our children, the world out there was a war zone, and they were feeling the brunt of it. Adults have a way of hiding behind their masks of politeness and not showing how they really feel about things or people. But children are straight and frank, and their directness can sometimes be cruel. Amanda and Dinayi were now victims of that frankness and directness.

"I don't want to go to school," announced Dinayi one morning. "I hate it."

"Dinayi, you've always loved school Why don't you want to go now?"

"Because."

"Because what?"

"Because of that stupid, mean Chalekwa!"

"I thought you and Chalekwa were very good friends. Why don't you like her now?"

"She said terrible things! So I … I … I hit her, right on her bad mouth yesterday. Teacher said, if I fight again, she will talk to you. But I don't care! If she says those stupid things again, I'll hit her."

"No. No fighting, Dinayi. You'd better tell me what is going on. What terrible things did Chalekwa say to upset you?"

After giving a few more evasive answers, Dinayi broke down and started crying. Everything came out. She was being teased by other kids who taunted her that she would "never have a real daddy. Only that *muzungu* (the white one) who has married your mummy."

Then Amanda came out with her own stories about her daddy being a 'nigger lover' and about Amanda having 'a black, niggery stepmother.'

We felt helpless. Absolutely helpless. We had been married for nine months, and our poor, little children had borne the brunt of harassment and teasing from their peers. For months they had tried to protect David and me, but what was bothering them had come out in their behaviour. We had put it all to adjustment problems, to bringing two different families together in a new marriage. But ours was more than just two families being brought together. It suddenly dawned on us that, blinded by love, we had plunged not only ourselves, but our children, into a small boat that had to withstand a very rough sea. We were furiously paddling away, trying to deal with wave after wave, but would our little boat survive the rigorous journey?

David and I had our own problems to deal with. Our relationship was under a lot of strain. We still behaved like widowed individuals, who had their own way of doing things. When one is young and naive, it is easy to be flexible and to be moulded, or to compromise. But when one has been married before and has children, one has set ways of doing things. We both placed our deceased spouses on high and idolized them to the point where they were now the perfect angels. We used them as the measuring stick. For me, it was, "Musa never used to mind if I … ," while David would say,

"Nancy was so good at ..." Our cultural differences also became huge mountains, looming above us.

My extended typical African family believed in giving us a 'nice surprise' by dropping in 'just to say hello.' It didn't matter what time of day or whether we were sitting down to dinner. At first David was friendly, but it soon got on his nerves. So he would excuse himself and retire to the study to 'do some work.' We also clashed over time-keeping. He believed in being very strict about time, while I saw nothing wrong in a little flexibility. I accused him of being too obsessed with time. The result was screaming at each other.

One day he started shouting at me as I was getting ready for our outing.

"Likande, this is not being flexible. It is downright sloppiness, and lacking any sense of time, which seems the norm in this country!"

"I see, first I was the one who was sloppy about time, and now it is the whole country, is it?" I shouted. "My country?"

He walked to our bed and slumped down. He looked tired and stressed. Slowly, and in a quiet voice, he said, "Likande, this is no good. I love you, but we'll surely drown if we don't do anything to salvage our marriage. It will sink into something we may never be able to retrieve it from. I'm willing to work at it, if you are."

I went towards him and, with my arms around him, said, "You're right, sweetie, I'm sorry about what's been happening. I love you, too, and I want to work at saving our marriage."

It was the turning point in our relationship. After that, we both worked at it, and we were determined to build a happy and secure home for our children. It was amazing how 'friendly' the rest of the world became. We couldn't please everybody in the world, and that was not the task we had set out to do. But both Amanda and Dinayi made lots of friends. Questions of colour seemed to disappear overnight from their conversation.

I also found more time to be with them after quitting my job. Both David and I had been so busy with our careers and jobs that we had no idea what was happening in our children's lives. Our contacts with them had been short periods of time – during supper, and before they went to bed, and then at breakfast. That was a typical weekday. During the weekend we were too busy catching up on some shopping.

But after I stopped working, I had more time for them, took them to various activities and had them involved in swimming classes. At the pool I met other parents, mostly mothers, and our circle of friends widened. Some were local, while many more were from several other countries. I also started doing volunteer work, helping out during the hours my children were at school and being home when they returned. Whenever David took time off from work, we went around the country to game parks, out on picnics and accompanied him on his diving trips. I started learning more about our country's rural areas and the beautiful landscape.

Within two months of quitting work, I became pregnant. I had not been on any contraceptive during the first year of our marriage, but all the same I could not conceive. I suppose the strain and tension were too much for my system. In a way, it was a blessing in disguise. We were not ready then for an additional child in the family. But now we all were, and everyone waited in anticipation for the baby to come.

However it wasn't just one. During a check-up, my doctor said, "Mrs. Scott, I think you're expecting twins. But we'll do further tests to make sure. I keep getting two heartbeats."

I nearly fell off the chair. Twins? Oh, God, a family with two instant children, and now twins? David often mentioned that the ideal British family was one child. What would he do once he learnt that we would now have four children!

But he started laughing when I told him the news. Then he said, "I'm not surprised."

"Not surprised?" I asked, not comprehending what he was getting at.

"There have been twins on my mother's side. I should have warned you," he said.

XIV

I gave birth to two lovely identical twins. They were a double delight, especially for David, because they were boys. He was very happy and said, "Now we are equal. This had been a female-dominated household!" We called them Patrick and Donald.

But they were hardly two months old when we moved from Zambia. It was now the end of David's employment contract. We moved to Peru, where he was hired as an adviser to one of their Ministries.

We loved Peru and its people and, as we had done in Zambia, spent any time we could during holidays and vacations visiting interesting places. Lima, the capital city, was a huge, sprawling megapolis with a bustling business and social life. The difference in living standards between the rich and poor was far worse than anything I had seen before.

I immediately got involved in volunteer work three mornings a week. We were privileged and were living so comfortably that the least I could do for our host country was give some of my time. I loved working with women and children in the 'Pueblos Jovenes,' their equivalent of our African shanty compounds.

I also enrolled at a language school, as most of the people I was working with spoke nothing but Spanish and I was getting frustrated at having to communicate through interpreters. The people became my best language teachers. Our children adored our new home and thrived in it. They had so many international friends in Peru that they settled to the new culture like fish to water.

We travelled outside Lima to historic places, rich in Incan and other pre-Spanish cultures: the Incan ruins in Machupichu, Cusco, Huaraz, Lake Titicaca, Huancayo, Arequipa and so on. I found the varied nature of the country fascinating, ranging from the Amazon jungle in Iquitos, to the snow-capped Andean mountains in Huaraz, where tourists went skiing, down to the desert areas by the coast.

The food was as varied as the climatic regions. Dinayi will always remember Peru, because it was the place where she learnt to really enjoy seafood. Every week, she would ask our cook whether she could prepare those '*mariscos, muy delicioso*.' The fish and seafood were indeed delicious. We also used our stay in Peru to visit neighbouring countries like Chile, Brazil and Argentina. All of them are interesting, in their own way as we discovered.

By our third year in Peru, we were all fluent in Spanish, with the children, of course, being much better at it than David and I. The twins, Patrick and Donald, were more fluent than any of us. They spoke Spanish like natives and grew so close to their nanny, Vilma, that when it was time to leave, they cried their hearts out. She had seen them grow from infancy and had become a part of the family.

Our next move was to lovely, sunny Jamaica and its beautiful beaches. We spent two happy years there and again enjoyed the friendliness and hospitality of its people. We were there only a short time, but long enough to appreciate its culture and traditions, the lovely music and vivacious nature of the people.

From Jamaica we went to England, back to where David and Amanda had come from when Dinayi and I first met them. We had visited England twice since then, but never for a long time. Now we had gone to stay, at least for some time, and to see our children through school. Moving around from country to country was fun, but it had its drawbacks, especially with regard to the children's schooling and their need for continuity and stability.

The important lesson our children had learnt through our travels was to appreciate the diversity of the people who live on this planet. They now see the world like a garden full of beautiful flowers of different colours and shapes. There is, of course, a thorn here and there, as well as a few prickly shrubs and sharp stones. But these don't take away the overall beauty of the garden. The children proudly talk of friends they met through our international travel, some of whom kept it touch with them for some time afterwards.

XV

The feeling of security, self-esteem, and general openness and warmth towards others which our children have shown, have been a beacon of light to other children. Our home is like a railway station, with children from the neighbourhood coming and going. Some of them are friends of our children; each of them has their own special friends. Others are just hangers-on, the so-called latch-key kids, who come home to empty houses after school and virtually fend for themselves, while both their parents are out working.

David teases me about them and says that I have adopted neighbourhood kids as my new social work project, the same way I did in the countries where we were before. He smiles when he hears kids greet me, when we are out walking or shopping, with shouts of, "Hello, auntie Lee." Once he said to me, "That's very English. Too lazy to pronounce strange-sounding names, so they give you a new name!"

But later that night, as we were in bed, he pulled me towards him and said, "Darling, you've done wonders with these cold, reserved English people. The number of times people ask after you when I'm out shopping or at the green grocer's! It's always, 'Please say hello to Limonde', or 'Leek-Andy', as some pronounce it. I bet you they never ask about me!"

All I could do was smile. Our family was home, at last. We had reached the peak and could look back over the years and say, "Yes, we've had our share of problems, and there may still be others on the way, but we shall fight them as a united family."

Our children have been a source of pride and pleasure for us. Amanda is now seventeen years old, Dinayi sixteen, and Patrick and Donald are ten years old. Amanda wants to be a musician and loves playing the piano. Dinayi wants to be a lawyer and loves getting into arguments "just to show the other side." Patrick wants to be a "scuba diver and find treasures from old ships," while Donald just wants to grow up fast so he "can go to the jungle in Peru to study butterflies." Although he was only three years old when we left Peru, everything is still clear in his mind, kept alive by all the artifacts which we collected from there and, of course, the family albums which he brings out to show his friends. His tales about the Amazon jungle get wilder and more exaggerated each time. But he has a captive audience in his little friends, who listen with their mouths open.

For me, the most touching and rewarding moment came one evening when we went to a recital in which Amanda was performing. We sat and listened as her long, dainty fingers moved over the piano keys, going from side to side, up and down, as her body moved and swayed to the rhythm of the piece she was playing.

She was fully engrossed in the music.

When she finished, the room resounded with applause, and nods and murmurs of approval. She bowed several times in acknowledgement, and when the applause died down, she said, "My next piece is a very special one for me. I would like to dedicate it to my parents, especially my mother, who has been a pillar of strength to me and a great support. Encouraging me when I first started, driving me to and from piano lessons, wherever we were. One of the first things she used to do, as soon as we moved to a new place, was ask around about piano lessons and who was the best teacher. Mum, thanks for everything. This is for you."

My eyes were filled with tears, and everyone before me looked blurred and hazy. I felt David's strong arm around me as we stood up to acknowledge the audience's applause. When we sat down, we felt the arms of our other children linking each other and over our shoulders. It was the best prize I could ever have wished for. How long ago it seemed, those terrible first months of our marriage! We were then, them and us, but now we were one happy family. Without any prompting on our part, both Dinayi and Amanda had started calling us "mummy and daddy."

When I now look back, they seemed to have started doing it when I was expecting the twins. Then they were feeling secure and happy, and had started identifying themselves with the family we had formed.

There have been moments when I have wondered whether I should have quit the fast career train. Times when I felt I was missing something, from a professional perspective and when I thought I had lost out. It was as if I wasted all that training and let down people who had such high hopes and expectations from me. When I see what Chilufya and Tengani are doing, I ask myself, "What have I done?"

But reflecting on my life has helped me see things in their right perspective. Life is not just about careers or making money. We all have the right to choose what is best for ourselves and those we love. If a woman wants to be a career woman and not to be "tied down by children and a husband," then her choice should be respected. If, on the other hand, a woman wishes to juggle her time between the two, a job and a family – "the mummy track," as someone once called it, then they, too, should be respected. Such a combination might mean working only a few days a week, not taking on demanding jobs which might interfere with children and family. Those who opt for full-time housewife and mother deserve as much respect for their decision. I have done both, first a career, then combining the two, and finally spending most of my time at home with the children.

People who think that women who stay home to rear children are doing nothing, don't really know what they are talking about. This is a twenty-four-hour job, with multiple tasks. If the world were to place a monetary value on what full-time mothers and wives do around the world, national coffers would go bankrupt within hours, if not minutes or seconds! Those downward plunges on Wall Street, the London Stock Exchange, and in Tokyo, would be 'baby stuff!' Just think of all those peasant women in the rural area whose working day begins before dawn and ends long after the sunset! Neither the World Bank nor the International Monetary Fund could find money to pay for such work. You bet these are services that no money can buy!

Did I say, at the beginning, that our reunion might be like Judgement Day for me? Because I had not really done anything worthwhile in my life? Well, I take that back. All of us, in our own way, small or big, have done something. I am now ready for our proposed reunion. I can't wait to see who will turn up and to hear what has happened to my classmates since we left school.

Printed in the United States
By Bookmasters